Praise for Elmore Leonard
Bestselling author of *Up in Honey's Room*

"Leonard's uncanny sense of plot, pace, and his inexhaustible flair for the nervous rhythms of contemporary urban speech have caught the spirit of the eighties. . . . Leonard is a superb craftsman, and his writing is pure pleasure."

—*Los Angeles Times Book Review*

"Everything Leonard touches turns to gold. He has a wonderful ear for the way the kind of people you'd never want to meet talk, and his own prose is lean and shifty. . . . He writes a love scene even better than he writes a murder, and when it comes to plotting, he has more moves than Bobby Fischer."

—*Boston Globe*

Praise for *Swag*

"When Mr. Leonard is observing, satirizing, plotting, working up suspense, thickening the air with menace, discharging it in lightning flashes of violence, exposing the black holes behind the parts people play . . . he gives us as much serious fun per word as anyone around."

—*New York Times Book Review*

"[*Swag* is] a brutally up-to-date crime novel and a good one."

—*The New Yorker*

About the Author

ELMORE LEONARD has written more than forty novels, including such bestsellers as *Up in Honey's Room, The Hot Kid, Mr. Paradise, Tishomingo Blues, Pagan Babies,* and *Glitz*—and nearly as many short stories. Many of his books have been made into movies, including *Get Shorty* and *Out of Sight*. He lives with his wife, Christine, in Bloomfield Village, Michigan.

Also by Elmore Leonard

Fiction

Road Dogs
Up in Honey's Room
The Hot Kid
The Complete Western
  Stories of Elmore Leonard
Mr. Paradise
When the Women Come Out
  to Dance
Tishomingo Blues
Pagan Babies
Be Cool
The Tonto Woman and
  Other Western Stories
Cuba Libre
Out of Sight
Riding the Rap
Pronto
Rum Punch
Maximum Bob
Get Shorty
Killshot
Freaky Deaky
Touch
Bandits
Glitz

LaBrava
Stick
Cat Chaser
Split Images
City Primeval
Gold Coast
Gunsights
The Switch
The Hunted
Unknown Man No. 89
Fifty-Two Pickup
Mr. Majestyk
Forty Lashes Less One
Valdez is Coming
The Moonshine War
The Big Bounce
Hombre
Last Stand at Saber River
Escape from Five Shadows
The Law at Randado
The Bounty Hunters

Nonfiction

Elmore Leonard's 10 Rules
  of Writing

ELMORE LEONARD

SWAG

formerly titled *RYAN'S RULES*

HARPER

NEW YORK • LONDON • TORONTO • SYDNEY

HARPER

A hardcover edition of this book was published in 1976 by Delacorte Press, and a mass market edition was published in 1988 by Dell Publishing. Delacorte Press and Dell Publishing are both divisions of Bantam Doubleday Dell Publishing Group, Inc.

This work was previously published under the title *Ryan's Rules*.

HarperCollins books may be purchased for educational, business, or sales promotional use. For information please write: Special Markets Department, HarperCollins Publishers, 10 East 53rd Street, New York, NY 10022.

FIRST HARPER PAPERBACK PUBLISHED 2009.

Library of Congress Cataloging-in-Publication Data is available upon request.

ISBN 978-0-06-174136-4

11 12 13 DIX/RRD 10 9 8

for Jane

_____

1

THERE WAS A PHOTOGRAPH OF Frank in an ad that ran in the *Detroit Free Press* and showed all the friendly salesmen at Red Bowers Chevrolet. Under his photo it said *Frank J. Ryan.* He had on a nice smile, a styled moustache, and a summer-weight suit made out of that material that's shiny and looks like it has snags in it.

There was a photograph of Stick on file at 1300 Beaubien, Detroit Police Headquarters. Under the photo it said *Ernest Stickley, Jr.,* 89037. He had on a sport shirt that had sailboats and palm trees on it. He'd bought it in Pompano Beach, Florida.

The first time they ever saw each other was the night at Red Bowers Chevrolet on Telegraph when Stick was pulling out of the used-car lot in the maroon '73 Camaro. Frank walked up to the side window as the car stopped before turning out on the street. He said, "You mind if I ask where you're going?"

The window was down. Stick looked at the guy who was stooped over a little, staring at him: nice-looking guy about thirty-five or so, long hair carefully combed, all dressed up with his suit and tie on. A car salesman. Stick could smell the guy's aftershave lotion.

Stick said, "I could be going home, I could be going to Florida." Which was his intention, the reason he was taking the car. He said, "What do you care where I'm going?"

Frank's first impression of Stick was a guy off the farm who'd come to town and somebody had sold him a genuine Hawaiian sport shirt, he wore with the collar spread open, showing a little bit of white T-shirt. Frank said, "Since you didn't buy the car, I mean pay for it yet, I wondered."

"Uh-unh," Stick said. "I come here to price a new one."

Frank kept staring at him. "You always shop for a car after the place's closed?"

"Yeah, that's what I found out. The showroom's all lit up but it's closed. Hey," Stick said, "maybe you think this is one of yours because you got one like it."

"Maybe that's it," Frank said. "Even down to the Indiana plates. It was parked over there where there's an empty space now." He said, "You say it's yours, you want to show me the registration?"

"Fuck no," Stick said, and took off, leaving Frank standing there in the drive.

Frank went into the used-car office, called the Detroit police, and gave them a description of the car. He didn't do it right away. He took his time, thinking the guy must be a real farmer to try and steal a car off a lot that was all lit up. The guy had been very cool about it, though. Slow-talking, relaxed, with the trace of a Southern accent. But he might have been putting it on, acting sincere. Frank himself would give customers a little down-home sound every once in a while and grin a lot. It wasn't hard.

He didn't give a personal shit if the guy got away with it or not. The car belonged to Red Bowers Chevrolet. He wasn't out anything. But there was something personal about it if the guy was driving down Telegraph grinning, thinking he'd aced him. That's why Frank called the police. Also he called to see how the police would handle it. To see if they were any good.

They weren't bad. A squad car turned on its flashers as soon as the Camaro was spotted on the Lodge Freeway. It took another twenty minutes, though, and three side-swiped cars on Grand River, before they got him. They found the wrinkled Camaro in a parking lot and Stick sitting in the bar next door with a bottle of Stroh's beer.

The next time Frank saw Stick was at Detroit Police Headquarters on Beaubien, looking through the one-way glass at him standing in line with the five plainclothes cops who stood patiently staring into the light glare. It was funny. Frank hesitated again before saying, "Second one on the left."

"You're sure he's the one?"

"I'm sure it isn't one of those cops," Frank said.

Out in the office he asked the detective sergeant about the guy, who he was and if he'd been arrested before, and learned the following:

Ernest Stickley, Jr. No aliases. Address: Zanzibar Motel, Southfield, Michigan. Born in Norman, Oklahoma, October 11, 1940. Occupation: truck driver, transit-mix operator. Marital status: divorced; ex-wife and seven-year-old daughter residing in Pompano Beach, Florida.

The sheet also listed previous arrests. The first time for joyriding; sentence suspended. Arrested two years later on a UDAA charge—unlawfully driving away an automobile—and received one-year probation. The final one, arrested for grand theft, auto—transporting a stolen motor vehicle across a state line—and convicted. Served ten months in the Federal Correctional Institution at Milan, Michigan.

Frank said to himself, Well well well well. An auto thief named Ernest, with a record. Maybe a hick but a fairly nice-looking guy. Mid-thirties. Had nerve. Didn't seem to get excited. Obviously knew how to steal cars. In fact,

Frank was pretty sure, the guy had stolen a lot more cars than were listed on his sheet. Four arrests now and most likely another conviction.

The third time Frank saw Stick was at the pretrial examination on the fourth floor of the Frank Murphy Hall of Justice. It was an air-conditioned, wood-paneled courtroom with indirect lighting and enough microphones placed around so the people in the audience could hear the proceedings. There were a few cops in off-duty clothes, some cute young black ladies and skinny guys in modified pimp outfits who were either pimps or pushers or might be felony suspects—B and E, robbery or assault—out on bond. There were a few spectators, too: mostly retirees who came up to watch felony exams and murder trials because they were more fun than movies and they were free.

Frank was surprised when he saw the assistant prosecutor: a young black guy in a tight sport coat. Young and short and fat. He had thought all young black guys in Detroit were at least six-seven and went about a hundred and a half. Frank decided the black guy was very smart and had passed the bar in the top ten. He looked like he was enjoying himself, shuffling papers, moving around a lot to talk to the judge and the court clerk and the defense lawyers; then turning away from them, smiling at some inside remark, having fun being a prosecuting attorney.

Frank had a feeling the people watching the guy were probably thinking. Look at that little mother. Little kiss-ass with the big horn-rim glasses on to show how smart he is. Everybody in the courtroom was black except Frank, a couple of Jewish lawyers in their sixties, and the off-duty cops waiting to be called as witnesses.

Stick hadn't been able to make bond. They brought him in through a side door and sat him at the end of a table facing the witness stand as the judge, a black guy with graying hair and a neat gray moustache, called a number and read Stick's name from a big file folder he was holding. Then the prosecutor called Mr. Frank Ryan, and he went through the gate and over to the court clerk, who swore him in and told him to sit down in the witness chair, take the mike off its stand, and hold it in front of him. They didn't waste any time. The little prosecutor asked him if he would please tell what happened the night of May twenty-second in the used-car lot at Red Bowers Chevrolet.

Frank told it. Most of it.

Then he was asked if he had, the next day, identified the same man in a show-up at Detroit Police Headquarters.

Frank said yes, he had.

The little prosecutor said, "And do you see that same man in this courtroom?"

Frank said, "No, I don't."

"And would you point—" The little prosecutor stopped. "What'd you say?"

"I said no, I don't see him."

"You *ident*ified him. Didn't you point him out at a show-up?"

"I thought he was the one," Frank said. "But now I see him again, I'm not sure."

Ernest Stickley, sitting about fifteen feet away, was staring at him. Frank met his gaze and held it a moment before looking at the prosecutor again.

"I mean maybe it's the same person, but I have to tell you I've got a reasonable doubt it isn't. I can't *swear* it's the same person."

"You're sure one day," the little prosecutor said, "now today you're not?"

"I didn't say I was sure. The police officer asked me if

he was the one and I said, I think so. I said, He's certainly not any of those other ones."

The little prosecutor didn't seem to be having fun anymore. He began trying to put words in Frank's mouth until Stick's lawyer, appointed by the court, felt he had better object to that and the judge sustained it. Then Stick's lawyer put a few words of his own in Frank's mouth the way he slanted his question and Frank repeated no, he could not positively identify anyone in the courtroom as the person who'd driven off in the '73 Camaro. The prosecutor wouldn't let go. He went at Frank again until the judge told him to please introduce a new line of questioning or else call another witness.

The prosecutor thanked the judge—Frank wasn't sure why—and the judge thanked Frank as he stepped down. The judge was quiet, very polite.

Watching all this, especially watching the guy from the used-car lot, Frank Ryan, Stick kept thinking. What the hell is going on? He couldn't believe it. He sat very still in the chair, almost with the feeling that if he moved, this Frank Ryan would look at him again and squint and say, Wait a minute, yeah, that's the one.

The guy from the used-car lot went out through the gate. Stick didn't turn around, but he had a feeling the guy was still in the courtroom.

He watched the officer who had arrested him take the stand, wearing slacks and a black leather jacket that was open, his holstered Police Special on a direct line with Stick's gaze.

The patrolman recited in Official Police how he and his partner had noted the Indiana license plate on the alleged stolen vehicle and had pursued the suspect, witnessing how he had apparently lost control taking a corner upon entering Grand River Avenue and proceeded to sideswipe three cars parked along the west side of the street. Because of the traffic they were not able to keep the suspect in sight, but did locate the vehicle in a parking lot adjacent to the Happy Times Bar located at Twenty-nine twenty-one Grand River. Upon entering the premises the patrolman asked the bartender who, if anyone, had come in during the past few minutes. The bartender pointed to the person later identified as the suspect. When approached, the suspect said, "What seems to be the trouble, Officer?" The suspect was placed under arrest and informed of his rights.

"And is that person now in this courtroom?"

"Yes sir," the patrolman said to the smart little prosecutor. "He's sitting right there in front of me."

Stick didn't move; he stared back at the policeman. Finally his lawyer leaned toward him with his cigar breath and asked in a hoarse whisper if he would be willing to take the stand, tell what he was doing in the bar and how he got there, show them he had nothing to hide.

Stick whispered back to him, "You out of your fucking mind?"

He didn't have to go up there and testify to anything if he didn't want to. They'd have to prove he had gotten out of the '73 Camaro and walked into the Happy Times Bar, and there wasn't any way in the world they could do it.

The prosecutor tried for another few minutes, until the judge called both attorneys up to the bench and politely told the prosecutor to please quit mind-fucking the court, produce some evidence that would stand up in trial or else everybody was going to miss lunch today. That was how Stick got off.

2

AFTER HE WAS RELEASED HE didn't see the guy from the used-car lot in the courtroom or in the hall. He saw him on the steps outside the building, lighting a cigarette, and knew the guy was waiting for him to come over.

"You want one?"

"I'm trying to quit," Stick said. He hesitated. "Yeah, I guess I will," he said then and took a Marlboro from a pack the guy offered.

Holding a lighted match, the guy said, "I'm Frank Ryan. I wasn't sure if you heard my name up there."

Stick looked at him. "I heard it." Neither of them offered to shake hands.

Frank said, "You're lucky. That judge seemed like a nice guy. No bullshit."

"I guess I was lucky, all right," Stick said, looking at the guy's neatly combed hair. He was an inch or so taller than Stick, about six feet even, slim build in his green, lightweight, shiny-looking summer suit, with the coat open. Stick had on the same yellow, green, and blue sport shirt he'd worn for almost a week. He said, "It's funny how sometimes you get lucky and other times everything goes against you."

"It is funny," Frank Ryan said. "You want to get a drink or something?"

"I wouldn't mind it. I was in that Wayne County jail six days and six nights and they didn't serve us any cocktails or anything. I guess that's when you were deciding I wasn't the guy after all."

"You were the guy," Frank said.

Looking at each other, squinting a little in the sunlight, they were both aware of the people passing them on the steps and could feel the Frank Murphy Hall of Justice rising above them with its big plate-glass windows. Stick said, "You got a place in mind?"

They walked down St. Antoine toward the river and over a side street through Greektown to the Club Bouzouki. Stick had never heard of the place or the drink Frank ordered once they were sitting at the bar. Ouzo. Frank said why didn't he try one; but Stick said he'd just as soon go with bourbon, it seemed to do the job. He looked around the place, a big, flashy bar, mirrors and paintings, a dance floor and bandstand, bartenders in red vests, but only a few customers in here at eleven thirty in the morning. It was dim and relaxing. Stick wasn't in a hurry. It was up to Frank; it was his party. He didn't seem to be in a hurry either. He sipped his milky-looking drink and said to Stick he ought to try it sometime. It tasted like paregoric, so it ought to be good for the stomach. Here he was, after six days in jail, sitting in a bar shooting the shit with the guy who'd put him in then gotten him out. Even though it didn't make sense, Stick wasn't going to rush it.

"You know, the whole thing was," Frank said, "I had a feeling you thought I was a cluck. I catch you dead nuts in the middle of the act, you don't even act nervous or anything."

"What was I supposed to do?" Stick said. "You walk up to me—you think I'm going to get out and run? I got the thing in *Drive*."

"I know, but it was what I felt. Like you're thinking I'm too dumb to do anything about it."

"I wasn't thinking so much of you as just getting out of there."

"See, I go to the show-up," Frank said, "and I'm still a little pissed off. So I identify you. As far as I know, the cops have you nailed down, so it doesn't make any difference. Then I find out I'm the only eyeball witness they got. Also I find out your name's Ernest."

"That's it," Stick said, "Ernest. But I didn't pick it."

"I started thinking about that old saying about being frank and earnest," Frank said. "You be frank and I'll be earnest."

Stick waited. "Yeah?"

"It seemed to fit."

"It seemed to fit what?"

"Also I learned a few things about your record, about doing time at Milan. You want a cigarette?"

"I got to buy some, I guess, if I'm going to keep smoking," Stick said.

Frank struck a match and held it for him. "Something I was wondering," he said. "If you got a gun. If you ever carried one."

"A gun?" Stick looked at him. "You don't need a gun to pick up a car. You don't *want* a gun."

"Well, I didn't know if that was all you did."

"I'll tell you something," Stick said, "since you'll probably ask me anyway. The other night—I hadn't picked up a car in over five years. That's a fact."

"But you picked up plenty before that, uh?"

"You could be a cop and I could give you places and dates, but it wouldn't do you any good. Time's run out."

"Well, you know I'm not a cop."

"That's about all I know," Stick said, "so I'll ask you a

question if it's okay. What're you besides a used-car sales-man and a sport that drinks a white Greek drink that looks like medicine?"

"I don't drink it all the time," Frank said. "Only when I come here."

"Is that your answer?"

"I'm not ducking the question. It's not so much what I am," Frank said, "as what I want to be."

"Yeah, and what's that?"

Frank hesitated, drawing on his cigarette, then took a sip of the milky-looking ouzo. "What do they call you? Ernie?"

"You call me that, I won't answer," Stick said. "No, I used to be Ernie, a long time ago. Still once in a while peo-ple call me Ernest. It's my name, I can't do anything about that. But usually they call me Stick. Friends, guys I work with."

"Because you stick up places?"

"Because of my name, Stickley, and I was skinny, like a stick in high school, when I was playing basketball."

"Yeah! I did, too," Frank said. "Was that down in Ok-lahoma you played?"

"Up here. I was born in Norman," Stick said, "but I guess you know that, uh?"

Frank nodded. "I don't detect much of an accent, though."

"I guess I lost most of what I had," Stick said, "moving around different places. We come up here, our family, my dad worked out at Rouge twenty-three years."

Frank seemed interested. "We got a lot in common. My old man worked at Ford Highland Park. I was born in Memphis, Tennessee, came to Detroit when I was four, and lived here, I guess, most of my life, except for three years I spent in LA."

"You married?" Stick asked him.

"Twice. And I got no intention right now of going for thirds. Let's get back," Frank said. "I want to ask you, you never stuck up a place? Used a gun?"

Stick waited a moment, like he was trying to see beyond the question, then shook his head. "Not my style. But since we're opening our souls, how about you?"

"Uh-unh, me neither," Frank said. "Well, years ago I was into a little burglary, B and E. Me and another guy, we didn't do too bad. But then he went into numbers or something—he was a black guy—so I quit before I got in too deep. In and out, you might say."

"You never used a gun during that time?"

"We didn't have to. We only went into places there wasn't anybody home."

"But now you got a sudden interest in guns, it seems."

"Not a sudden interest." Frank came around on his stool, giving it a quarter turn. "I've been studying the situation for some time now, ever since I got back from LA, reading up on all the different ways people break the law to make money. You know why most people get caught?"

"Because they're dumb."

"Right. Or they're desperate. Like a junkie."

"Stay away from junkies," Stick said. "Don't have any part of them."

Frank raised his eyebrows, impressed. "You believe that, uh?"

"It's the first rule of life," Stick said. He finished his drink, making sure he got it all, shaking the ice in the empty glass. "I'd buy a round," he said, "but I got eight bucks on me and it's got to last till I find out where I'm at."

Frank looked over at the bartender and made a circular motion for a couple of more. He said to Stick, "Don't worry about it. Listen, I was going to ask you what you had in mind. The cop I talked to said you were unemployed."

"Not in Florida. I can get all the work I want in Florida. Cement work. I was going back there to see my little girl."

"I understand you're divorced, too."

"Finally. Listen to this, you want to hear something? We're living in Florida, my wife starts bitching about the hot weather, how she doesn't see her old friends anymore, how her mom's driving her crazy? Her mom lives down there. Wonderful woman, old lady's never smiled in her life. She's watching television, that commercial used to be on a couple years ago about brotherhood, working together and all? It shows all these people standing in a field singing that song—I can't think of how it goes now. All these people singing, and in there you start to recognize some celebrities, Johnny Carson . . . lot of different ones. Her mom squints at the TV set and says, 'Is that niggers?' I'm taking her to the eye doctor's, the car radio's on. Every Friday I'd take her to the eye doctor's. She listens to this group playing some rock thing and says, 'Is that niggers?' We come back up here, sell this house we got that's right off the Intercoastal—come back, my wife's still bitching. Now it's the cold weather, busing, the colored situation, shit, you name it. We're arguing all the time, so finally we separate. Not legally, but we separate. Now what does she do? She goes back to Florida and moves in with her mom. Divorce was final last month."

"Listen, I believe it," Frank said. "Man, every word."

"I don't know what's going to happen there," Stick said, "but I like to see my little girl once in a while."

"Fortunately," Frank said, "neither of my wives had any children. Or any of my acquaintances, I mean that I know of."

Their drinks came and Frank stirred his, watching the clear liquid turn milky as it mixed with the ice cubes. Stick waited for whatever was next and Frank said, "It's funny you mentioned staying away from junkies as a *rule*. That's one of my rules. Don't have anything to do with them. Don't even go to a place where they're liable to hang out."

"You never get in trouble doing that," Stick said.

"I got some other rules, too," Frank said. "In fact, I've got ten rules. I mean, written down."

"What? How to live a happy life?"

"Sort of. How to be a success in a particular undertaking. Which could certainly lead to a happy life."

"You going to tell me," Stick said, "or I got to ask you what they are?"

The bartender rang up their tab and put it on the bar. Frank waited until he moved away.

"I told you I've been studying, well, different ways of making money. I'm not talking about anything tricky like embezzlement, you know, or checks. I've hung a little paper, not much, there's no excitement in it. Christ, it's like work. No, I'm talking about going out and picking up some dough. You know how many ways you can do that?"

"I don't know—auto theft, B and E, burglary, strongarm—" Stick paused. "There's probably a hundred ways. Some that haven't even been thought up yet."

"What you mentioned, you're talking about things you can take," Frank said. "Yes, cars, TVs, silverware, fur coats, household shit. But you got to convert it into money, right? You've got to sell it to somebody, and he knows you didn't get the stuff laying around your basement or out in the garage."

"It's unavoidable if you got to fence it."

"That's what I'm talking about," Frank said. "The

thing you do first, you eliminate the secondary party. You only take money. And money you can get rid of anywhere. Man, you spend it."

"So then you're into mugging, strong-arm, I mentioned that," Stick paused. "Bank robbery—is that what you want to do, rob a bank?"

Frank looked around and then at Stick again. "I'll tell you something. Nobody's going to rob banks as a career and get rich *and* stay out of jail. Not both. Not with the time locks, the alarm systems. The teller doesn't even have to press a button. You lift the money out of the drawer and a bell rings at the Holmes Protection Agency. They got the TV cameras. You pull a gun, you're on instant replay. The odds are lousy, less than fifty-fifty. Like the average take on a bank job in New York City last year was eleven thousand two. Not bad. But those are the guys that got away. Half the clowns didn't make it."

Frank paused to draw on his cigarette and take a drink. "Let me ask you something. What do you think pays the most? Wait a minute, let me rephrase it. What do you think is the fastest and, percentagewise, safest way to make the most money?"

"Not the horses," Stick said. "I used to spend weekends I wasn't working at Gulfstream or Hialeah."

"No, not the horses," Frank said patiently. "Think about it. What's the fastest and relatively safest way to do it?"

Stick was thoughtful. "Big payoff? Maybe kidnapping."

Frank was losing some of his patience. "Christ no, not kidnapping. FBI, you don't have a fucking chance kidnapping."

"Are we talking about something I never heard of?"

"You heard of it."

"All right," Stick said, "you tell me. What's the best way to make a lot of money fast? Without working, that is."

Frank held up the palm of his hand, his elbow on the edge of the bar. "You ready for this?"

"I'm ready."

"Armed robbery."

"Big fucking deal."

"Say it again," Frank said, "and put it in capital letters and underline it. Say it backwards, robbery comma armed. Yes, it can be a *very* big deal. Listen, last year there were twenty-three thousand and thirty-eight reported robberies in the city of Detroit. Reported. That's everything. B and E, muggings, banks, everything. Most of them pulled by dummies, junkies, and still a high percentage got away with it."

"Going in with a gun," Stick said, "is something else."

"You bet it is." Frank leaned in a little closer. "Ernie . . . Ernest—"

"Stick."

"Stick . . . I'm talking about simple everyday armed robbery. Supermarkets, bars, liquor stores, gas stations, that kind of place. Statistics show—man, I'm not just saying it, the *statistics* show—armed robbery pays the most for the least amount of risk. Now, you ready for this? I see how two guys who know what they're doing and 're businesslike about it"—he paused, grinning a little—"who're frank with each other and earnest about their work, can pull down three to five grand a week."

"You can also pull ten to a quarter in Jackson," Stick said.

"Listen," Frank said, his voice low and very serious, "I read a true story about two guys who actually did it. Two, three hits a week, they had to keep getting a bigger safe-deposit box. Lived well, I mean *well*, had all the clothes, broads they wanted, everything. It was written by this psychologist or sociologist, you know? who actually interviewed them."

"They told him anything he wanted to know?"

"They trusted him."

"Where was this, where he talked to them?"

"Well, at the time they were in Lucasville, Southern Ohio Correctional, but they went three and a half, four years straight, without ever being arrested. Oh, they were picked up a couple of times, on suspicion, but not for anything nailed down. See, any business will fail if you fuck up. I agree the end result is slightly different here. You don't just go broke, you're liable to give up a few years of your life, confined, you might say. But I don't see any reason to get caught. And that's where my ten rules for success and happiness come in. I see this strictly as a business venture. What I'm wondering now, if you're the business partner I'm looking for."

3

FRANK RYAN'S TEN RULES FOR success and happiness were written in blue ink on ten different cocktail napkins from the Club Bouzouki, the Lafayette Bar, Edjo's, and a place called The Lindell AC. Some of the rules, especially the last few, were on torn napkins with crossed-out words and were hard to read. The napkins said:

1. ALWAYS BE POLITE ON THE JOB. SAY PLEASE AND THANK YOU.
2. NEVER SAY MORE THAN IS NECESSARY.
3. NEVER CALL YOUR PARTNER BY NAME—UNLESS YOU USE A MADE-UP NAME.
4. DRESS WELL. NEVER LOOK SUSPICIOUS OR LIKE A BUM.
5. NEVER USE YOUR OWN CAR. (DETAILS TO COME.)
6. NEVER COUNT THE TAKE IN THE CAR.
7. NEVER FLASH MONEY IN A BAR OR WITH WOMEN.
8. NEVER GO BACK TO AN OLD BAR OR HANGOUT ONCE YOU HAVE MOVED UP.
9. NEVER TELL ANYONE YOUR BUSINESS. NEVER TELL A JUNKIE EVEN YOUR NAME.
10. NEVER ASSOCIATE WITH PEOPLE KNOWN TO BE IN CRIME.

The angle of the venetian blinds gave Stick enough outside light. He sat by the window in his striped undershorts, placing the cocktail napkins on his bare leg as he read them again, one by one, concentrating on making out some of the blotted words. He was smoking a Marlboro and taking sips from a can of Busch Bavarian that sat on the metal radiator cover beneath the window. He didn't look up until the groaning sound came from the bed and he knew Frank was awake.

"What's that noise?"

"Air conditioning," Stick said. "You want a beer?"

"Jesus Christ." Frank got up on an elbow, looking at the window, squinting. "What time is it?"

"About nine thirty. My watch's over on the TV." Stick took a swallow of beer as Frank got his feet on the floor and finally stood up. He was wearing jockey shorts and black socks.

"Where'd you sleep?"

"Right there in bed with you," Stick said, "but I swear I never touched you."

He waited until Frank went into the bathroom, then reached over and pulled the cord on the venetian blinds, raising them and flooding part of the room in morning sunlight. He wanted to get Frank's reaction when he came out and saw the bright pink walls.

He didn't notice them right away. When he came out, he said, "There's four cans of beer in the washbasin."

"Three for you and one for me," Stick said. "I've already had a couple."

Frank was looking at the pink walls now. "Jesus, where in the hell are we?"

"Zanzibar Motel. You're about a mile and a half from where you work. You can walk it if you want."

Frank stooped over a little, squinting, looking across the room at the sunlight filling the window. There wasn't much to see: empty asphalt pavement, and beyond that, a four-lane highway with a grass median, Telegraph Road. A few cars and a semi went past. They could hear them above the humming sound of the air conditioning.

"Where's my car?"

"You couldn't remember where you parked it."

Frank went into the bathroom and came out with a Busch.

"Then how'd we get here?"

"You remember looking for your car?"

"'Course I do." Frank took a drink of beer and let his breath out, feeling a little better.

"You lost your parking ticket," Stick said.

"I know, that's why I couldn't find the car. All those streets over there look alike. At night, shit, you can't tell."

"You remember trying to get that waitress to take her clothes off?"

Frank hesitated, then drank some more of the beer. "We had a pretty good time, didn't we?"

Stick said, "You remember standing in front of the J. L. Hudson Company, in the middle of Woodward Avenue, taking a leak?"

"I really had to go, didn't I?"

"Eileen sure got a kick out of that."

Frank looked at him. "Eileen, uh?"

"The one you picked up at the Lafayette Bar. Wasn't she a size?"

Frank managed to grin and shake his head. "Yeah, she sure was."

"I was surprised she didn't get sore, you started calling her Fatty."

"Just kidding around," Frank said. He went over to the dresser, opened his wallet, and fingered the bills inside. "Yeah, I guess we had a pretty good time." Looking at Stick he said, "I must have paid for the cab, uh?"

"Taxicab? We didn't take any cab anywhere."

"All right, you win," Frank said. "How'd we get here?"

"In a 1975 Mercury Montego." Stick watched Frank look toward the window again. "You remember we're standing in front of the Sheraton-Cadillac?"

Frank's expression began to open and show signs of life. "Yeah, they wouldn't let us in the bar because you didn't have a coat on."

"We're standing out in front," Stick said, "when the Merc pulls up and the guy gets out, looking around. You remember?"

Frank seemed happier as he began to recall it and could see the Mercury—dark brown, shiny—in front of the hotel and Stick walking over to the guy who got out, and now Frank was grinning. "Yeah, you went up to the guy and said something—"

"I said, 'Good evening, sir. Are you a guest at the hotel?'"

"Right. And he said he'd only be about an hour and handed you the keys."

"And a dollar tip," Stick said.

Frank was still grinning. "Sure, I remember it. Where's the car?"

"Up the street, in the Burger Chef parking lot. You go out, don't look at it. Don't even walk past it." Stick held up the ten cocktail napkins. "You remember these?"

"Sure I remember them. What do you keep asking me that for? I remember everything that happened." Frank took the napkins over to the dresser, spread them out, and stood there idly scratching his jockey shorts as he looked at them.

Stick watched him. After a moment he said, "I been reading your rules for success and happiness. And you know what?"

Frank kept scratching. "What?"

"I think you got an idea."

Frank looked over now. "Yeah? You think so, uh?"

"I think it might be worth looking into. It's a wild-ass idea—two guys who don't know shit going into the armed-robbery business. But you never know, do you?" He watched Frank go into the bathroom again and raised his voice. "I'm thinking maybe it's the way to make a stake. Be able to put a down payment on something that'll carry you. Instead of working all your life. That's what I been doing, working. What have I got? Eight bucks in my pants, nothing, not a cent in the bank."

"Working is for workingmen," Frank said, coming out with two cans of Busch. He walked over to Stick and handed him one, raising his own. "To our new business, uh? What do you say?"

"To the new business." Stick raised his beer and took a sip. "I'll tell you a secret, buddy, put your mind at rest."

Frank seemed interested. "What's that?"

"Last night, you didn't take a leak in the middle of Woodward Avenue."

"I didn't?"

"Uh-unh. I did."

First they had to find Frank's car, which wasn't actually his, it was a demo.

Frank called a friend of his at Red Bowers Chevrolet, a salesman, and got him to drive them downtown to look for it. On the freeway the friend kept asking, "But how can you lose a car? Not have it stolen, *lose* it. A car." Frank told him it could happen to anybody. Get turned around, forget exactly where you parked it. "See, this guy here had the ticket, with the address on it and everything, and he lost it." Stick didn't say anything. They found the car, paid six and a half to get it out, and Frank bought them a couple of drinks at the Greek place.

After the friend left, Frank said, while they were downtown, they might as well look up Sportree and see about the guns. Right?

Stick hesitated. This was the part he wasn't sure of.

"Look," Frank said, "you got to have a gun or it isn't armed robbery, is it? You don't have a gun, the guy says go fuck yourself and you're standing there, your hand in your pocket, pointing your finger at him."

"I'm not talking about the guns," Stick said. "I'm talking about the source." He'd been thinking about it and his idea was maybe they ought to run down to South Carolina or someplace.

"Buy them?" Frank said. "Fill out the papers? Registered in whose name, yours or mine?" No, Frank said, the only way to do it was to talk to Sportree, his old B and E associate.

Stick said how did they know they could trust this guy Sportree? Where was he getting the guns? Were they used before? Get caught with the goddamn piece and they check it and find it killed some colored guy the week before. "I never dealt with a colored guy," Stick said, "on anything important, and I don't know if I want to."

Frank told him to quit thinking about it. Sportree wasn't going to sell them the guns. All he'd do was set it up so they could put their hands on a couple of clean pieces. Once they found him.

Frank hadn't seen Sportree in a few years. When he tried to call, he got an operator who told him the number was no longer in service. Stick said why didn't he look in the phone book. Frank said, Jesus, that'd be like looking up Gracie's Whorehouse. Stick said why didn't he try it anyway.

That was how they found the listing for Sportree's Royal Lounge on West Eight Mile.

In the late afternoon and early evening Sportree's offered semidarkness and a sophisticated cocktail piano and was a spot for Southfield secretaries who worked in the new modern glass office buildings for companies that had moved out of downtown Detroit. They'd stop in after five and let guys buy them drinks. Or a secretary might come in with her boss, or with a salesman who called on her boss. A good-looking black girl with red hair and horn-rimmed glasses played cocktail Cole Porter from five to eight, getting the secretaries and the executives in the mood. Then she'd cover the piano keys and take her sheet music upstairs to the apartment over the Lounge.

Also at eight the two white bartenders, who had come on at noon, went off, and two black bartenders took over. By nine, the executives and the secretaries were out of there. By ten, the clientele was solid black and the cute redheaded piano player came down without her sheet music and played soul on and off until two A.M.

When Frank and Stick got there a little before seven, it was cocktail time and the secretaries were sitting around in the moody dimness with bosses or salesmen or waiting for live ones to come in. Walking in, Frank liked the place right away. He said, "Hey, yeah." A few of the girls looked up and gave them a quick reading, without showing any interest. Nothing. A guy who slept in his clothes and a garage mechanic off duty—probably what they thought. It bothered Frank. He felt seedy and needed a shave and imagined he had rotten breath. He wanted to go home and change, come back later. He wasn't disappointed at all when the bartender told them Sportree wouldn't be in till around ten.

They drove out to Stick's motel, the Zanzibar, picked up the ten cocktail napkins, the can of Busch Bavarian left over, and Stick's suitcase that looked like it had been through a lot of Greyhound bus stations and held nearly everything he owned. After that they went to Frank's apartment on Thirteen Mile in Royal Oak.

Frank told Stick to unpack and make himself comfortable while he took a shower. Stick looked around; it was a small place, one bedroom, not much. He didn't unpack but took a pale-green sport coat out of the suitcase and draped it over the back of a chair. He wondered if Frank had an iron. Probably not, the place was pretty bare, a few magazines lying around and ashtrays that hadn't been emptied. The place didn't look lived in; it looked like a waiting room in a hospital.

Frank put on a clean shirt, a dark-blue shiny suit, and asked Stick if he was going to change.

"I already did," Stick said, "this morning." He had on a faded blue work shirt.

Frank looked at the sport coat on the chair. "I guess you couldn't wear it anyway till you had it cleaned."

"I haven't worn it in a month," Stick said. "What do I need to get it cleaned for?"

"I mean pressed," Frank said. "Let's get out of here."

They stopped for something to eat and got back to Sportree's a little after ten.

As soon as they were inside the door, Stick said, "What's going on?" He kept his voice low. "What the fuck is going *on*?"

He followed Frank over to an open space at the bar, seeing the young black guys with their hats and hairdos turning to look at them.

Frank said to the bartender, "Bourbon and a Scotch, please. Splash of water."

He looked over his shoulder at the tables. There wasn't another white person in the place. The light was off where the redheaded black girl had been playing the piano. The heavy chugging beat of West Indian reggae was coming from a hi-fi. The place seemed darker.

Frank waited for the bartender to put their drinks down. He said, "Where's Sportree? Tell him Frank Ryan. He knows me."

The bartender looked at him, didn't say a word, and moved away.

Stick said, "What's going on?"

"I got an idea," Frank said. "I don't know, but I got an idea."

When Sportree approached a few minutes later, Frank saw him coming in the mirror behind the bar. He looked over his shoulder at Sportree, at his open body shirt and double string of Ashanti trading beads, and said, "Where you going, to a drag party?"

Frank could feel the people near them watching, and felt good seeing the warm, amused expression in the man's eyes. He hadn't changed; he still knew who he was, in control. A good-looking, no-age black man with straightened long hair glistening across his forehead, a full, curled-down moustache, a little bebop growth beneath his lower lip, and liquid, slow-moving eyes.

Sportree said, very quietly, "Frank, how you doing? It's been awhile."

Frank said, "I'd like you to meet my business associate,

Ernest Stickley, Jr., man, if you can dig the name. Stick Stickley. And this is Sportree in the Zulu outfit, in case anybody doesn't know he's a jig."

Sportree didn't change his expression. He said, "You come down to learn some new words? Don't know whether you're Elvis Presley or a downtown white nigger, do you?"

"Well, you know," Frank said, "it's hard to keep up with all that jive shit living with honkies. Actually what we're looking for is a cleaning lady."

Sportree's expression held, then began to relax more, and he almost smiled. "A cleaning lady. Yeah, why don't we go upstairs, be comfortable? Talk about it."

They went outside to the entrance and up a flight of stairs to the apartment over the Lounge. The good-looking young black girl with red hair was sitting on the couch smoking a homemade cigarette. Sportree said, "A bourbon and a Scotch, little water." Stick could smell the cigarette. He watched the girl get up without a word and go into the kitchen: little ninety-six-pounder in a white halter top and white pants.

As they sat down Sportree said, "You all want to smoke?"

Frank said, "Hey, don't start my partner on any bad habits. He's straight and I want to keep him that way."

Stick didn't say anything. He listened to Frank ask the black guy how the numbers business was, and the black said numbers, numbers was for little children. He was in the saloon business now. You mean in front, Frank said, with a pharmacy in the rear. The black guy said well, maybe a little coke and hash, some African speed, but no skag, uh-unh, he wouldn't deal shit to a man he found in bed with his lady.

The redheaded black girl brought the drinks in and left the room again, still without a word or change of expression.

Stick listened to Frank talking about the car business, LA, smog, traffic on the Hollywood Freeway, how he'd worked in a bar in North Hollywood, screwed a starlet once, and finally, after thinking awhile, remembering the name of the picture she was murdered in, which Stick and the black guy had never heard of. Stick went out to the kitchen and made himself another drink. The redheaded black girl sitting at the table reading *Cosmopolitan* didn't look up. He went back into the living room, which reminded him of a Miami Beach hotel, waited until Frank got through saying no, he wasn't in jail out there, and said, "You having a nice visit?"

Frank gave him a deadpan look. "Why, you in a hurry?"

"I thought we were looking for a cleaning lady."

Sportree was watching them both with his lazy, amused expression. He said, "Yeah, I believe somebody mentioned that." His eyes held on Frank. "Your business associate know what he's doing?"

"Cars," Frank said. "He's very good with cars. Many, many years at it, one conviction."

"If that's your pleasure, what you need with a cleaning lady?"

"That's his credentials. I'm saying we're all friends," Frank said. "Kindred spirits. Birds of a feather."

"Man," Sportree said, "you do need some new words."

"I'll take a side order," Frank said, "but for the entree how about a nice cleaning lady with big brown eyes?"

"You going back in the business? It's hard work, man. For young, strong boys with a habit."

Frank shook his head. "No, we got something else in mind. But first we got to locate a couple of items."

"Like what items we talking about?"

"Well, what this cleaning lady should look for are, you know, color TVs—"

"Yeah."

"Fur coats."

"Yeah."

"Watches. Jewelry."

"Go on."

"Silverware maybe, you know, silver stuff. And firearms."

Sportree grinned. "You almost forgot to mention that. Any particular firearms you got in mind?"

"Well, like the kind you might find in the guy's top drawer," Frank said. "Underneath his jockeys."

"No hunting rifles, anything like that."

"No, I had more in mind the smaller models you can hold in one hand."

"Put in your pocket, or in your belt."

"Yeah, that kind."

"You remember my cousin LaGreta?"

"That's right, your cousin."

"She used to have big eyes. I can talk to her," Sportree said. "Seems to me the rate was twenty bucks a house. I mean a house, you know, there's goods in it. She give you the plan, where everything is, twenty bucks."

"That's fine," Frank said. "Twenty dollars, if that's the going rate, fine."

"She's with this Rent-A-Maid and also a catering service," Sportree said. "Work parties, weddings, you understand? and does some cleaning jobs, too. She don't do floors, though. I remember her saying she don't do floors."

"Long as she gets in the house," Frank said, "I don't care what the fuck she does in there."

"Nice thing," Sportree said, "she gets around. You know, doesn't work for the same people all the time. That wouldn't be so good."

"Listen, that sounds fine," Frank said. "In fact it's exactly what we're looking for. If LaGreta's got the eyes you say she has."

"Nice big eyes," Sportree said.

"Can I ask you if she's on anything?"

"She smoke a little, that's all. Vacuum that big house, clean the oven, polish the furniture, she like to visit friends and have a little something. But what she make you know, she ain't on any hard shit."

"You think you can set it up?"

"I'll talk to her. You give me your telephone number."

Frank hesitated. "I better call you. We're in and out a lot. Maybe we're not there when you call."

Sportree said, "Frank, I hope you still the same person I used to be associated with." His gaze moved to Stick. "Just as I hope your friend here is pure."

"I'll tell you something," Stick said to him. "I enjoyed the drinks, but I don't know a rat's ass about you either, do I?"

It was the quiet way he said it that jolted Frank. He couldn't believe it—the first time Stick even opened his mouth. Frank said, "Hey, let's not have any misunderstandings," and looked over at Sportree.

"It's all right," Sportree said, his tone a little cooler than before. "You call me in a couple of days. Maybe I'll have something for you, maybe I won't."

When they were outside Frank said, "What're you trying to prove? The guy's doing us a favor, you come on like you're some dangerous character."

"All I said was I didn't know him very well."

"But I do." Frank was tense. "I've known him a hell of a lot longer'n I've known you. You don't like the way I'm handling it, go back working cement, maybe I'll see you around."

"You're handling it," Stick said. "You made up the rules. It seems to me one of them, it says don't even tell a junkie your name. The first guy we talk to, it happens, runs a dope store."

"You don't know anything about him."

They got in the car and drove off and didn't say anything for a while, each feeling the other's presence. Finally Frank said, "Listen, this is kind of dumb. We got something going or we haven't. We don't blow it over a few words."

"I'll tell you the truth," Stick said, "I thought the guy was all right. I probably wasn't talking so much to him as I was to you."

Frank looked over. "I don't follow you."

"There you are," Stick said. "And I don't follow you around either, you say go pee-pee, I do it. You don't say to the guy I don't want a smoke. If I don't want it, I tell him."

Frank glanced away from the windshield again. "Is that all that's bothering you?"

"That's all," Stick said. "I thought I might as well mention it."

4

THEY SPENT THE WEEKEND ON a slow tour of some of Detroit's industrial suburbs on the northeast side—Clawson, Madison Heights, Warren, Roseville—Stick driving. Frank taking notes, writing down the names and locations of bars, supermarkets, liquor stores, with a few words to describe the traffic and the fastest way out of each area. There was a liquor store in Warren that Frank especially liked and said maybe ought to be the first one. The liquor store was on a four-lane industrial street that was lined with machine and sheet-metal shops, automotive supply houses. Hit the place on a Friday, payday. How'd that sound? Stick said if they were going to start, the liquor store was probably as good a place as any.

Monday, Frank went back to Red Bowers Chevrolet and told the sales manager he was leaving the end of the week. The sales manager didn't seem too upset about it. Frank looked around the used-car lot and gave himself a good deal on a tan '72 Plymouth Duster that needed a ring job and some transmission work. If they had any luck at all, they wouldn't have the car very long.

After he got home he drove Stick around downtown Royal Oak until Stick spotted Al's Plumbing & Heating on South Main and said, "There. I think I like that one." He liked the way they parked the panel trucks behind the building with no fence or spotlight to worry about.

Tuesday, Stick took his green sport coat to the cleaner's, then stopped at an auto parts store and had some clips made for shorting and hooking up electric wires. The guy at the place didn't ask him any questions. He bowled and drank beer most of the afternoon, rolling a one eighty-six he felt pretty good about.

Wednesday, Frank called Sportree, who told them to come down, he had something they might like.

What it was: a sheet of Ace tablet paper, lined, with the addresses of two homes in Bloomfield Hills and a list of the goods they'd find in each place. The words looked like they'd been written by a child, in pencil, but that was all right. They could read the words without any trouble. Especially the one that said GUNS.

"This one place, LaGreta say the man's got a gun collection in his recreation room, down in the basement," Sportree explained. "The whole family's out to the lake for the summer. Sometime the man stop off home, but usually he drive out there from his work. How's that sound to you for forty dollars? Whole mother collection to pick from."

Thursday night, they went to a ten o'clock show in Royal Oak, watched Clint Eastwood kill some people, and at twelve walked out of the movie theater, across the street, and down two blocks to Al's Plumbing & Heating. Frank waited on the corner while Stick went around the back. A few minutes later a panel truck with Al's name on the side stopped at the corner and Frank got in.

"That was pretty quick."

"It used to take me less than a minute," Stick said, "but with these newer models, I got to figure things out."

"You jump the wires?"

"Not under the hood." Stick patted the dashboard.

"All the work's done underneath here. You look, you see some clips I had made."

Driving out to the gun collector's house in Bloomfield Hills, he told Frank what he used to do when he spotted a certain car he liked that had the dealer's name on it. Get the serial number off the car, then go to the dealer and tell them you lost the key and have one made. Simple.

They found the address and Stick pulled into the side drive of the big Colonial.

It was Frank's turn now. "They all do the same thing," he said, "leave two lights on downstairs and one up, and you're supposed to think somebody's home."

Stick sat in the truck while Frank rang the bell at the side door and waited. He rang it again and waited almost a minute before he broke a pane of glass in the door, reached in, and unlocked it. Stick got out of the truck and went inside, down a hallway past the kitchen to the family room, where a lamp was on. Frank was looking at the TV set, a big Motorola that was like a piece of furniture.

"What do you think!" Frank said. "Use the top for a bar, get rid of that little black-and-white I got. Except it's a big mother, isn't it?" He looked at Stick. "You think we can handle it?"

"If I remember right," Stick said, "we come here for guns."

There was a locked cabinet full of them down in the recreation room. Three rifles, three shotguns, and an assortment of handguns: several new-looking revolvers, a couple of Lugers, a Japanese automatic, and a Frontier model Colt .44, the kind Clint Eastwood had carried in the movie.

Stick had a feeling Frank would pick it up first. He did—pulled the hammer back and sighted and clicked the trigger, then hefted it in his hand, feeling the weight and looking at it from different angles. Frank held the Colt .44 against his hip, then threw it out in front of him and did it again.

"Fastest gun in Royal Oak," Stick said. "You know how to shoot?"

"Pull the trigger," Frank said. "Isn't that what you do?"

Stick considered a P-38 Walther, it looked pretty good, but chose a Smith & Wesson .38 Chief's Special with a two-inch barrel. After Frank finished fooling around, he picked a big Colt Python 357 with a ventilated rib over its six-inch barrel. They found boxes of cartridges for both revolvers and got out of there.

The next day, Friday, Frank bought the Deluxe Anniversary Edition of *Gun Digest* and read off the vital statistics of the two revolvers, his forty-seven-ounce number and Stick's stubby little fourteen-ouncer. The Colt Python listed for a hundred and ninety-nine dollars and ninety-five cents new. Stick's little Smith only cost ninety-six. Stick said, "But I don't have to carry four pounds of metal around in my pants, do I?"

At noon Frank reported in at Red Bowers Chevrolet for the last time, sold two late-model used cars and made eighty-six bucks in commission. A good sign, everything was working. Stick got his sport coat from the cleaner's and had it on with a starched white shirt and a green-and-yellow-print tie when Frank got home. Frank didn't say anything about the coat or the tie. He changed and they each had a couple of drinks. At six thirty they couldn't think of anything else they had to do, so they went out to hold up the liquor store.

Stick got a car from a movie theater parking lot in Warren, a '74 Olds Cutlass Supreme, drove it up the street to where Frank was waiting in the Duster, and picked him up. Frank asked if he had any trouble and Stick said, "What'd it take me, two minutes?"

Frank felt pretty good, anxious and a little excited, until they were approaching the liquor store. Then he wasn't sure. They came even with the building that was in a block of storefronts. There was plenty of parking space. Stick slowed down but kept going, his eyes on the rearview mirror.

"I wanted to look at it again," Stick said.

They went around the block, past vacant lots and plant-equipment yards.

"What we have to consider," Frank said, "what if we don't get much? Like fifty, sixty bucks, something like that. The guy could have most of his dough locked up somewhere, hidden. Then what do you do, he refuses to tell you where it is, shoot him?"

Stick was looking around. His eyes kept going to the rearview mirror. "Or try another place," he said. "There's plenty around."

"What I mean is," Frank said, "maybe it's more trouble than it's worth. Nobody's forcing us. We go in a place because we want to. We try it or we don't. What're we out? Nothing. We could sell the guns. Maybe even the car, dump it off on somebody."

They were on the four-lane street again, with very little traffic going either way. A quiet, daylight-saving-time early evening in the summer. A car pulled away from the liquor store, leaving the curb empty for at least sixty feet.

"Well," Frank said, "what do you think?"

Stick swung the Olds in to the curb. "What do I think about what?" he said. "Let's do it."

He pulled up a little past the store entrance and put the

lever in Park, then accelerated to make sure the engine was idling.

As Stick opened his door, Frank said, "What's Rule Number One?"

Stick paused. "Always be polite. Say please and thank you."

Frank said, "You know, when I worked at the dealership a man came in to teach us how to sell cars over the phone. Call up people, find out if they're in the market. He says to me, 'What's your name?' I tell him Frank Ryan. He says, 'No, it's not.' He says, 'Not over the phone. You call a prospect, you say, "Hi, I'm Frank Duffy of Red Bowers Chevrolet." Duff-*ee*. You always use a name that ends in *y* or *i-e*. Because when you say it you got a smile on your face.'"

Stick waited, staring at Frank for a moment before he got out of the car.

The counter and shelves of liquor ran along the left wall. Down the middle of the store were wine bins and displays of party supplies. Along the right-hand wall the beer and soft drinks were in coolers with sliding glass doors. Two guys were standing over there.

Frank and Stick walked up to the liquor counter. The guy behind it was about sixty but big, over two hundred, with tight curly gray hair. He laid his cigarette in a chrome ashtray and said, "Can I help you?"

Frank wanted to look around, but he didn't. He hesitated and said, "Yes sir, you can," unbuttoned his suit coat, took out the Colt Python, and rested the butt on the counter so that the gun was pointing directly at the man's wide expanse of stomach. The man closed and opened his eyes and seemed tired.

"You can empty your cash register," Frank said.

"But sir? I see anything in your hand's not green and made of paper, I'll blow you right through the fucking wall."

It was happening. Frank watched the guy punch open the cash register without a word. Maybe it had happened to him before. He held the gun on him and his hand was steady. He motioned with his head then.

Stick walked around the rack of potato chips and Fritos to the two guys standing by the beer cooler. They were hunched over, trying to decide, one of them reaching in then for a six-pack of Stroh's.

Opening his sport coat, Stick said, "Excuse me, gents." When they looked at him he said, "You see what I got here?" They didn't right away, until they saw he was holding his coat open.

The one with the six-pack said, "Jesus," and dropped it on the floor. Stick kept himself from jumping back.

The other one didn't say a word, his eyes on the butt of the .38 Special sticking out of the waistband.

"You don't want to get hurt," Stick said, "and I certainly don't want to hurt you. So let's march to the rear, see what's in back."

Past the potato-chip rack he could see Frank holding open a paper bag and the man behind the counter dropping bills into it.

There was a young clerk in the storeroom, sitting on a stack of beer cases holding a sandwich and eating from a half-pint container of coleslaw. He looked surprised to see three men coming in, but he was also polite. He said, "Can I help you?"

Stick spotted the big walk-in reefer and said, "No thanks, I guess I can handle it myself."

He walked over, opened the door to the refrigerator, and nodded for the two customers to go inside.

The clerk said, "Hey, you can't go in there. What do you want?"

"You, too," Stick said. He held open his coat again. "Okay?"

When he came out into the store he thought the place was empty and got an awful feeling in his stomach for a moment. Then, near the cash register, Frank rose up from behind the counter with the paper bag.

As he came over the counter, the bag in one hand—the top of it rolled tightly closed—and the Python in the other, Stick said, "Where's the guy?"

"On the floor." Frank looked over the counter and said, "Stay down there, if you will please. Because if you raise up too soon, if you see me again, then I'll see you, won't I? And if I see you again, I won't hesitate to shoot and probably kill you."

Stick said, "Tell him the other people're in the icebox."

"You hear that, sir?" Frank looked over the counter again. "In the icebox."

"Tell him much obliged," Stick said.

"Yeah, much obliged. Maybe we'll see you again some-time."

Neither one of them wanted to look anxious. They walked out, taking their time.

In the car Stick put the gear into Drive and waited, looking at the rearview mirror, until he saw the big guy with the gray curly hair appear suddenly in the doorway and stop dead. Stick got out of there then, tires squealing as he peeled away from the curb.

Frank turned around to look straight ahead again. "He saw the car, I'm sure. Maybe even the license."

"You bet he did," Stick said. "Now I drop you off at your car, head back to the picture show, and you pick me up there."

"It seems like a lot of trouble," Frank said.

"Yes, it does," Stick said. "But it sure keeps the police busy, looking for a '74 Cutlass Supreme, doesn't it? How much we get?"

Frank held the bag on his lap, the top tightly folded. "Rule Number Six," he said.

As soon as they were in the apartment Stick took off his sport coat. He was sweating. The Duster didn't have air conditioning. He looked at Frank, who was sitting on the couch lighting a cigarette like he had his lunch in the bag and there wasn't any hurry getting to it.

Stick said, "You going to count it or you want me to?"

"Why don't you make us a couple of drinks?" Frank said.

Stick went out to the kitchen. He poured Scotch in one glass and bourbon in another, then got a tray out of the refrigerator and began filling the glasses with ice. It was all right that Frank counted it, but he wanted to watch, at least. He put a splash of water on the drinks and went back out to the living room.

"I don't believe it," Frank said.

He was hunched over the coffee table, looking down at the neatly stacked piles of bills, like a guy playing solitaire. He laid a twenty on one pile, a fifty on another. As Stick approached he was peeling off tens from the wad he held in his hand.

"Jesus," Stick said. "How much?"

"Don't talk, I'll have to start over."

Stick put the drinks down carefully, got a cigarette and lit it and walked over to the window that looked out on the parking area behind the building. It was quiet back there, sunlight on the cars and long shadows, the end of

the day. The cars looked hot. The tan Duster without air
conditioning was parked there. A VW and a Pinto wagon
and a Chevy pickup and a bike, a big Harley that made a
racket every morning at seven fifteen—

"All right, how much you think?"

Stick turned from the window. "Why don't you
tell me?"

Frank was sitting back with the Scotch in his hand, all
the bills stacked in front of him, now in five neat piles.

"How about six grand?" Frank said. "How about six
thousand two hundred and forty-eight fucking dollars,
man? Tax free."

Stick came over to the table and stared at the money.

"Six, comma, two four eight," Frank said. "Most of it
was in a box under the counter."

"Jesus, what a business," Stick said. "One day he
makes that much?"

"You mean one day *we* make that much. No, what it
is," Frank said, "the guy cashes paychecks."

"Yeah?"

"See, to get the hourly guys to come in, working in the
shops. So he's got to have a lot of cash on hand payday.
Keeps it in the box with the checks he cashes, from all different companies around there."

Stick looked up at him. "Endorsed? I mean the checks
were signed?"

"I thought of that," Frank said, "but I figure it's not
worth all the trouble, unless you know somebody likes to
buy checks."

"Yeah, I guess so," Stick said. "Then you're dealing
with somebody else."

"I figure we hit him earlier, we could've gotten even
more. You know? Around three thirty or so, before the
first-shift guys start coming in."

"You complaining?" Stick said. "First time, Christ. I don't believe it."

Frank started to grin. "Guy took one look at the Python—you see him?—I thought he was going to shit. I say to him, very polite, 'You can empty the cash register, sir. But I see anything in your hand isn't green or made of paper, I'm going to blow you right through the fucking wall.'"

Stick was grinning, too, shaking his head. He said, "I gave the two guys over by the beer cooler a flash of the Smith. I didn't take it out, I just showed it to them. I said, 'Hey, fellas, you see what I got here?' Just the grip sticking out. The guy drops his six-pack. The fella out in back's eating his lunch. He says, 'Can I help you?'"

"We're home counting our wages," Frank said, "they're still looking for the car. Or they got it staked out. The guy comes out of the show and they bust him."

"It's the only way to do it," Stick said. "Takes a little longer, but you keep your car clean, off the sheet. Yeah, it's a very good rule. In fact, that told me right away you had it pretty well thought out."

"You think it's worth it then, uh, all the trouble?"

"What trouble?"

"That's the way I see it," Frank said. "If they're all this easy, I believe we found our calling."

5

FRANK WOULD STAND AT THE bar in the living room with one leg over a bamboo stool, pick up his Scotch, and say, "Well, here we are."

Stick would say, "You sure?"

And Frank would say, "You look out and see if the broads are still there. I'll go count the suits."

It was a ritual after three months in the business and twenty-five armed robberies—after they'd bought the clothes and the new car and moved into the apartment building where nearly half the occupants were single young ladies. Frank liked to strike his pose at the bar and say, "Well, here we are."

During the first few weeks, when they were still in the small, one-bedroom place, he'd say, "You believe it?" He'd finish laying out the stacks of bills on the coffee table, look up at Stick, and say, "You believe it? They're sitting out there waiting for us. Like they want to get held up, dying for it." Going in, Frank had told himself over and over it would be easy—if they observed the rules and didn't take chances—but he never thought it would be this easy.

After the first few weeks he began to take it in stride. They were pros, that's why it was easy. They knew exactly what they were doing. Look at the record: twenty-five armed robberies, twenty-five stolen cars, more money coming in than they could spend, and they had yet to get on a police sheet, even as suspects.

Frank would say, "Partner, what do you want? Come on, anything. You want it, buy it."

Frank didn't waste any time getting five new suits, a couple of sport outfits, slacks, shirts, and a safari jacket. Stick bought a suit, a sport coat, and three pairs of off-the-shelf pants for sixteen dollars each, studied the pants in the mirror—clown pants, they looked like—and had the store cut off the big bell-bottom cuffs before he'd buy them. They traded the Duster in on a white '75 Thunderbird with white velour upholstery, air, power everything, and went looking for a bigger apartment.

The third place they looked at was the Villa Monterey, out in Troy: a cream-colored stucco building with dark wood trim, a dark wood railing along the second-floor walk, a Spanish tile roof, and a balcony with each apartment overlooking the backyard where shrubbery and a stockade fence enclosed the patio and swimming pool. There was also an ice machine back there, a good sign.

Stick said he thought it looked like a motel. Frank said no, it was authentic California. He told the manager, the lady who showed them the apartment, okay, gave her the deposit and three months in advance to get out of signing a lease, and that was it. They got two bedrooms, bath, bar in the living room with bamboo stools, orange-and-yellow draperies, off-white shag carpeting, off-white walls with chrome-framed graphics, chrome gooseneck lamps, chrome-and-canvas chairs, an off-white Naugahyde sectional sofa, and three dying plants for four and a half a month, furnished. Stick didn't tell Frank but he thought the place looked like a beauty parlor.

The first Saturday they were in, Frank went out on the balcony. He looked down at the swimming pool and said,

"Holy shit." He said it again, reverently, "Holy shit. Come here and look."

There were five of them lying around the pool in their skimpy little two-piece outfits. Nice-looking girls, none of them likely to be offered a screen test—except one, who turned out to be a photographer's model—but all of them better than average, and they were right there, handy. Frank and Stick went to the pool just about every afternoon they weren't working—Frank in a tank suit with his stomach sucked in, and Stick in a new pair of bright blue trunks—and got to know the regulars pretty well. Frank called them the career ladies.

There was a nurse, Mary Kay something, an RN who worked nights on the psychiatric floor at Beaumont Hospital. Dark hair, very clean looking. Also very skinny, but with wide hips. A generous pelvic region, Frank said. Mary Kay was a possible. Stick said, Maybe, if you looked sincere and told her you loved her.

There was a redheaded girl, frizzy red hair and bright brown eyes, who wore beads and seven rings with her bikini. Arlene. She was a little wacky and laughed at almost everything they said, whether it was supposed to be funny or not. Somebody was paying Arlene's rent, a guy in a silver Mark IV who came twice a week, Tuesday and Thursday, at six, and was usually out by ten thirty. Arlene said he was a good friend.

There were several Jewish career ladies. Frank was glad to see that. He told Stick he liked good-looking Jewish girls because they had a lot of hair, big tits, and usually pretty nice noses once they had them fixed. He told Stick he'd been out with plenty of Jewish girls, including the little starlet in LA. Stick said he wasn't sure if he ever had. He asked Frank if it was all right to mention the word *Jew* in front of them or refer to them as being Jewish in any way. Frank said, "You dumb shit, that's what they *are*. Don't you think they know it?"

There was a schoolteacher named Karen who didn't talk or look like a schoolteacher. Stick didn't think she looked Jewish either. Karen said some funny things about her sixth-graders being sex-crazed and how the little girls stuck out their training bras for the horny little boys. Frank started taking Karen out and sometimes he spent the night at her apartment. Stick didn't think she seemed too impressed with Frank, though. She was off all summer with nothing to do.

There was a dental hygienist by the name of Donna who had a boyfriend but wasn't going to marry him until he made as much as she did. She told them how much a dentist with a good practice could make and referred to net and gross a lot. Donna was way down at the bottom of Frank's list of things to do.

Sonny, the photographer's model, was the winner of the group. But she was unresponsive to drink offers. She seldom came up to their apartment with the others. She'd lie there behind her big sunglasses and hardly ever laugh when they said something funny. Frank said she was battery-operated. You pressed a little button on her can and she'd say, "Hi, I'm Sonny. I'm a model. So fuck off."

Stick noticed that Frank watched her, studied her, more than he did the others. Sonny was the only one Frank had trouble talking to.

There was a girl in the next apartment—a career lady but not one of the group—who they found out was a pro. Stick called her Mona because sometimes, through the wall, he'd hear her in there with a guy, saying things to him and moaning like she was about to die it was so good. Frank called her what's-her-name. He was polite to her but not interested. He said a guy would be out of his mind to pay for it at the Villa Monterey. Stick never mentioned it to Frank, but he liked her. He liked her straight dark hair parted in the middle. He liked the calm expression in her eyes and the quiet way she talked, though she never said very much. She was fragile-looking, a thin little thing with bony shoulders sticking out of her sleeveless blouse. When he'd see her outside he couldn't believe she was the same girl he'd hear moaning and carrying on through the wall. Maybe sometime, when Frank wasn't around, he'd get talking to her in private and find out which one was the real Mona.

They both liked the cocktail waitress, Jackie, who worked at a place called The Ball Joint and wore a kitty outfit with little ears and a tail. Jackie wasn't the smartest girl there, but she was very friendly. Also she had the biggest pair at the Villa Monterey, even when they weren't pushed up by her kitty outfit. She showed the group one time, in her bikini, how she placed drinks on a table, bending her knees and keeping her body straight so they wouldn't fall out. Frank said if they ever did and hit some-body, they'd kill him. Jackie worked nights and usually didn't drink in the afternoon, but was liable to bang on their door when she got home, two thirty in the morning, if she saw a light on and heard the hi-fi playing. It wasn't unusual.

Their apartment had become a little social center, with the best-stocked bar in the building. Frank started it, inviting people up, especially on weekends. After a while they could count on people dropping in whenever there was a sign of something going on.

There'd be a good selection of career ladies.

There might even be some of the young married set. Frank would lure them away from their cookouts with Chivas Regal and talk about car prices and inflation with the husbands while he appraised the cute little house-wives.

There might be two or three young single guys, somebody's date, and Barry Kleiman for sure. The career ladies called Barry the Prince. Stick thought because he looked like Prince Valiant with his hair, but that wasn't the reason. Barry was successful, owned a McDonald's franchise, wore bright-colored sport outfits with a white plastic belt and white patent-leather loafers, and was only about twenty pounds overweight. Barry would stand with his elbows tucked in close and his wrists limp and say, "Listen, when I was a kid, the neighborhood I grew up in? It was so dirty I'd sit out in the sun for two hours and get a nice stain." Then he'd wait for their reaction with an innocent, wide-eyed expression. Karen said he used to do Jerry Lewis imitations.

"Not a bad guy," Frank said. "He could be a pain in the ass, you know? But he's not a bad guy."

"You go for Barry, you must really like the place," Stick said.

Frank seemed surprised. "Yeah, I like it. You don't?"

"It's all right, I guess."

"All *right*? You ever had it like this, pouring cement?"

No, he'd never lived in a place with a swimming pool and had a party going most of the week with two guns in the closet and fifteen hundred bucks in an Oxydol box under the sink. It was funny, he never had.

When Frank recited his line—"Well, here we are"— instead of saying, "Are you sure?" he should say, "Where, Frank? Where exactly are we? And for how long?"

It was like getting excited and moving to Florida and having the Atlantic Ocean down the street and palm trees and a nice tan all year and wondering. Now what? Sitting in a marina bar, watching gulls diving at the waves and seeing the charter boats out by the horizon, it didn't make the beer taste better. He'd tell himself this was the life and go home and have to take a nap before supper.

He wondered if he missed working, putting in a nine-ten-hour day driving the big transit mix and pouring the footings for the condominiums that would someday wall out the ocean from Key West to Jacksonville Beach. There was plenty of work down there. It was on his mind a lot and he wasn't sure why, because the thought of going back to hauling cement bored the shit out of him.

He'd say to himself, What do you want to do more than anything?

Go see his little girl.

All right, but what do you want to do with your *life*?

He'd think about it awhile and picture things.

He didn't see himself owning a cement company or a chicken farm or a restaurant. He never thought much about owning things, having a big house and a powerboat. He didn't care one way or the other about clothes. He'd never been much of a tourist. The travel brochures made it look good and he could see himself under a thatched roof with a big rum drink and some colored guys banging on oil drums, but he'd end up thinking. Then what do you do? Go in and get dressed up and eat the American Plan dinner and listen to the fag with the hairpiece play his cocktail piano and get bombed for no reason and go to bed and get up and do it over again the next day. He could picture a girl with him, on the beach, under the thatched roof. A nice-looking, quiet girl. Not his ex-wife. He never pictured his ex-wife with him and he never pictured the girl as his wife.

Maybe, Stick told himself, this was the kind of life he always wanted but never realized it before. Hold up one or two places a week, make more money than he could spend, and live in a thirty-unit L-shaped authentic California apartment building that had a private swimming pool and patio in the crotch of the L and was full of career ladies laying around waiting for it.

It sounded good.

Didn't it?

Yeah, Stick guessed it did.

6

THEY LIKED SUPERMARKETS. GET A polite manager who was scared shitless and not more than a few people in the store, that was the ideal situation, worth three or four gas stations even on a bad day. The only trouble with supermarkets, they were big. You never knew who might be down an aisle somewhere.

They hit the Kroger store in West Bloomfield early Saturday morning.

It looked good. No customers yet. The checkout counters were empty. The only person they saw was a stockboy stamping prices on canned goods. Stick asked him for the manager, saying he'd been called about a check that'd bounced and he wanted to cover it. He followed the boy to the back and waited, holding the swinging door open, seeing the manager back there talking to a Budweiser deliveryman and a few of the checkout girls drinking coffee. When the manager and the stockboy came out, Stick let the door swing closed. And when the manager said, "May I have your name, please?" Stick said, "No sir," taking the Smith from inside his jacket, "but you can give me your money."

The manager said, "Oh my God," and the three of them paraded up to the front where Frank was waiting. Frank got the cash register key from the manager and headed for the checkout counters. Stick and the manager and the stockboy went into the cashier's enclosure, Stick bringing a Kroger bag with him.

The manager kept saying, "Oh my God." He told Stick he'd only been manager here one week. Stick said well, he was getting good experience, wasn't he? The stockboy was a heavy-boned, rangy kid who kept staring at him, making him nervous, until Stick told him to lay on the floor, facedown. He told the manager to clean out the cash drawer and open the safe. The manager had to get a piece of paper out of his wallet with the combination written on it, then kept missing numbers as he turned the dial and would have to start over again; but finally he got it open and pulled out a trayful of bills and personal checks. When he started to count the bills, Stick told him never mind, he'd do it later. The manager thanked him.

"What about these?" the manager said, picking up the checks.

"Keep 'em," Stick said.

"I appreciate that very much," the manager said. "I really do."

"Just the bills," Stick said, "no change. You can keep that, too."

"Thank you," the manager said. "Thank you very much."

Frank was at the third checkout counter, digging the bills out of the cash register and stuffing them in a Kroger bag. He looked up to see a woman with hair curlers pushing a cart toward him. He was taken by surprise and his hand went into his jacket for the Python. He'd looked down the aisles and hadn't seen anyone in the store. The woman began unloading her cart—coffee, milk, bread, and a few other items—not paying any attention to him. Frank brought his hand out of the jacket. The best thing to do was get rid of her, fast. He said, "How're you this morning?" and began ringing up the groceries, not looking at her. She was a pale, puffy woman with a permanent scowl etched in her face. And the hair curlers—in case anyone thought she wasn't ugly enough she had light-blue plastic curlers wrapped in her light-blue hair.

The woman squinted at him. "You're new."

"Yes, ma'am, new assistant manager."

"Where's your white coat?"

He was going to say that a jacket and sunglasses was the new thing for assistant managers, you cluck, you dumb, ugly broad, but he played it straight and told her they were getting him a white coat with his name on it. He punched the total and said, "Four sixty-eight, please."

The woman was digging in her purse, looking for something. She took almost a minute to bring out a piece of newspaper, unfold it, and hand it to him.

"Coupon for the coffee," the woman said. "Twenty cents off."

Frank took the coupon and looked at it. "Okay, then that's four forty-eight. No, wait a minute." He noticed the date on the coupon. "This offer's expired. It's not, you know . . . redeemable anymore, it's no good."

"I couldn't come in yesterday," the woman said. "It's not my fault. I cut the coupon out and there it is."

"I'm sorry," Frank said. "It says, see? Thursday and Friday only. Big letters."

"I've been coming here fifteen years, using the coupons," the woman said. "My husband and I. We buy all our groceries, our dog food, everything here. I'm one day late and you're going to tell me this is no good?"

"I'm sorry, I wish there was something I could do about it."

"Yesterday Earl took the car, had Timmie with him. All

day he's gone, didn't even feed Timmie the whole while, and I had to sit home alone."

"All right—" Frank said.

"After all the money this store's made off us," the woman said. "I could've been going to Farmer Jack, Safeway. No, I come here and then get treated like I'm somebody with food stamps."

Frank was about to give in, but he changed his mind. He looked right at the lady now and said, "I got an idea. Why don't you take the coupon—okay?—and the one-pound can of Maxwell House coffee and shove 'em up your ass."

When they were in the stolen car, the Kroger bags on the floor, turning out of the parking lot, Frank said, "That fucking Earl. He stays out with their car all day, their dog, his old lady gets pissed off and makes life miserable for everybody. Jesus."

Stick wasn't listening. He was anxious. He waited for Frank to finish and said, "The manager, you know what he says when I'm leaving? Honest to God, he says, 'Thank you very much, sir, and come back again.'"

"That poor fucking Earl," Frank said. "I sure wouldn't want to be him."

They got a little over seventeen hundred at Kroger's. The story in the paper said "about three thousand." Typical. Four days later, to show you how it could go, they hit a place and didn't get anything. The guy wouldn't give them the money.

It was a good thing it didn't happen on their first job. They would have quit. The guy was Armenian, a little bald-headed, excitable Armenian who ran a party store. No liquor, but imported beer and wine and expensive gourmet items, and the store was in a good location, out North Woodward near Bloomfield Hills. They went in on a Saturday night at ten. Frank took out his Python and Stick turned the OPEN sign around to CLOSED and pulled the shade down on the glass door.

Right away the little Armenian said, "What do you want to do this to me for? I never done nothing to you. I never saw you before." He stood there with his hands raised in the air.

Frank said, "Sir, put your hands down, will you?"

"I don't want this happening to me," the Armenian said in his high, excitable voice. "Since I move out here it never happen before. Never. Good people live out here. Why aren't you good people? You don't have to do this to me."

"It won't hurt at all, you do what I tell you," Frank said. "You understand? Now put your fucking hands down!"

Stick found the guy's wife in the back room, a little dark-haired lady with a moustache, clutching her hands in front of her like she was praying. Stick said, "Everything's going to be all right, Mama. Nothing to worry about." He moved her into the toilet compartment, closed the door, and poked around the storage room that was stacked high with beer and soft-drink cases.

Frank looked up from the cash register when Stick came back out.

"He's got a safe or he hid it somewhere."

Stick shook his head. "Not out there."

"Thirty-eight bucks and change," Frank said. "For tomorrow. He's cleaned out the drawer."

Stick went over to the Armenian, turned him around to face the shelves, and felt the pockets of his white store coat.

"Nothing."

"It's somewhere," Frank said.

"All the money I have, in the cash register," the Armenian said to the shelf of canned smoked oysters and clams. "I don't have no more than that."

"Hey," Frank said, "come on. All day you make thirty-eight bucks? Where is it? You hide it someplace?"

"I took it to the bank."

"No, you didn't. You been here all day."

"My wife took it." His voice went higher as he said, "Where is my wife—what did you do to her!"

"This guy here raped her," Frank said.

Stick made a face like he was going to get sick.

"Now *I'm* going to rape her, you don't tell us where the money is."

The Armenian didn't say anything. He was considering whether he should give up the money or let his wife get raped again.

"Come on," Frank said to him, touching the back of the Armenian's head with the Colt Python, "where is it! You don't get it out by the time I count three, I'm going to blow your bald head apart. . . . One."

"Do it!" the Armenian said in his high voice.

"Two."

"Kill me! You take my money, kill me!"

"Three."

Frank clicked the hammer back with his thumb. The Armenian's shoulders hunched rigid and held like that. Stick waited, feeling his own tension.

After a moment Frank said, "Shit."

There was no point in wasting any more time. They could tear the place apart and not find anything.

Frank said to the Armenian, "You're lucky, you know that? You're dumb fucking lucky, that's all."

After they left and were driving away, Stick said, "Shit, we forgot the thirty-eight bucks."

There weren't any textbooks on armed robbery. The only way to learn was through experience.

They found out gas stations weren't as good as they looked. Hand the kid a twenty and watch him go over to the manager or owner who'd take a wad out of his pocket and peel off change. But it didn't amount to that much: a bunch of singles and fives. There were too many people using credit cards now. Also, the high-volume service stations, where the money would be, always had five or six guys working there, using wrenches and tire irons, some hard-looking guys, maybe not too bright, who might see the gun pointing at them and decide to take a swing anyway. In their three gas station hits they went in and got out fast, the best take seven-eighty, which they figured was about as good as you could do.

They crossed off gas stations and altered a couple of their ten rules for success and happiness, finding it was all right to be polite, but you still had to scare the guy enough so he'd know better than to try and be a hero. It was all right, too, to dress well, look presentable. But they realized they'd better not become typecast or pretty soon the police would be writing a book on the two dudes who always wore business suits and said please and thank you. So they wore jackets sometimes, and raincoats. Stick had a pair of coveralls he liked he'd bought at J. C. Penney. They were comfortable and no one seemed to bother looking at him. Frank liked his pale-tan safari jacket with the epaulets. Very sharp, big in California. He liked the way the Python rested in the deep side pocket and didn't show. Usually, after a job, they kept the guns locked in the glove compartment of the T-bird. Stick thought they should put them away somewhere, hidden. But Frank said it was better to have them handy; they saw a place they liked, they were ready. Keep them in the apartment, some inquisitive broad could be snooping around and find them. Ho *ho*, what're these two business types doing with loaded firearms? Stick wasn't convinced, but he couldn't think of a better place to keep them.

Speaking of rules, Stick said maybe there was one more they should add. Number Eleven. Never try and hold up an Armenian.

They had taken in, so far, close to twenty-five thousand, spent a lot, but still had ninety-six hundred in a safe-deposit box at the Troy branch of Detroit Bank & Trust and about fifteen hundred or so spending money in the Oxydol box under the sink. They didn't divide the money. Except for major purchases—like the car and an eight-hundred-dollar hi-fi setup Frank picked out for them—the money went from the bank safe deposit to the Oxydol box, usually a thousand at a time, where it was available to both of them for pocket money and personal expenditures. There was no rule as to how much you could take; it was whatever you needed.

Two months ago, when they'd moved in, Stick had questioned the arrangement. He'd see Frank dipping in every day or so for fifty, a hundred, sometimes as much as two hundred. Finally he'd said, "Don't you think it'd be better, after a job, we divvied it up?"

Frank said, "I thought we were partners."

"Equal partners," Stick said. "We divvy it up, then we know it's equal."

"Wait just a minute now. You saying I'm cheating you?"

"I'm saying it might be better to split it each time, that's all. Then we know where we stand, individually."

"You know where the dough is," Frank said, "right? Under the sink, that's where we keep it. And you know you can go in there and take as much as you need, right? So how am I cheating you?"

"I understand the arrangement," Stick said. "I'm only asking, you think it would be better if we each took care of our own dough?"

"What're you, insecure? You want to hide it?"

"If half the dough's mine, why can't I do anything I want with it?"

"Jesus," Frank said, "you sound like a little kid. Nya nya nya, I got my money hidden and I'm not gonna tell you where it is. What is this shit? We partners or not?"

Stick let it drop.

From then on, he took two hundred dollars a week out of the Oxydol box, over and above what he needed, and put it away in his suitcase.

7

STICK WAS ON THE BALCONY, looking down at the empty patio. It was quiet, the pool area in shadows. He turned when he heard Frank come out of his bedroom and watched him walk over to the bar in one of his new suits and finish a drink he'd made and forgotten about.

"You taking the car?"

"No," Frank said, "we're going to walk. Broads love to get taken out to dinner and have to walk. You going out?"

"How?"

"What do you mean, how? You going out?"

"I mean *how*. What am I supposed to do, hitchhike?"

Frank took his time. He said, "It seems to me I remember I said maybe we better get two cars. You said, Two cars? Christ, what do we need with two cars? You remember that?"

"How come you figure it's yours?" Stick said. "Take it anytime you want."

"Jesus Christ," Frank said, "I don't believe it. You want a car, steal one. You want it bad enough, *buy* one, for Christ sake. Take it out of the bank thing."

"Have a nice time," Stick said.

Frank was shaking his head, a little sadly, patiently. "Sometimes, you know what? You sound like a broad. A wife. Poor fucking martyr's got to sit home while the guy's out having a good time."

"I'll wait up for you," Stick said. "Case you come in, you fall and hit your head on the toilet when you're throwing up."

"How long you been saving that?"

"It just came to me, you throw up a lot."

"You're quite a conversationalist," Frank said. "I'd like to stay and chat, but I'm running a little late." He went out.

There was a junior executive group at the Villa, a few guys with friends who were always coming over. Sometimes in the evening, after they'd changed from their business outfits to Levi's and Adidas, they'd sit on the patio and drink beer. If Stick was out on the balcony he'd listen to them, see if he could learn anything.

Usually it was about how stoned one of them got the night before. Or the best source of grass in Ann Arbor. Or why this one guy had switched from a Wilson Jack Kramer to a Bancroft Competition. Or how a friend of one of them had brought back eight cases of Coors from Vail. Then he wouldn't hear anything for a minute or so— one of them talking low—then loud laughter. The laughter would get louder as they went through the six-packs, and the junior executives would say *shit* a lot more. That was about all Stick learned.

This evening he didn't learn anything. They had two beers and decided to go to the show. Stick wondered what Mona was doing. Frank was gone. It'd be a good time if he was going to do it. He liked her looks and could picture her clearly in his mind, but he couldn't see her making all those sounds.

He wondered how much she charged.

He went out past the Formica table at the end of the living room to the kitchen and got a can of Busch Bavarian, came back in, sat down on one of the canvas chairs, and stared at an orange-and-yellow shape on the wall, a mess of colors, like somebody had spilled a dozen eggs and framed them.

He put the beer on the glass coffee table, went over and got Donna Fargo going on the hi-fi. He listened to her tell how she was the luckiest girl in the U.S.A., how she would wake up and say, "Mornin' Lord, howdy sun," and studied himself in the polished aluminum mirror on the wall. He looked dark and gaunt, a little mean-looking with his serious expression. Howdy there. I'm your next-door neighbor. I was wondering—

Going out the door and along the second-floor walk, he was still wondering.

I was wondering, if you weren't busy—

I was wondering, if you were free—had some free time, I mean.

He said to himself, Shit, let her do it. She knows what you want.

He knocked on her door and waited and knocked a couple more times. Still nothing, not a sound from inside the apartment. Stick went back to his own place, picked up the can of Busch, and walked out on the balcony. It was still quiet, with a dull evening sky clouding over. A lifeless expanse of sky, boring.

But there was somebody down there now. In the swimming pool. A girl doing a sidestroke, trying to keep her head up and barely moving. She was actually in the water, and Stick couldn't recall any of the career ladies ever actually swimming before. He thought she had on a reddish bathing cap, then realized it was her hair—the redheaded one with the frizzy hair the guy in the silver Mark IV came to visit a couple of times a week. That one.

* * *

Arlene saw him standing there with her purple beach towel as she came out of the pool in her lavender bikini, her beads, and her seven rings. She said, "Hi," and laughed.

Stick handed her the towel, asked her how she was doing, and learned, Just fine.

He said, "Your friend coming over tonight?"

"He's tied up," Arlene said. "Had to go to Lansing." She began drying her wiry hair, rubbing it hard, and Stick couldn't see her face for a while. He watched her little boobs jiggling up and down. They were small but well shaped, perky. She had freckles on her chest. Stick figured she was a redhead all the way.

"What're you supposed to do when he doesn't show," Stick said, "sit around, be a good little girl?"

She answered him, but he couldn't hear what she said under the heavy towel.

"Do what?"

She peeked out at him through the purple folds. "I said he never told me I had to sit and twiddle my thumbs."

Stick gave her a little grin. "Don't you like to twiddle?"

Arlene grinned back and giggled. "I don't know as I ever have, tell you the truth. Is it fun?"

"You're from somewhere, aren't you?" Stick said. "Let me guess. Not Louisville. No, little more this way. Columbus, Ohio."

"Uh-unh, Indianapolis," Arlene said.

"Close," Stick said. "You take Interstate 70 right on over to Indianapolis from Columbus. Used to be old U.S. 40." He wasn't going to let go of Columbus that easy.

"I was Miss NHRA Nationals last year," Arlene said. "You know, the drag races? I was going to go out to

California—a friend of mine lives in Bakersfield—but I was asked to come here instead, to do special promotions for Hi-Performance Products Incorporated. You know them?"

"I think I've heard the name."

"They make Hi-Speed Cams. That's their main thing. Also Hi-Performance Shifters. Pretty soon they're going into mag wheels and headers."

"It must be interesting work," Stick said.

"You'd think so. But what it is," Arlene said, "it's a pain in the ass. Those drag strips are so dirty. I mean the dust and grease and all. The noise, God. The first thing I do I get back to the motel is dive in the pool. I love to swim."

"I noticed, I was out on the balcony there," Stick said, glancing up at the apartment. "You're like a fish in the water."

"I love it, the feeling, like I don't even have a body."

"I guarantee you got a body," Stick said.

Arlene laughed, raised closed eyes to the dull sky, and shook her wiry hair. It barely moved.

Stick was looking at her mouth, slightly open, her slender little nose and the trace of something greenish on her eyelids.

"I was thinking," he said, "after all that swimming how'd you like a nice cool drink now to wet your insides?"

Arlene loved the apartment. She said it was cool, it looked like it would be in California. Stick thought Arlene looked pretty cool, too, on the bamboo barstool in her little swimming suit, bare feet hooked on the rung and her legs sloping apart. He fixed her Salty Dogs, once she told him how, kept the vodka bottle handy, and sipped a bourbon over ice while she told him what it was like to put on a little metallic silver outfit with white boots and pose for camshaft promotion shots, with the hot lights and all. She said it wasn't any picnic and Stick said he bet it wasn't. He watched her rubbing her eyes and blinking, but didn't say anything about it until she'd put away three Salty Dogs and was working on number four.

He said, "It's that chlorine in the pool. What you ought to do is go in and take a shower."

"You mean here?"

"What's the matter with here?"

"But I don't have anything to put on after," Arlene said, "except this wet swimming suit."

If that was all she was worried about, Stick knew he was home. He said, "I'll get you a robe or something. How'll that be?"

That was how he got her in the shower. He put her drink on the top of the toilet tank, adjusted the spray to nice and warm, and went out, closing the door.

Stick didn't own a robe. Maybe Frank had one, but he didn't bother to look. He went into his bedroom and got undressed, put his shoes and socks in the closet, hung up his new pants and shirt, got down to his striped boxer shorts, thinking he could have taken her to dinner, spent twenty bucks. He could have taken her to a movie and then to a bar, hear some music, then coming home ask her if she wanted a nightcap at his place. He could have gone through all that and then have her say thanks anyway, she was tired. Find out first, then take her out after; that was the way to do it. He couldn't figure out why he had hesitated going to Mona's, trying to get the words right. Mona was a pro, whether she looked like one or not. Arlene was a—what? Hot-rod queen. A flake. Part-time camshaft model and kept lady. But he really didn't know her or how she'd react.

She might scream. She might say, Now wait a minute, or, Get the hell out of here, or threaten to call the police, or be so scared she couldn't say anything.

What Arlene did say, when he pulled the curtain back and stepped naked into the shower with her, was, "Hon, get me another Salty Dog first, will you?"

They were in bed, dried off and smelling of Mennen's talcum powder, when Mona started.

That faint sound through the wall, a caressing sound without words.

Stick hadn't heard her come in. Probably while they were in the shower. He was on an elbow right now, half over Arlene with a leg between hers, giving her a little knee, feeling strong with his gut sucked in, giving her nice tender kisses and feeling her hands moving over the muscles in his back.

Arlene opened her eyes.

"What's that?"

"What?" He put his mouth on hers to keep her from talking.

"Like somebody's in pain."

"I doubt it's pain," Stick said. He got back to it and Arlene began to squirm and press hard against him.

Mona, in another bed in another room, said, "Oh Jesus. Oh God. Oh Jesus."

Arlene's eyes opened again. "Listen."

"Oh please—"

Arlene slid around him and sat up. "Where's it coming from, next door?"

"I guess so."

"Who lives there?"

"The one—I don't know her name."

Arlene frowned. "The mousy one with the straight hair?"

"I don't know as she's mousy. A little plain maybe. Not what you'd expect—"

Arlene stopped him. "Listen."

She got out of bed, carefully climbing over him, and followed the faint murmuring sound to the wall where the dresser stood. Stick watched her crouch there—a naked redhead who looked especially naked to him because her skin was white and didn't show tan lines—her face alert, pressed to the wall, her perky little boobs hanging free.

"You want to learn how it's done. Is that it?"

"Shhhhhhhh."

"I thought you knew. You seemed to be doing all right."

Arlene didn't look over or change her expression. The room was silent. Stick could hear the sound again.

After a moment Arlene said, "Oh . . . *now*, please. Oh please, please, please," keeping her voice low.

"I'd be glad to oblige," Stick said.

Arlene was fascinated, glued to the wall, her eyes alive and mouth slightly open.

"Give it to me. Give me everything, oh please. Oh God, Jesus."

"Maybe what she's doing," Stick said, "she's saying her prayers."

"Uh-unh. She just said the word."

"What word?"

"I can't say it out loud. God, now she's saying it over and over."

"Spell it," Stick said.

He got a Marlboro off the night table with the Chinese

figurine lamp and sat up in bed to smoke and watch Arlene and tried to imagine what was going on in the bed on the other side of the wall. He could picture Mona's face, her eyes closed; but he couldn't picture her saying anything or picture the guy with her. He didn't want to picture the guy. Arlene's eyes opened a little wider. It wouldn't be long now. Arlene looked good. He wondered if he could like her seriously. Studying her he realized she was very pretty. Delicate features. Slim body. Flat little tummy. Not at all self-conscious about standing there naked. But she couldn't say the word.

Arlene must have been thinking about it, too. When she came back to bed and crawled over him she said, "I could never say that. I can do it, God, no trouble at all. But I can't say it. Isn't that strange?"

Stick said, "I was thinking, why don't you take your rings off? So nobody'll get hurt."

8

THE BAR IN HAZEL PARK was on Dequindre, only a few blocks from the racetrack. They had been in once before and watched a couple of big winners buy rounds for the house. They weren't sure if bars were worth it and picked this one as a good place to find out.

When they went in at 1:30 A.M., a half hour before closing, it was filled with the sound of voices and country music playing on the jukebox. The bar section was still very much alive, though the tables were empty now and the waitress was standing by the service station counting her tips.

Once they pulled their guns, Stick would cover the people at the bar and put them down on the floor while Frank concentrated on the bartender, a woman, and got her to empty the cash register. Before Frank could get his Python out, Stick touched him on the arm.

"Let's sit down."

They got a table. The waitress brought them a couple of draft beers and left.

"The guy with the hair," Stick said, "at the end of the bar."

The guy was at the curved end nearer the door, facing the length of the bar: thick hair over his ears, big arms and shoulders in a dull yellow-satin athletic jacket. Frank drank some of his beer as the guy's head turned toward them.

"What about him?"

"He eyed us when we came in. Watch him, keeps looking around."

"Maybe he's waiting for somebody."

"Or maybe he's a cop, staking the place out. You read about it? They been doing that."

"A cop," Frank said. "He looks like a bush leaguer never made it."

"Cops put on these outfits now, play dress-up," Stick said. "You never know anymore."

"If you don't feel right about it," Frank said, "let's go. Maybe it's not a good idea anyway. Six, seven, nine with the waitress, that's a lot of people to keep track of."

"Wait," Stick said. "I think he's leaving."

They watched the guy in the yellow-satin jacket slide off the stool and pick up a leather case that must have been leaning against the bar on the other side of him.

"He's got pool cues," Frank said. "I thought he was a jock. He's a poolhall cowboy."

"Going to the can," Stick said.

There was an inscription on the back of his jacket. They watched it go into the men's room.

"Port Huron Bullets," Stick said. "He's one of the famous Port Huron Bullets. You ever heard of them?"

"We'll wait'll he leaves," Frank said. He finished his beer. When he took a cigarette out Stick did, too, and got a light from him.

Dolly Parton was singing on the jukebox. Stick had been in love with Dolly when he used to watch the "Porter Waggoner Show" and paused to listen before he said, "You want to do it, huh?"

Frank looked at him. "What's the matter, you nervous?"

"No more than usual. You bring a bag?"

"Shit, I forgot," Frank said. "They probably got something behind the bar. Wrap it in the broad's apron or something."

"She doesn't have an apron on."

"We'll put it in *some*thing, okay?"

"I don't know," Stick said. "I don't feel we're a hundred percent this time. You know what I mean?"

"When're we ever a hundred percent sure?"

"I don't mean sure. I mean ready, wanting to do it. We come in, right away we hang back."

Frank was looking past him. "Here he comes."

Stick saw the change in Frank's expression and heard him say, "Jesus Christ," softly, with a sound of awe. He heard that and heard Loretta Lynn now saying they didn't make men like her daddy anymore, as he turned and saw the guy in the yellow-satin jacket and the door of the men's room behind him, the guy raising a pump-action shotgun level with his waist.

"Don't nobody move! This is a holdup!"

The guy shouted it, drowning out Loretta Lynn. "I'll shoot the first one moves!"

When he swung the shotgun at their table, Frank and Stick were looking right at him about fifteen feet away. "You two—don't make a move. Don't anybody. I'm warning you. I'll shoot to kill."

"Wants everybody to know he means business," Frank said.

They watched him move hesitantly toward the bar, telling people who were looking over their shoulders at him to turn the fuck around. Loretta Lynn was finished and it was quiet in the place now as he got around behind the bar and moved down to where the woman bartender was standing at the cash register.

"How come he doesn't make 'em lay on the floor?" Stick said. "You believe it?"

"He doesn't know what he's doing," Frank said. "Dumb poolhall cowboy. Tells everybody on his jacket where he's from."

"That shotgun'd be a pain in the ass," Stick said, "wouldn't it? You imagine carrying a shotgun around?"

"Keep your hands on the bar!" the guy shouted at somebody.

"He's pretty nervous," Frank said. "Maybe it's his first time."

"He's more nervous than I am. Look at him wave that scattergun," Stick said. "Doesn't know where to point it."

"What he ought to do," Frank said, "is put it on the waitress. Tell 'em he'll blow her off if anybody moves, or if the broad doesn't give him the money."

"Yeah, get 'em laying down first, they don't see where he's at." Stick shook his head. "Dumb cowboy, I wouldn't be surprised he had a horse outside."

"Runs out in the street waving his shotgun," Frank said. "Or you suppose he puts it back in the case first?"

"He goes in the toilet," Stick said, "and comes out again pretending he's got pool cues in it. Now he's getting the change off the bar. What'd she put the money in? The broad."

"Looked like her purse."

"Runs out with a shotgun and a purse," Stick said. "That'd be a sight, wouldn't it? How much you think he got?"

Frank was silent for a moment, watching the guy as he moved carefully toward the end of the bar.

"He isn't out of here yet."

Stick looked at Frank, then back to the guy, who was coming around the bar and now backing toward the door.

"It's an idea, isn't it?" Stick said.

"If we see the chance."

"I think when he goes to open the door," Stick said.

The guy seemed more nervous than before. He glanced over at their table but was concentrating on the people at the bar. "Don't nobody move," he said. "I go out, I'm liable to come back in to make sure. Anybody I see moved gets a load of twelve-gauge, and I *mean* it."

"He talks too much," Stick said.

The guy turned to the door, raising the shotgun barrel straight up in front of him, and started to push it open.

"Drop it," Frank said.

The guy hesitated, his back to them and the shotgun upright against the door. He had a moment, but when he finally turned, it was too late. Both Frank and Stick, standing away from the table, ten feet apart, had their revolvers on him, aimed at arm's length.

"Come on," Frank said, "put it down."

When the shotgun was on the floor, Stick walked over to the guy and took the purse from him.

He said, "Much obliged, partner. We appreciate it."

The story in the *Detroit News* the next day described how for six hours the would-be holdup man and the bar patrons were locked up together in a storeroom where all the liquor and bar supplies were kept. When they were found the next morning, the newspaper account stated, the would-be holdup man appeared to have suffered a severe beating, while the bar patrons were in a festive state of intoxication.

"Can you see it?" Stick said. "The Port Huron Bullet comes out, blood all over him, can't open his eyes. Hasn't got any idea what happened to him. Keeps asking himself, over and over, 'What went wrong?'"

"A customer comes out," Frank said, "absolutely fried.

Cop says to him, 'Sir, you want to tell us how much you had stolen? Any valuables?' The guy, the customer, looks at him with these bleary eyes and says, 'Who the fuck cares?' "

They got a kick out of the Hazel Park bar robbery, plus a little better than eleven hundred in cash.

They decided they didn't like bars, though: too many people and too unpredictable with booze involved. So they crossed off bars along with gas stations and would concentrate on other types of establishments.

9

THREE OF THE CAREER LADIES were at the pool when Frank and Stick came down: two of them lying face up, eyes closed—Mary Kay, the skinny nurse with the wide hips, and Jackie, the cocktail lounge kitty—and one on her stomach, face hidden in an outstretched arm. Frank knew by the short, dark hair and deep tan it was Karen, the schoolteacher. Karen had her bra strap unfastened, out of the way, and there was no line. Her brown skin glistened with oil, smooth and bare all the way down to where the little bikini bottom almost covered her can.

Stick, with his towel and a rolled-up magazine, eased into the first empty lounge he came to, near the edge of the grass.

Frank made a production out of it. He stood with his gold beach towel over one shoulder, looked at his watch, checked the angle of the sun, then dragged a lounge chair around—with the sound of aluminum scraping on cement—to catch the direct rays.

Without opening her eyes Jackie said, "Frank's here."

"I'm sorry, honey, the chair wake you up?" He brought a tray table over for his towel, his watch, and for the drinks he'd have later on.

"You're supposed to lift it," Jackie said. "It leaves marks."

"Yeah, I always forget."

Karen's face rose from her arm.

"Frank, while you're up, you want to do my back?"

"I'll force myself," Frank said.

Stick had his magazine, the latest issue of *Oui*, folded open. He had looked at the pictures already, the boob and crotch shots. Now he was reading about Alex Karras and what Alex thought about Howard Cosell and doing NFL color on TV. Looking over the top of the magazine, he watched Frank sit down on the edge of Karen's lounge.

The nurse, Mary Kay, was watching them, too. Mary Kay usually didn't say much. She listened; sometimes she laughed.

Stick wondered what she thought of them. Probably nothing. She probably saw so many weird things up in that nut ward nothing down here would shock her.

"Cut it out," Karen said.

"What am I doing?"

Stick looked over there again. As Frank's hands caressed her back, one of them slid into the space between her arm and body.

"*Fra*-ank!"

"What's the matter? I'm not doing anything."

"That's enough."

"Little more right . . . *there*."

"Frank—"

As he stood up and moved about idly, wiping his hands on his chest and stomach, Stick said, "Sure is full of the devil, isn't he?"

Frank looked up at the sun, raising his arms and stretching.

"Oh, man. Perfect day, isn't it? Sun, the sky's clear, little breeze so it's not too hot . . . Jackie, you got a perfect navel, you know that? Anybody ever tell you?"

She pressed her chin to her chest to look down at it.

"What's so different about it?"

"It's round," Frank said, "like a bullet hole. Pow, right in the navel."

"I don't know, Frank," Jackie said, "sometimes I wonder about you."

"What do you wonder?"

"If you're all there."

"I'm all here. Hey, look at me. Jackie, look. You see anything missing?"

"The exhibitionist," Karen said. "You ever see him go out with his raincoat on? Sunny day, he's wearing a raincoat. We heard about guys like that, Frank. Our moms told us a long time ago."

Frank looked over at Stick, and Stick said mildly. "He's insecure is all. Wears drawers under his pajamas, and socks to bed."

"See, I'm right," Jackie said. "He's a little strange."

Frank liked it there in the center of things, playing around with the career ladies. He looked over at the nurse, to get them all involved.

"Mary Kay, honey, you got room for me in your psycho ward? Maybe I better have some tests."

"We're overcrowded," Mary Kay said. "We don't have enough beds the way it is."

"How about if I stood up?"

Stick felt sorry for her—put on the spot and not having a smart-ass reply ready. Everybody had to be a smart-ass, get a laugh and make it look easy. It wore you out, thinking, just staying in a conversation.

He said to Mary Kay, "How about giving him a shot, then, to quiet him down? Case anybody wanted to take a nap?"

Mary Kay smiled but didn't say anything.

Stick let it go. It looked like too much of a job to bring

her out. And if he got her out, then what? There had to be something better to do. He went up to the apartment, poured a half bottle of vodka and a quart of tonic into a plastic pitcher, threw in some limes and ice and carried it down on a tray with a half dozen plastic poolside glasses.

Arlene was in his lounge chair, looking at the magazine. She didn't notice him right away. Frank was talking to Karen.

"It's funny nobody ever asked before. What'd you think we were, retired?"

"Are you kidding?" Karen said. "We thought you were out of work."

Frank looked up at Stick and moved his towel, making room on the table next to him.

"You hear that? She thought we were out of work."

"It just looks like it sometimes," Stick said. He picked up the glasses as Frank poured them. Mary Kay shook her head and said no thanks. Jackie took a sip and made a little sound of appreciation. Karen was snapping her bra and he had to wait for her to take the glass. Arlene smiled at him. She said, "Here, there's room. Come on."

Stick sat down on the edge of the chair, feeling the aluminum tube beneath his thighs. He saw Mary Kay watching and then look away.

"What we are," Frank said, "we're sales motivators. We go in a place, say a car dealership, okay? We motivate the salesmen, get them off their cans, by actually showing them how to cultivate prospects and close deals. I demonstrate what we call the *frank* approach, how to appear open and sincere with customers, sympathetic to their needs. Then Ernest here, better known as Stick, shows them how an *earnest*, confident attitude will close the sale every time."

Arlene gave Stick a little poke. "You must travel a lot. You ever been to California?"

Frank answered her. "Many times. Write us care of the Continental Hyatt House, Sunset Boulevard."

"I'd love to go out there," Arlene said. "I've got a friend in Bakersfield."

She went into the pool after a while and Stick got a chance to stretch out again with his magazine, half-listening to Frank bullshitting the ladies. Finally he heard Frank say, "Which reminds me, partner. We got a sales meeting this afternoon." As Stick got up Frank was telling the ladies they hated to leave but would see them again real soon. Stick kept trying to think of something to say, something a little clever.

Walking away from the patio with the pitcher and tray and magazine under his arm, he glanced back and said, "You all be good now."

10

THERE WAS A SIX O'CLOCK wedding at the Shrine of the Little Flower, on Woodward in Royal Oak. Stick took a Chevrolet Impala that was parked in line at the side of the church—washed, key in the ignition, ready to go.

Frank was waiting in the T-bird, in the lot behind the Berkley Theater on Twelve Mile Road. They changed from their suit coats to lightweight jackets, took off their ties, and got their revolvers out of the glove box. Frank put on sunglasses; Stick, a souvenir Detroit Tiger baseball cap. They left their suit coats and ties in the T-bird, got in the Impala, and drove over to the A&P on the corner of Southfield and Twelve. On the way, Stick said he almost took the car with the pink-and-white pompoms all over it. He didn't because he was afraid Frank might feel a little funny riding in it.

It was a good-looking A&P, in a high-income suburban area. But Frank didn't like all the cars in the parking area. Too many.

They drove back to a bowling alley-bar on Twelve in Berkley to kill some time and had a few vodkas-and-tonic in the dim, chrome-and-Formica lounge. Sitting in a bar in the early evening reminded Stick of Florida. He didn't like the feeling.

"I was thinking," Stick said, "you could tell them the truth and nobody's believe it. Girl says, 'What do you do

for a living?' And you say, 'Oh, we hold up stores, different places.' And Jackie or one of them would say, 'I believe it.' Only she wouldn't. None of them would."

"You think that'd be funny, uh?" Frank said.

"You'd think it was funny if you'd thought of it," Stick
said.

"You heard what Karen said about wearing the raincoats?"

"She thinks you're queer, that's all."

"That's what she does," Frank said, "thinks. She's got
those big knockers, she's got nothing to do all day, she sits
around and thinks."

When they got back to the A&P, there were only about
a dozen cars in the lot. Stick pulled up, almost at the front
entrance, where there was a NO PARKING—PICKUP ONLY
sign.

"I'll see you," Stick said.

Frank slid over behind the wheel when Stick got out.
He lit a cigarette and took his time smoking it, five or six
minutes, then left the motor running and went into the
store.

The manager was inside the cashier's enclosure. Frank
could see his head and shoulders through the glass part of
the partition. Stick wasn't in there.

Another employee, maybe the assistant, was working
the Kwick-Check, eight-items-or-less, counter, where several people were lined up waiting. Only one other checkout counter was open. A woman was unloading a cart
with a week's supply of groceries while a checkout girl in
a red A&P smock rang them up.

The assistant, or whoever it was at the Kwick-Check
counter, looked over at Frank, then down at the counter
again.

Frank got a cart and pushed it down to the end of the

store, turned left at baked goods, stopped at dairy products for a wedge of Pinconning cheese and some French onion dip, found the potato-chip counter, and was two aisles over before he ran into Stick.

Stick was putting two boxes of Jiffy Corn Bread Mix in his cart. He already had lettuce, cucumbers, tomatoes, a sackful of potatoes, and four cans of Blue Lake mustard greens.

"Hi there," Frank said. "It certainly does save to shop at A&P, doesn't it?"

"It saves your ass if you got your eyes open," Stick said. "You see the guy at the counter?"

"I thought he might be the assistant."

"He might've been," Stick said, "if he hadn't gone into police work instead."

"You sure?"

"There's one just like him over in produce weighing tomatoes. You know the look, their face, when they look at you? Like they see clear through and can tell you what color drawers you got on."

"I don't know," Frank said. "You thought the guy in the bar was a cop."

"I could be wrong," Stick said, "but I got no intention of finding out if I'm right. I think we ought to get out of here."

Frank shrugged. "Well, if you don't have your heart in it, I guess that's it."

"Go over and look at the guy in produce," Stick said. "Big, hardheaded-looking guy. He might just as well have his badge pinned on his apron."

"I'm not doubting your word," Frank said, "you want to go, let's go."

"I'll be right behind you." Stick turned his cart around and started back up the aisle.

"Where you going?"

"Get some salt pork for my mustard greens."

They cruised down Southfield looking for another store and passed two shopping centers, one with a Wrigley, the other with a Farmer Jack, before Frank said anything.

"You didn't like either of those?"

Stick was driving. "I don't know. The parking, all the stores there, it looked congested. I see us trying to get out and some broad in a Cadillac's got everything fucked up."

"How about over there?" Frank said. "Nice neat little post office." It was a red-brick Colonial with white trim. "You ever hear of somebody knocking down a post office?"

"There's a good reason," Stick said. He saw determined-looking, clean-cut guys in narrow suits who never smiled. "It's called the Federal Bureau of Investigation."

Frank looked back as they passed it. "It might be an idea, though. U.S. Post Office. Save it for around Christmastime when business's up."

Stick didn't bite. He realized now what Frank was doing.

Coming to Ten Mile Road, Frank said, "Hey, there we are. What do you say?"

Stick looked at the bank on the southwest corner. Michigan National. He didn't say anything.

"You don't like it?"

"I like it," Stick said. "It's just I don't love it."

"How about the Chinese place? All right, you guys, give me all your fucking egg rolls. You like egg rolls or you love them?"

"The next one," Stick said, "I think I might go for."

It was a Food Lanes supermarket. Stick turned in and

pulled to a stop facing the building. He liked the location, the alley running next to the store, the ample parking on two sides. Or they could park across the alley at the Chinese place. That might be better.

"It's up to you," Frank said. "Go in and look it over. I'll wait here."

He was still playing his game. Stick didn't say anything. He went in and took his time walking around the store and bought cigarettes. Frank had a bag of potato chips open when he got back in the car and drove out.

"You still like it?"

"Not bad," Stick said. "The only thing, you notice the doors? The cashier's place's in the front, in the corner, and there's doors on both sides. Two doors to watch. Also there's a magazine rack. So from the cashier's place you can't see much of the store."

Frank put a potato chip in his mouth and crunched it between his teeth.

"But no cops in there dressed up like grocery boys?"

"Fuck you," Stick said.

"You want a chip? Lay's. They dare you to try and eat just one."

"You didn't like the looks of the guy any more than I did," Stick said. "I said he looked like a cop, you agreed."

"I said you also thought the guy in the bar looked like a cop, with the fucking shotgun."

"You're trying to make it look like it's my fault we didn't hit the place," Stick said. "Like I'm chicken or something. You want to hit the post office? How about that bank there. All that shit."

"Watch the road," Frank said.

"Watch your ass. You don't like the way I drive, get the fuck out."

"You know, it's funny," Frank said, "you come on as a

very easygoing person. Then bang, no reason, you get a hard-on like you want to kill somebody."

"No reason, no, none at all," Stick said.

"I was being funny, for Christ sake, you get pissed off. Like the other day you're pissed off at me using the car. Think about it," Frank said. "You got this down-home, you-all delivery like nothing in the world bothers you, but you know what? I think you could be a pretty mean son of a bitch underneath it all."

Frank was turning it around again, making it all his fault. There was no sense arguing with him when he did that. Stick kept his eyes on the road and didn't say anything. It always irritated him and he would begin to think about how he'd got into this and wonder if he should get out, now, while he still had a choice and could walk away.

But he had to admit they were doing better than he'd expected, and maybe it was natural for two guys as different as they were to rub each other the wrong way sometimes. So what, right? He could live with it, as long as they kept the jobs simple and didn't overextend themselves.

Frank offered the potato chips again and he took some.

"You want to do one or go home or what?"

"Well, long as we're out," Stick said, "we may as well. You got a hundred on you?"

The hundred-dollar bill usually worked. It was something they had thought of after the experience with the Armenian and could save a lot of threatening and gun waving. Make a purchase and hand the guy the bill. He would always hesitate, then look in the cash register, then hesitate again. Then, with Frank standing there looking prosperous and honest in his suit, the guy would fish a roll out of his pocket or say, Just a minute, and step into the back-room. Stick would come in and they'd find the guy taking his excess cash out of a safe or wherever he kept it hidden.

They stopped by the T-bird to put their suit coats back on, cruised around for a while and found a drugstore with a liquor department. Frank bought a bottle of J&B and handed the guy the hundred-dollar note. This led them back to the prescription department where the pharmacist was making change out of a drawer. Stick tied up the clerk and pharmacist with Ace wraps and one-inch adhesive—the same tape he had used to do his ankles before a basketball game—while Frank hit the cash registers and the secret drawer for sixteen-fifty, their all-time record drugstore take.

They stayed out, had dinner, and closed the bar at the Kingsley Inn, singing along with the piano player, talking and making friends but not seeing anything worth picking up; all too old. Driving home, going through the business section of Birmingham, they noticed an appliance store holding its Annual Twenty-four-Hour Marathon Sales Spectacular. They looked at each other, full of drinks, and grinned.

The two guys who ran the store were dressed up in flannel nightshirts, still smiling and friendly at two thirty in the morning. Frank and Stick each got a free-gift yard-stick with the store's name on it for coming in. They looked around for a few minutes. Then Frank picked out a couple of ice trays that were sale priced at two ninety-eight each and handed the hundred-dollar bill to the cluck behind the counter in his nightshirt. The cluck looked at Frank and at the bill and finally shook his head and said gee, he was sorry but he didn't have enough cash in the store to make change.

Walking out, Frank said, "Bullshit."

11

THE TIME BEFORE HE HAD looked for Mona and found Arlene. Tonight it was the other way around.

Arlene wasn't in her apartment. He went there twice and knocked and waited.

Frank was out for the evening, with the car and probably Karen. Stick didn't bring up the car again. If he wanted a car he'd get his own. He didn't feel like going out, though. He made a drink and went down to sit by the pool for a while.

He liked the darkness and the lights beneath the clear water and the sound of crickets in the shrubs. The bourbon was good, too. It was nice, sitting by himself having a drink and a cigarette.

It could be his own private patio and swimming pool. He wondered if he'd enjoy it any more if it was.

Mona appeared out of the darkness, without a sound, and sank into a lounge chair by the deep end of the pool. He wondered if she had seen him, the glow from his cigarette. She sat with the backrest up, her legs stretched out, staring at the illuminated water. She didn't move. He wondered if her eyes were closed, staring at the water but not seeing it.

Stick said, "How you doing?"

Mona looked over.

Stick said, "You cheap bastard, why didn't you pick out a radio or something?"

"Don't worry," Frank said.

A half hour later they met the cluck down the street, at the local bank's night-deposit box. They pressed a free-gift yardstick into his back, relieved him of a little more than seven hundred in cash, and left the cluck standing there in his nightshirt.

Frank could be a pain in the ass sometimes, but they usually had a good time and it was a pretty interesting way to make a living.

"Hi. How're you?" She said it quietly, without putting anything extra into it.

She reminded him of somebody. Her face was pale in the reflection of the underwater lights. Her hair seemed darker. It was her nose and her mouth and the way her hair hung close to her face. She reminded him of somebody in the movies he used to like.

He almost told her that—bringing the aluminum chair over next to her lounge—but it would sound dumb, like he was making it up. It didn't make sense, did it? Trying to think of something to say to a hooker that wouldn't sound dumb. Hooker or call girl or whore, prostitute, whatever she considered herself. That might be something to talk about—if there was a difference between them. Get in a conversation about it, like he was making a study. When did you first consider turning pro? First accept money? What do you think got you doing it? Is it true whores really don't like guys? And all that bullshit.

He had been with whores in Toledo, Findlay, Ohio, Columbus, Fort Wayne, Terre Haute, Rock Island, Illinois, Dubuque, and Minot, North Dakota. Most had been nice, a few had had no personality at all. But he had never met a whore with a nose and mouth like Mona's. And he couldn't look past her nose and mouth and see her as a whore. Also she seemed too small and frail to be a whore—even though he had read that women were better than men at withstanding pain or punishment. He pictured her taking her blouse off, no bra, and asking for the money; then imagined a guy punching her in the mouth, threatening to do it again, and getting it for nothing. It could happen, a guy who didn't have any feeling. It must be a pretty tough life. He wanted to get into it with her, but didn't know how.

What had he said to all those other whores from Toledo to Minot? He'd said, "How much?"

He said to Mona, "You want a drink? I can get you one."

"No, thank you, though."

"How about a sip then? It's bourbon."

She hesitated. "All right."

As she was taking a drink he said, "No trouble to get you one. Salty Dog, anything you want."

"No thanks." She handed the glass back. "I'm going up in a minute."

He wanted to say something so there wouldn't be a silence, but it came. She was staring at the pool again.

"You know, you remind me of somebody. I can't think of who it is."

"Is that so?"

"Somebody in the movies."

He said it and it didn't sound as bad as he thought it would.

"My dad used to say I reminded him of a Labrador retriever we had. His name was Larry. The dog, I mean."

"You sure don't look like a Labrador retriever," Stick said. "Maybe the hair."

"It was when Larry was a puppy. I think the feet had something to do with it," Mona said. "We both had big feet."

Stick looked at her legs, at the white sandals pointing out of her white slacks.

"They don't look very big."

"Seven and a half quad." She looked down at them and wiggled her toes. "I have trouble getting fitted, except sandals, something like that."

There was a silence again.

"You sure you don't want a drink?"

"No, I think I'll go up."

"I still can't think of who it is you look like."

"Somebody in the movies, huh?"

"Dark hair, really pretty."

"Oh, it's a girl?"

"Sure it's a girl. She was in—I know she was in one John Wayne was in."

"I don't know who it could be," Mona said. "I don't go to the movies much."

"It was on television. I think the Monday night movie about a month ago."

"I guess I was out."

Stick hesitated. "Working?"

"Could've been."

"How much you charge?"

"Fifty," Mona said. "How's that sound?"

Mona squeezed her eyes closed and said, "Oh, God. Jesus."

Stick said, "Hey, don't do that, okay? Unless you really mean it."

12

STICK DIDN'T KNOW WHY HE expected her to be different. He realized now the person in there, behind the calm expression, was predictable and he'd met her before, many times. She wasn't a mystery person at all; she was really kind of dumb. She had never heard of Waylon Jennings or his hit record *Midnight Rider*. She hadn't even heard of Billy Crash Craddock or Jerry Reed, the Alabama Wild Man. She liked Roger Williams and Johnny Mathis. She also liked Tab with Jack Daniel's. Stick was disappointed, then relieved. He fixed himself some greens with salt pork and ring baloney and Jiffy Corn Bread Mix, fell asleep watching the late movie, woke up, and went to bed. He didn't know what time Frank got in.

The way he knew he was home was seeing the colored girl in the kitchen the next morning.

He got the paper in and came into the kitchen in his striped undershorts, scratching the hair on his chest, reading a headline about Ford and not sure which Ford they were talking about. A pan of water was boiling on the range. The colored girl was looking in the refrigerator. She had on a bra and panties, that's all, and was barefoot.

She looked over at him and said, "I don't see no tomato juice."

Stick saw her as she spoke and maybe he jumped, he

wasn't sure. It was pretty unexpected. Good-looking colored girl standing there in her underwear, he walks in the same way, like they were married or good friends. He felt funny, aware of his bare skin.

"What'd you say?"

"Tomato juice." She was relaxed, like she was in her own kitchen.

"In the cupboard," Stick said, "if we got any."

He watched her open the cupboard, look over the shelves, and reach for the gold can of Sacramento: slim brown body and white panties very low, legs stretched, on her tiptoes. He really felt funny. He didn't know if it was because she was black or because she was in her underwear. He tried to seem at ease and sound casual.

"You the maid?"

"Yeah, the cleaning lady," the girl said. "But I don't do floors or any ironing."

"LaGreta," Stick said. "Are you LaGreta?"

The girl turned and looked at him. "You know somebody that name?"

"I don't know her. I think I heard of her."

"Uh-huh. Where's your opener, love?"

"In the drawer there."

He watched her get it out and pry two holes in the top of the can.

"You and him work together, huh?"

"You left me," Stick said. "I thought we were talking about LaGreta."

"She's my mother."

"Oh." Stick nodded.

"You see it now?"

"Well—not exactly. You might think we're somebody else you heard about, I don't know."

"Yeah, that's it," the girl said. "You're somebody else."

"You and...my friend, you meet each other at Sportree's, I bet."

"Hey, baby, don't worry about it. Just tell me where I can find the vodka."

"I'll get it." Stick went out to the bar, still holding the newspaper in front of him, still not at ease talking to the girl. Young little colored girl, and he felt awkward. He came back in with a bottle of vodka. The girl was lacing a glass of ice with Lea & Perrins and Tabasco.

"He like it hot?"

"Probably."

"I hope so. It's the only way I fix it." She took the vodka bottle, poured in a couple of ounces, and filled the glass with tomato juice.

"You work with your mama?"

"I told you I was a cleaning lady."

"Come on, really. What do you do?"

"I suppose you'll learn sooner or later anyway," the girl said. "I'm a brain surgeon." She moved past him with the Bloody Mary.

Stick watched her tight little can cross the living room and go into the hall, then heard her voice.

"Come on, sport. Time to open those baby blues and face the world."

Stick made bacon and fried some eggs in the grease.

When the girl came out again she was dressed in slacks and a blouse and earrings, a jacket over her arm. She didn't care for fried eggs, asked if they had any real coffee and settled for freeze-dried instant. Stick got up the nerve to ask her a few questions while she drank her coffee and read Shirley Eder and Earl Wilson. Her name was Marlys. She was twenty years old, not a brain surgeon, she worked in the office of a department store as a secretary.

Marlys grabbed her jacket and purse, yelled into the bedroom, "See you, sport," and was gone.

When Frank came out in his jockeys with the empty glass, looking like he'd been through major surgery the night before, Stick said, "What's Rule Number Nine?"

Frank said, "For Christ sake, lemme alone."

He looked terrible first thing in the morning, his hairdo mussed up and needing a shave, sad, wet eyes looking out of a swollen face. Stick could understand why the colored girl was anxious to leave. Frank's bedroom probably smelled like a sour-mash still.

"Don't feel so good, uh?"

"I'm all right. Once I have some breakfast."

"You throw up yet? Get down there and make love to the toilet bowl?"

Frank didn't answer. He turned the fire on under the pan of water.

"Rule Number Eight," Stick said. "Never go back to an old bar or hangout. You go to Sportree's."

"An old hangout. I've been there twice, three times."

"Rule Number Nine. Never tell anyone your business. You pick up a broad, her *mother* knows what you do."

"She doesn't know me," Frank said, "not by name. We never met."

"Never tell a junkie even your name," Stick said. "The place is a dope store, full of heads. Rule Number Ten— you want another one? Never associate with people known to be in crime. Your friend Sportree—into many things, right? beginning with dope—and probably everybody else in the place."

Frank jiggled the pan of water to make it boil faster. "The guy's a friend of mine. I talked to him for a while, then Marlys came in, we been getting to know each other."

"Marlys," Stick said. "I thought you went out with Karen."

"I went out with Sonny, since we're keeping records. I ran into her coming in, waited an hour while she changed into an identical outfit, and we went out, had dinner."

"Yeah?"

"Yeah what?"

"What happened?"

Frank looked over from the range. "It's a long, boring story. For your record, Sonny doesn't kiss and hug on the first date. Maybe not on the second or third or fourth, either. Maybe she never does. Maybe not even if you married her."

"What'd you do, try and rape her?"

"I bought her dinner. Forty-eight bucks with the tip. She takes a couple of bites of filet and leaves it. We come back here, it's nighty-night time, that's it."

"What'd you talk about?"

"Her. What do you think? She's in a couple of Chevy ads, you'd think she was a fucking movie star. I told her I'd been there already, used to take out a girl was in the movies. She isn't even listening. You tell her something, she's thinking about what she's going to say next about herself. It's not worth it. Forty-eight bucks—I say, You want to go somewhere else, hear some music? No. How about, I know a place we can see some interesting characters. No."

"So you went alone."

"I couldn't find anybody and it was just as well I didn't," Frank said, "since I ran into Marlys."

"She must be pretty good."

Frank looked over again as he took the water off the fire.

"Buddy, it's all good. Like chili, when you're in the mood. Even when it's bad it's good."

"I guess so," Stick said. "Matter of degree." He waited a moment, then said it. "I never done it with a colored girl."

"Or a Jewish girl, as I recall," Frank said. "Only White Anglo-Saxon Protestants."

"No, my wife was a Catholic at one time, when we first got married. There was another girl I used to go with when I was about eighteen, she was a Catholic, too."

"That's interesting," Frank said. He poured a cup of instant and took it over to the table. "You certainly talk about interesting things." Stirring the coffee, he began looking at the morning paper.

"You want to see something interesting," Stick said, "page three. Another guy shot knocking down a liquor store." He watched Frank turn the page.

"Where?"

"Down near the bottom. Bringing the total to six in the past week. You see it? Six guys shot, four killed, in attempted robberies. What does it tell you?"

Frank was looking at the news story. "The cop, it says Patrolman William Cotter, called out, 'Freeze! Police officer!' The suspect, Haven Owens—a jig," Frank said, "you can tell by the name—pointed his revolver at Patrolman Cotter, then turned and attempted to run from the store. He was shot three times in the back . . . wounds proved fatal . . . pronounced dead on arrival at Wayne County General. I like that wounds proved fatal—hit three times in the back with a fucking thirty-eight."

"What does it tell you?" Stick said. "Doesn't come right out and say, but the cop's waiting there, isn't he?"

"Of course he is. I know that. Christ, a little kid'd know it."

"So you go in a place now, since they're cracking down," Stick said, "how do you know it isn't staked out?"

"Because we don't work in Detroit. These suburban places, Troy, Clawson, for Christ sake, they don't have cops for stakeouts."

"You know that for a fact?"

"Hey, have we seen any? I don't mean feel it, as you say, imagine it, like the A&P. Have we actually seen any stakeouts?"

"All we need is one," Stick said. "We won't see any more for ten to twenty-five years."

13

THE BRIGHT-GREEN REPAINTED CHEVY Nova stalled three times before they were out of the shopping center.

"The idle's set too low," Frank said. "I don't want to seem critical but how come, all the cars, you pick this turkey?"

"I think what sold me was the key on the visor," Stick said. "It's just cold."

"*Cold*? It's seventy degrees out."

"It was probably sitting there all day. Belongs to some kid works in one of the stores." When they were stopped at a light and the engine stalled again, Stick said, "Or else the idle's set too low."

It was eight twenty now, almost dark. Stick turned onto Southfield and eased over to the right lane, in no hurry, the store would be waiting.

Frank said, "You go any slower, this thing is going to roll over and die."

Stick didn't say anything. Maybe he was putting off getting there and that's why he didn't mind the car stalling. They were both stalling. He'd watch the approaching headlights, then shift his eyes to the rearview mirror. Police cars were black and white with blue-and-red bubbles. Oklahoma State Police were also black and white. And Texas. Texas Department of Public Safety. Black and white with three flashers on top—count 'em, three—in case anybody didn't know they were cops. He thought of something else, what an old boy from Oklahoma had said. "Do you know why there's a litter barrel every mile going down the highway in Texas?" "No, why?" "To dispose of all the shit they hand you in that state."

In Missouri they were cream-colored.

They drove past the bank, parked on the dark side of the Chinese restaurant, and walked across the alley to the Food Lanes supermarket.

Stick went in the front entrance and took a shopping cart as he moved along the aisle past the checkout counters—only two of them busy with customers. He'd circle through the store before coming back to the checkouts.

Frank went in the side door. Past the magazine rack Stick had mentioned, he looked toward the brightly lighted produce department, then glanced over at the cashier's enclosure and saw two heads, one bald, one a tall blond beehive.

Frank walked through the empty produce department to the back of the store, to the double doors with the little glass windows, and looked into the storage area. A couple of stockboys were loading cases onto hand trucks. By the time Frank got back to the front, Stick was at one of the checkout counters with a few grocery items in his cart, waiting behind a customer. A man in a sport shirt was standing at the magazine rack. He picked out a copy of *Outdoor Life* as Frank walked past him, to the cashier's window.

Frank looked over his shoulder. The guy was leafing through the magazine. He turned to the window again and the blond girl with the beehive, a two-hundred-pounder, was waiting for him.

"Can I help you?"

"Yes, you can," Frank said. He took the Python out of his safari jacket and rested it in the opening. "You can unlock the door if you will, please, and let me in."

Stick watched him go around, wait by the door a moment, then slip into the enclosure. He could see three heads in there now, the blond one higher than Frank's and the bald one. No one else seemed to have noticed Frank. The two checkout girls looked tired and probably wouldn't give a shit if the place caught fire, long as they got out.

Stick's turn came and the checkout girl began ringing up his groceries, a few things they needed anyway.

She said, "You like these buckwheat flakes?" pausing to study the box.

"I sure do," Stick said. "They're honey-flavored."

"I'll have to try them," the checkout girl said. She tore off the tape and gave him the total. Four oh nine.

Stick opened his poplin jacket and showed her the Smith sticking out of his pants. Like a dirty old man in front of a little kid.

"You see it?"

"Oh my," the checkout girl said. She was in her forties and seemed like a friendly, easygoing person. "I've never been held up before. Lord, this is the first time."

Stick was pretty sure she wouldn't do anything dumb. "Something to tell your friends about," he said.

"I sure will." She tensed up then. "I mean I won't if you don't want me to."

"No, it's okay. Put the money in a bag. Just the bills." He got his own bag from the end of the counter and put the groceries in it while the checkout girl emptied the cash register. "Then get those other ones down there," Stick said, "the other cash registers."

The checkout girl at the next counter was busy with a Jewish-looking lady who was unloading a cart piled with groceries and telling the girl how a hundred dollars a week used to take care of everything, her hair and her cleaning woman, and now it barely covered food the way prices were, but she wasn't going to cut down or skimp because her husband insisted on only prime sirloin, filets or standing rib and also liked his snacks and that's where the money went, on meat like it was from sacred cows and the snacks, pastries, ice cream, he loved peanut brittle, something sweet to snack on watching TV.

The checkout girl was concentrating on ringing up the items, then would pause and lay on a buzzer for a few seconds to get a carry-out boy who never appeared. She probably didn't hear anything the woman said. That was fine, she was busy and had things on her mind.

"I'll tell you what," Stick said to his checkout girl. "On the other cash registers, take out the tray inside—you can carry four—and take them over to the cashier's place." He picked up his groceries and the shopping bag with the money in it. "I'll be right behind you."

If the Jewish lady ever finished and left, he'd come back for that cash register. He hoped he wouldn't get involved with her and have to tell her to lie down on the floor or something. The woman looked like she'd scream. The last thing he wanted was a screamer. That's why he liked his checkout girl—following her along the front of the counters as she stepped into each one and collected the cash register tray—she was excited and naturally scared, but she was probably already thinking how she was going to tell it after, the biggest thing that ever happened to her.

Stick noticed the guy at the magazine rack, half turned away from it. He wondered if the guy had looked down, just then, at his magazine.

Frank opened the door to the cashier's enclosure. Stick and the checkout girl stepped inside with her trays.

"Come on in," Frank said. "Mr. Miller here's having a little trouble with the safe."

The manager was down on his knees, fooling with the dial of the safe built into the counter. The big girl with the beehive was watching him, biting her lower lip.

Stick handed the checkout girl the bag of currency. "Put everything in here, will you? Except checks and silver." He touched Frank on the arm then and nodded toward the magazine rack.

"I saw him," Frank said.

The big girl glanced over.

"Honey, get down there by Mr. Miller, will you, please? Tell him he doesn't open the safe right now, I'm going to cause him pain and suffering."

"The guy just looked over," Stick said.

Frank's head rose. He studied the guy, not saying anything.

"He knows something's going on," Stick said. "Five people in here having a convention."

"Take it easy," Frank said.

Take it easy? Stick looked at him. He was taking it easy, his voice was calm, what the fuck was he talking about, take it easy.

Frank was stooped over the manager again, touching the big Python gently to the man's head.

"I'm going to count to three, Mr. Miller."

"I can't help it," the manager said, "I'm trying. I can't see the numbers with these glasses, they're my old pair. My regular glasses that I use, the frames broke—"

"Okay," Frank said.

"—and they're in being repaired. I was supposed to have them the next day, but they didn't have the frames—"

"Hey," Frank said, "I believe you, no shit, I really do. Just get out of the way." He glanced at the big girl's name tag. "Let Annette get in there. Give her the numbers."

Stick watched the guy close the magazine and put it under his arm. The guy hesitated but didn't look over. He got himself ready and started for the side entrance.

"Hey—" Stick said.

Frank looked up. The guy was going through the door, hurrying now as he moved through the breezeway to the outer door.

"He saw us," Stick said.

"Mr. Miller," Frank said to the manager, "a guy just walked out with a magazine without paying for it—the cheap son of a bitch."

"We better move," Stick said.

Frank looked at him. "Take it easy, okay?"

It got to him again, hooked him. Stick waited, making sure his voice would be calm, and moved closer to Frank.

"The guy's out, and if he's got a dime in his pocket we're going to be seeing the fucking colored lights in about three minutes."

"Or maybe he didn't notice anything," Frank said. "We're here, man, we're going to get what we came for." Looking down again: "Annette, would you mind, please, opening the fucking safe?" Saying it calmly, for Stick more than for the big blond girl.

Stick knew it. He had to keep himself in control again. It was crowded in here, the checkout girl staring at him then looking away quickly, he wanted to take what they had right now and get out. But the big blond girl was saying something. She had the safe open and Frank was stooped down next to her, holding the grocery bag. Stick looked at the clock on the wall.

Frank told everybody to lie down and not move and if

he saw a head raise up he'd blow it off, giving them the farewell address in his cool-gunman voice. Stick took the bag from him. Going out, he glanced at the clock again. The Jewish-looking lady was still there, the checkout girl loading bags and buzzing the buzzer. Stick wasn't sure how much time had passed since the guy left with the magazine. Enough, though. He didn't see the guy outside anywhere. He didn't expect to. He kept a few steps ahead of Frank, who was holding back on purpose walking to the car. Fucking games.

They got in the Nova. Frank slammed his door, it didn't catch and he had to open it and slam it again.

"I hope it starts," Frank said, "and doesn't konk out. You think it's cold?"

Stick didn't say anything. He pushed the accelerator down halfway, held it, and snapped on the ignition. The engine caught at once with a good, heavy roar. Stick gave it a little more gas to be sure and listened to the idle. It was fine. But there was another sound, far away, a shrill, irritating sound that went *who-who, who-who*, and kept it up, getting louder, scaring the shit out of anybody sitting in a stolen car with a grocery bag full of money, scaring them way more than the old standard siren ever did.

Frank said, "Let's get out of here." Not quite as cool as before.

The blue-and-red flashers were coming down South-field, weaving through the traffic, still a couple of blocks away. They saw the flashers as they came out of the shadow and turned in front of the Chinese place. Stick glanced and saw enough, looked away to figure out where he was going, and saw the man coming out of the restaurant, the man with a magazine running out across the drive, then stopping dead as he saw the green Nova and the two guys inside. He was about five feet away from them when he ran back into the restaurant.

The red-and-blue flashing squad car with its awful *who-who* wail almost lost it taking the corner, got itself straightened out passing the bank and the Chinese place, and swerved into the Food Lanes parking lot as Stick eased the Nova around the far corner of the restaurant, cut through the open blacktop area behind the Michigan National Bank, and hit Southfield already doing thirty, not fast enough to attract attention but enough to get them out of there. Stick could picture the guy running over to the squad car, waving the magazine at them and pointing. *A green car!* Or if he knew anything—*A green '72 Nova went that way!* Shit.

Frank was hunched around, looking back. "Nothing yet." He spotted the flashers a half mile back as they were going through an amber past Michigan Bell. "There they are."

Stick edged over to the left and followed the curving ramp that led to the Lodge Expressway. He didn't take it, though. He ducked out on the spur that connected with the Northland service drive, followed it to the first overpass, crossed the expressway, and two minutes later was weaving through the mile-long parking area on the east side of the Northland shopping complex.

Stick felt better.

There was no hurry now, no red-and-blue flashers in sight. They were hidden among rows of shining automobiles, protected by the mass of the department store, Hudson's Northland, rising above the arcades of shops and stores and neon lights that formed a wall against the darkness and the police, wherever they were, over there somewhere.

Stick felt pretty good, in fact, realizing he was in control and had been in control from the time the cop car came fishtailing around the corner. He had used his head and timed it and got out of there without squealing the tires or doing anything dumb. That was a good feeling, once it was over and he could look back at it. Frank, Mr. Cool, was still tense, watching for cops.

Stick glanced at him. "How about a J&B?"

"How about a couple?" Frank said. He paused and got some of his calm back. "Since we got nothing else to do."

14

THE DINING ROOM WAS PANELED and brightly lighted. Not in there, Frank said. In the cocktail lounge that was marble and velvet and dark wood, with imitation gas lamps and waitresses in French-maid outfits. Stick said, You think we're dressed all right? Frank said, Relax.

He was getting it all back now.

"It's the same booze in the bottles," Frank said. "The rest of the shit is overhead. But not bad, uh? I used to come here."

He called the waitress with the dark-dyed hairdo and rosy makeup dear and ordered doubles, Scotch and a bourbon. It was funny, Frank was at ease now and Stick felt awkward, sitting in the booth with his poplin jacket on and the Food Lanes shopping bag next to him—the groceries in with the money, maybe two grand or more in there—afraid the manager or somebody was going to come over and ask them to leave because they weren't dressed right.

"Here's to it," Frank said. He raised his glass and took a drink. "You were right about the guy with the magazine. You see him outside?"

"See him—I almost ran over him."

"You should've. Teach him to mind his fucking business."

"Another half a minute," Stick said, "we wouldn't be here."

Frank sipped his drink. "Adds a little color. Otherwise it'd be routine, like a job. Same thing all the time."

"It was close," Stick said.

"Sure it was close, in a way it was. We're looking in the fucking whites of their eyes. But we did it. Suck in a little, let them go by, then take off. It's called timing. We don't have to put it down as a rule because we've got it, instinctively."

"You telling me you like it?" Stick said. "The flashers, that sound? That's a terrible sound to hear coming at you."

"It's part of it. You don't have to like it, no," Frank said. "You accept it, the possibility, and when it happens you keep it together."

"What're the odds?" Stick said. "One close one out of what, thirty? That's not bad, but maybe we've been lucky and it's starting to catch up."

"No, if you know what you're doing, each one is like the first time only better, because you've been there. Incidentally, it's thirty-one."

"But things can happen," Stick said. "In the grocery, I tell you the guy saw us. No, you're playing some fucking game, you're going to stay there till you get the safe. That's not going by instinct or rules or anything, that's so fucking dumb it's stupid."

"We're here, right? And we got what was in the safe."

"We're here—you want to do it like that every time?"

"All right—" Frank paused and lit a cigarette, then motioned to the waitress to do it again. "You're saying don't take unnecessary chances. I agree, up to a point. But the nature of the business, you play it as you come to it. The rules are basically good, *but* what I'm saying, you can't fit them into each and every situation."

"You're the one made them up," Stick said, "ten rules for success and happiness. Now you want to throw them out."

"Did I say that?"

"It's the same thing."

"Look, we start with the rules, fine. We obey them like the fucking Ten Commandments, nothing wrong with that, we're just starting out. But we also have experience now, instinct. We know as much about it, maybe more than anybody in the business."

"I don't know," Stick said, "thirty in a row—thirty-one in a row—maybe it's time to rest awhile. It doesn't seem like much at the time, but it's hard work, it takes it out of you."

"That's right, it's not the kind of work for somebody with a heart condition. Hernia, it doesn't matter. Picking up money never gave anybody a hernia. It's hard work but not hard labor." Frank paused. "Actually, the amount of effort to pick up one or two grand, it doesn't take any more to lift twenty or thirty or, say, fifty grand. You follow me?"

"I'm ahead of you," Stick said. "I can see it coming."

"Don't start shifting around, listen a minute. I'm talking about what if we do the same thing practically we've been doing, only we pick up, say, fifty times more. What's wrong with that? One shot, we take a trip, we don't work for months."

"It seems to me we discussed banks one time, savings and loan," Stick said. "What're the odds, fifty-fifty?"

"I'm not talking about a bank."

"You going to tell me, or I have to guess? I remember this other time we're in a bar you get me into a quiz game. What's the best way to make the most money? The simplest way."

The waitress came with the drinks, giving Frank a chance to sit back and take his time. He waited until she walked away.

"I've been giving this a lot of thought," he said. "I'm not talking about some half-assed stunt like we walk into the downtown branch of the National Bank of Detroit. This one's real."

"Okay, it's not a bank. How many more guesses do I have?"

"I wasn't going to tell you about it till I thought you were ready. I'm still not sure you are." Frank paused, but Stick didn't say anything. "I'm talking about your attitude," Frank said. "I want to lay something on you and be able to discuss it like I'm talking to a pro, man who's been there. But if this thing tonight shook you up, then I don't think you're ready and maybe it's possible you never will be."

"I drove the car," Stick said.

"Yeah, you drove the car." Frank waited.

Stick took a drink. He could see a couple of kids arguing. Unbelievable. You were the one was scared, I wasn't. You were, too. I was not. Were, too. Maybe not in those words, but it would be the same thing.

He said, "All right, when you think I'm ready. Then again, if you don't think I'll ever be ready, you know what you can do with your great idea."

"I'll tell you something else," Frank said, "since you're in a nice open frame of mind. There'd be some other people involved."

Stick shook his head, very slowly, watching Frank, the two of them staring at each other in the gaslit cocktail lounge.

"You're trying different ways—why don't you come right out with it?"

"With what?"

"You want to knock off this twosome shit, split up. All right, that's fine with me, any time you want."

"I say anything about splitting up?"

"You haven't said anything at *all* yet. Everything is what you *didn't* say, for Christ sake. You want to say something, say it, and quit jerking around."

"I'm considering something," Frank said.

Stick had the urge to punch him out, go over the table and give him one. The son of a bitch, sitting there doing his cool number.

"I've got a proposition," Frank was saying, "but I don't want to spring it on you prematurely. I want to be sure you've got the balls for it before I tell you the whole thing."

"Leak out a little at a time. That's what you're doing, trying to get me to bite."

"Uh-uhn, getting reactions."

"Why don't we talk about it again," Stick said, "sometime when a flasher's coming up behind us and you're pissing your pants."

Frank looked up at Stick as he slid out of the booth, the Food Lanes shopping bag in his hand.

"We're a little edgy, huh? I must've said something hit you where you live."

Stick was tired of it and didn't want to play anymore. "You going to stay or what?"

"No, I'm ready. I'll get the bill, you get the car." He looked for the waitress, then at Stick again. "A different one, right? In case they spotted that green turkey out there."

"I had that in mind," Stick said. His voice was calm, he wasn't going to let Frank rattle him anymore, not tonight. "You want any particular make or model?"

"One that doesn't stall'd be nice," Frank said. "See what you can do."

There was valet parking, but no board with keys on it by the entrance. The attendants probably parked the cars in the shopping plaza lot as close to the restaurant as they could and maybe even put the keys under the seat.

Stick rolled the top of the grocery bag a little tighter in his hand and walked out past the people waiting for their cars.

It would be easy to take one. If he didn't have to wait for Frank or swing back and pick him up—and see the owner of the car running out yelling for him to stop. Gee, I'm sorry, sir, is it yours? I guess I got the wrong one. And go through all that.

Frank complicated things. If he'd knock off the shit and stick to the rules, they could do very well in a year, shake hands, and dissolve the partnership.

He had told Frank about where he'd be, down toward the end of the lot, past the light poles and the car bodies shining in the darkness, and maybe over a couple of rows. He'd probably have to use the clips, do some rewiring under the dash. There were enough cars, a good selection, but he was tired and didn't feel like concentrating and getting himself into a calm-alert frame of mind. He shouldn't have let Frank bother him like that. He shouldn't have said he'd get a car, asking him what kind he wanted. That was dumb, playing Frank's game with him, like a little kid. Two kids playing chicken. Frank acting, talking about the big hit, fifty grand and some other people involved, trying to get a rise out of him with the big mystery hit. What he should do maybe, call Frank on it. Say, Come on, sure, I'm ready, let's go. Except the dumb shit might think he had to quit talking about it and do it and they'd walk in someplace for the big hit playing I-dare-you and get their fucking heads blown off.

He looked back, glancing over his shoulder, to see if he was far enough away from the restaurant.

Someone was coming along behind him.

Not Frank or a parking attendant, he was pretty sure. A guy taking his time. About thirty feet back, keeping pace, a thin, elongated figure against the lights of the restaurant. Not anyone he had noticed in front. He had a feeling the guy was black, and it tightened him up a little. The feeling just came, a reaction. There was no reason to be suspicious of the guy. The guy was going to get his car. A car he owned. That was kind of funny, he was out here to steal one, commit a crime, and he was worried about being robbed.

Stick moved through the rows of cars on his left, parked in two rows front end to front end, to the next aisle. He looked back. Nothing. He continued on toward the end of the lot. There were streetlights beyond the darkness and the sound of cars. When he looked back again, the guy was in the aisle, thirty feet behind him.

The second guy stepped into the open directly in front of him and stood waiting. Stick could see he was black. Tall like the one behind him, a couple of basketball players with easy moves. The guy's arms were folded, his hands beneath his biceps. He could be waiting for his friend, the guy following him.

Which was about as likely as waiting for a streetcar.

Stick moved out to walk around the guy, and the guy stepped out with him. He had to stop then or keep going and say excuse me or turn around and run. He stopped.

The black guy unfolded his arms so Stick could see the

revolver in his hand. He was pretty sure it was real. The black guy said, "How you this evening?"

"Pretty good," Stick said. "Well, no, I take that back." He grinned to show the guy he was easy to get along with.

"Where your car at?"

"You might not believe this," Stick said, "but I don't have one."

"You don't, huh? You out for a stroll?" His gaze shifted as the tall, skinny one who'd been following came up on Stick's left. "He say he don't have a car."

"Put your arms out," the skinny black guy said.

Stick did it, holding the grocery bag extended in his left hand. He felt the guy pat him down, his jacket pockets and then his hips and back pockets. The guy's hands didn't go around to the front. He lifted Stick's wallet, took out the money, and dropped the wallet on the pavement.

Stick said, "Thank you." It just came out. He thought of the manager at the Kroger store who'd thanked him and told him to come back again.

"Twenty and three singles," the skinny black guy said. "Man, where your keys?"

"He left them in the car," the black guy with the gun said. "Come on, man, show it to us."

"I'm telling you, I don't have a car. I got to get one myself."

"You going to steal it?" the skinny black guy said. He sounded amused.

Stick looked at him, at his sweatshirt with the sleeves cut off, showing his long, stringy muscles. Six-three or -four, with a nice outside jump shot and tough under the boards. They could go to some schoolyard with lights and play one-on-one.

"If all you want's a car, shit, help yourself," Stick said. "What one you want?"

"We'll take yours, man, anything you got," the black guy with the gun said. "What's in the bag? You got some booze?"

"Buckwheat flakes," Stick said. "Cereal, a few other things."

The guy motioned with the gun. "Hand it to him."

Stick turned a little to face the skinny guy, backing away and bringing the grocery bag up in front of him with both hands on it. He felt the rear bumper of the car behind him, against his legs.

He said, "You guys want groceries, why don't you go the store, help yourself?"

The black guy with the gun said, "Man, what you got in there you don't want us to have?" He motioned to his partner. "See what he's got."

Stick's right hand went under his jacket and closed on the butt of the .38. That was as far as he got. Before he could pull it or jerk the grocery bag out of reach, the skinny black guy got a grip on the bag, pushed him, grunted something, and threw a quick, hard jab into the side of his face. The grocery bag tore open between them, ripped apart, as Stick fell against the car, rolled to keep his balance, and held onto the trunk lid. He was dazed, his face numb, but he was still gripping the .38 under his jacket, like he was holding his stomach.

Both of the black guys were looking at the pavement, at the money scattered in a little pile with the cereal and the bread and boxes of Jell-O. The skinny black guy stooped down and began to pick it up, saying, Man, look, man, look at the motherfucking money the motherfucker's got, man, *look at it*—scooping it up as fast as he could and stuffing it in the torn remains of the grocery bag.

The black guy with the gun looked from the money to Stick lying against the trunk of the car. He said, "Man, you robbed some place, didn't you? Shit." He began to grin, looking at the money again, and laughed, getting happy-excited about it, like finding money in the street.

"Man *robbed* a place, put it in a bag—"

He stopped—because if the man was a holdup man, if he was an armed robber—

Stick had the .38 out, extended, pointed at the guy.

The black guy with the gun said, "Shit," the excitement gone out of his voice. He held his revolver in front of him but pointed at a down angle and away from Stick.

The skinny black guy hadn't looked up. He was down there, getting it all back into the torn-up bag, saying, "Look at it. Man, will you . . . look . . . at . . . it."

"Turn around," Stick said to the guy with the gun, "and let's see your arm. Throw it down there as far as you can."

The skinny black guy stopped talking and looked up from the pavement.

Stick could see him but kept his attention on the guy with the gun. When the guy didn't move, Stick said, "I don't know what you got, some Mickey Mouse piece. This one's a thirty-eight Smith. It'll go clean through you and break some windows down the street. Now turn the fuck around and throw it away."

The skinny guy crouched on the pavement said, "They two of us, man. How you going to get us both?"

Stick turned toward him a little but kept the .38 on the other one. "You worried about it," he said, "I'll do you first."

"Buuullshit. You ain't going to do nobody." The skinny guy got to his feet, holding the torn sack against his body. His free hand went into his pocket and came out with a clasp knife. Watching Stick, he opened the blade with his teeth.

"Shiiit, come on, man, hand me that thing. Let's cut out the bullshit."

"Do what he say," the black guy with the gun said. He was careful with the gun, not moving it, but he seemed confident again. It was in the tone of his voice.

Neither of them moved. The skinny guy waited, his hand extended with the knife in it—five, six feet away— patient, sure of himself. He said, "Man, you ever shoot that thing? You know how? Come on, give it to me. We let you go home with your buckwheat flakes."

He wasn't sure which one of them he should look at.

He wasn't sure if he could fire the gun at either of them. He didn't like the guy's sound, the skinny black guy hold- ing the money, but he didn't know if he could shoot him. He had had them for a moment and now he was losing it. He knew it and could feel it and he couldn't think of any- thing to say.

If he had had a little more time to make up his mind, maybe he would have said it wasn't worth it, shit no, and handed over the gun and taken his groceries and gone home. Maybe he looked like he was wavering, scared. Or he looked so easy the skinny guy couldn't resist going for him.

That's what the guy did, rushed him, pulling his knife hand back to throw it into him.

Stick shot him, not more than a yard away, and heard his scream with the heavy report of the gun.

The other black guy was caught by surprise, not ready until it was already happening, hurrying to get the re- volver on the man, firing once, too soon.

Stick shot him twice, he was pretty sure in the chest. The guy fired again, wildly, a reflex action, and made a gasping sound, like the wind was knocked out of him, as he fell to the pavement.

The skinny black guy was running, holding the grocery bag against his sweatshirt. Stick heard himself yell at the guy to stop, to hold it right there, seeing the guy running and knowing he was going to keep running, and he fired almost as he yelled it, one shot from the .38 that caught him in the middle of the back. The skinny guy bounced off a car and hit the pavement facedown.

Stick didn't roll him over or feel for a pulse. He pulled the torn bag out from under him, in a hurry to get it, knowing he was leaving some bills but not caring about them, not wanting to touch the guy. He remembered that. He remembered the sound of someone running on pavement, coming this way, a dark figure against the restaurant sign, the way the skinny black guy had appeared when he first saw him. That seemed like a long time ago. Some other night. But he had talked to the guy less than a minute ago and now the guy was dead. The black guy with the gun lay on his back with his eyes open, staring at nothing. Maybe he could've talked to them a little more. Said, Look, you know how it is. I went to a lot of trouble for this, man. You want some, go get your own. Talk it over with them, couple of guys in the same business. No, a different type of business, but they'd understand things he did. He felt like he knew them. Couple of guys, shoot some baskets, play a little one-on-one, have a few beers after. The sound of the running steps was close, almost on top of him. He could hear someone breathing, out of breath.

"Jesus Christ," Frank said. He looked at the two black guys on the pavement and at Stick holding the .38 tightly against the grocery bag, and said it again, "Jesus Christ."

15

IT WAS IN THE *NEWS* the next afternoon. Frank went out for beer and brought back a paper. He read the story through, twice, and had a beer open for Stick when he came out of the shower and sat down in his striped shorts.

Stick lit a cigarette first and drank some of the beer. He was anxious, but at the same time he wasn't sure he wanted to read it. Maybe it would be better not to know anything about the two guys.

"Nobody saw us?"

Frank shook his head. "Uh-unh. I figure we were in the cab before anybody found them."

"It say who they were?"

"Read it."

Stick looked down at the paper.

"Man, you did a job," Frank said.

There was a quiet tone of respect in his voice Stick had never heard before.

The one-column story referred to it as "The Northland Slaying" and related how Andrew Seed and Walter Wheeler, both residents of Detroit, had been found shot to death in the parking lot of the shopping plaza, victims of an unknown assailant. Police were proceeding with an investigation, though there were no witnesses to the shooting or apparent motive other than attempted robbery. Both victims were known to the police.

Seed had been arrested several times on charges of robbery, felonious assault, and rape, and had served time in both the Detroit House of Correction and the Southern Michigan Prison at Jackson. Wheeler had a record of narcotics arrests and a conviction in addition to a list of assault and robbery charges. Both were also described as having been outstanding athletes while in high school, seven years before. Both had won All-City basketball recognition, first team, and All-State honorable mention.

"I knew it," Stick said. "It was a funny feeling, the way they moved or something, I knew they'd played and I wondered, What're they doing out here trying to hustle somebody?"

"You played," Frank said. "What were you doing, trying to steal a fucking car?"

"I wasn't that good, All-City. Those guys made All-City, All-State honorable mention."

"You were good with the Smith," Frank said. "Jesus, I couldn't believe it. Bam, bam—that's it, no fucking around. I wish I could've seen their faces. They're going to pull this easy hustle in a parking lot. Guy comes along with a bag of groceries, going home to Mom and the kids. Yeah? That's what you think, motherfuckers. Man, next thing they know, they're fucking dead. That time just before, that few seconds, that's what I'd like to have seen. You should've waited for me. I'd have helped you."

"You could've done the whole thing," Stick said. "Any time. Listen, I think about it, I don't even believe it happened. I see the guy running away, I can still see him—this light-colored sweatshirt on with the sleeves cut off—I yelled at him to stop and I shot him, I mean I killed him."

"Because he wouldn't stop," Frank said. He sounded a little surprised. "What were you supposed to do, let him get away? He's got our twenty-three hundred, forty-eight bucks. Guy's a fucking thief."

"You don't kill somebody because he steals something."

"Bull*shit*, you don't. What do the cops do? They shoot you, man. You don't stop, they shoot you."

"I don't know," Stick said. "This is different."

"He was taking our money. You're supposed to let him take it? Sure, go ahead, any time. Bullshit, you're protecting our property."

"Frank, we stole it."

"Right, and that makes it ours. They weren't taking it from the store, going to all that work and getting their nerves stretched out, no, they think they're taking it from some meek, defenseless asshole who isn't going to do anything about it. Well, they made a mistake. And one's all you get."

Stick drew on his cigarette. He could see the skinny black guy running with his shoulders hunched. He should have gotten in between some cars, but he ran instead, already with one bullet in his side. The guy had nerve. He was holding all that money and he was going to keep it. Stick wondered if the guy was married and had a family. He wondered if he'd be listed in the death notices and if there'd be a funeral and if many people would attend. The two guys must've had friends. They'd gone to school in Detroit. He imagined a lot of black people at a cemetery. He thought about his little girl for some reason and wondered what she was doing.

"Maybe we ought to rest awhile," he said to Frank.

"What're we doing?" Frank said, "We're sitting down, we're resting. I was thinking we ought to have a party."

"I mean knock it off for a while," Stick said. "Make sure they don't have something on us."

"The police? How could they?"

"They said there weren't any witnesses, but they wouldn't say if there were, would they? I mean maybe there's a way we can be traced."

Frank shook his head. "No way. No car, no gun. We got the cab at least, what, a mile away from there. Nobody saw us or even knows it was two guys, right? And if there's no way they can even begin to trace us, we're clear."

"We're clear," Stick said, "but I still killed two guys."

"You sure did," Frank said. "Man. Listen, forget everything I said, we were talking in the bar, I said maybe you weren't ready for this thing I had in mind? I take it all back. You're ready."

"In the bar—you mean just before?"

"I told you I'd been working something out?"

"Yeah, I remember."

"Couple of days we'll know."

Stick wasn't sure he was following. He hadn't slept very well. All night he kept waking up and hearing the .38 going off and seeing the two black guys, not dreaming it but thinking about it, especially seeing the one who'd tried to run.

"Couple of days we'll know what?"

"Whether or not we can set it up. It's going to take a little doing."

"*We*," Stick said. "You mean more than just you and me. You mentioned in the bar, you said, since I was in a nice, open frame of mind—"

"That was a little smart-ass of me," Frank said. "I take it back. Forget it. But yes, there would be a few other people involved, because of the nature of the job. Couple of helpers, guys to watch more than anything else. And one on the inside. She's already there. In fact, it's because of her I got the idea. We've been talking it over."

Stick was listening, paying close attention now. He knew Frank was serious.

He said, "You mean one of the broads lives here?"

"No, no, those broads, Christ," Frank said. "This one's got it together and she likes the idea. You understand, she wouldn't be in on it, involved directly, so to speak, but she'd give us all the inside information we'd need."

"If she doesn't live here—" Stick said. He stopped then. "You mean the colored broad? What's her name? Marlys?"

"That's right, you met her. I forgot," Frank said. "Very smart and grown-up for her age."

Stick could see her again, in the white bra and panties. Cute little black girl, yes, very grown-up.

"She said, I think she said she worked downtown, in an office."

"She works at Hudson's," Frank said. "Up on the fifteenth floor."

Stick frowned. "That's a department store."

"You bet it is," Frank said. "The biggest one in town."

"You're crazy," Stick said, "Jesus," and shook his head.

Frank waited.

"You're out of your fucking mind. Hudson's."

"The J. L. Hudson Company," Frank said. "You know how many cash registers they got in the store?"

"I don't want to know," Stick said. "I don't give a shit if they got a thousand."

"You're close," Frank said.

16

AT ONE POINT IN THE evening there were fifteen people in the apartment. Frank found most of them; others dropped in. They'd come and go.

The way it started, Frank went out for a couple of hours in the afternoon—Stick didn't ask where—and when he got back he brought four of the career ladies up from the pool, Karen, Jackie, Mary Kay, and Arlene, and started making them drinks. Stick got out the grapefruit juice for the Salty Dogs and Arlene came over to help him. Even Mary Kay said she'd have one. It was strange to see four girls sitting around the apartment in swimming suits. Frank said they dressed up the place. Stick thought it looked like a Nevada whorehouse, the way he imagined one would look. Frank had had a few—wherever he'd gone—and was already a little high. He told Stick to come on and quit moping around. Stick decided, Why not? He'd have some fun and quit thinking about the two colored guys.

Then Frank told him Marlys was going to try and stop by later, and winked, and Stick thought about the two guys again. He wondered if Marlys knew them.

A little later Stick asked Mary Kay, didn't she have to go to work? And was surprised when she told him she was going to call in and say she was in bed with the curse. It was amazing, one and a half Salty Dogs.

Still a little later Frank went down to the ice machine, ran into Barry Kleiman in his white belt and white loafers talking to Sonny the Model and one of the young married couples, the Kaplans, and got them to come up. Frank went in and put on his safari jacket and wore it with a chain he borrowed from Arlene, no shirt. Barry Kleiman said, Hey, cool.

They weren't sure when Donna, the dental hygienist, and her boyfriend came in; but they were there and after a while seemed like they'd always been there. Donna's boyfriend, Gordon, was working on his PhD in something that had to do with clinical psychology and he spent a lot of time with Karen.

Every time Stick looked around, Arlene seemed to be watching him. That was the feeling he got. Like he was committed to her. She seemed to want to talk and finally steered him toward the balcony. But when they were out there, he spotted three of the junior executives down on the patio drinking beer and yelled at them to come up and be sociable.

The junior executives came in cautiously, like gunfighters in their tight Levi's, and slouched around awhile; but pretty soon they were mixing it up with the others and Stick was glad he had invited them. It didn't hurt to be friendly. He told Arlene to be nice to them. The poor ass-holes were giving their lives to IBM and the Ford Motor Company and they deserved a little fun.

They were good-looking young guys with families in Bloomfield Hills, two of them named Ron and one named Scott. Ernest Stickley, Jr., could see them jogging through life in their thirty-dollar Adidas, never knowing it was hard. But he didn't hold it against them. He didn't give a shit, one way or the other, what they did.

One of the junior executive Rons went down to his apartment and brought back a Baggie of grass and a pack of yellow cigarette paper. He said it was Nicaragua Gold, which impressed Karen and Jackie. Karen named a couple of other kinds she had smoked. Ron got a few joints going and pretty soon everybody was taking drags. Stick tried it. It was all right, but he didn't feel anything from the two drags and he didn't like the smell at all. Frank said, Man, you know what we used to call this, this kind of scene? Reefer madness. Ron, rolling the joints, said you could call it anything you wanted, but why get mad? Stick asked him if they let you smoke grass out at the Ford Motor Company. Ron looked at him and said, Ford Motor Company? I'm with Merrill fucking Lynch, man. How's your portfolio?

Frank was cruising on Scotch and reefer. He'd poke Stick and say, "Hey, are we having a party or we having a party?" Like he was celebrating something. Stick would say yeah, they were having a party.

Arlene was following Stick's instructions, being nice to the junior executive named Scott. She looked small and frail sitting next to him on the floor. Scott was studying the hammered silver pendant that hung between her breasts. Arlene told him it was a Navajo love symbol or else a sheep spirit, she'd forgotten which, and Scott was nodding, showing his interest in primitive art.

Stick went over to the eight-hundred-dollar hi-fi and put on a Billy Crash Craddock while he picked out a Loretta Lynn, an Olivia Newton-John, and a brand-new LP by Jerry Reed, the Alabama Wild Man.

Mary Kay said, "You like that music?"

He looked up to see her standing close to him with a smudged empty glass in her hand, blue eyes looking at him that he bet were blurry inside. Nice, clean-looking girl letting go. Why did that surprise him? Or what did clean-looking have to do with it?

Stick put the LPs down, took Mary Kay by the arm, and said some of the words along with Billy Crash Craddock, telling her perfect love is milk and honey, Captain Crunch, and you in the morning.

Stick said, "To answer your question, it's not one of my top ten favorites, but I guess I like it pretty well."

Mary Kay said, "I think it's a bunch of shit. Perfect love, milk and honey, and all that. It's a lot of bullshit."

A voice told Stick to get out, quick. If he hesitated, she'd tell him how she was the oldest girl in a family of ten kids and how she had to do all the housework and pay her own way through Blessed Sacrament because her dad drank and sat around the house in his undershirt reading paperbacks, and how she went to Mass regularly, prayed for a vocation, worked hard, always did what she was told, and now she was a registered nurse with her own apartment, a savings account, and five doctors who wanted to get her in bed. If he didn't listen to the voice, he'd ask her, What's the problem? and she'd say, What's the *problem?* What good was all the hard work and being good? *This?* Then they'd get in a half-assed discussion about the meaning of life and maybe he'd get her in bed and maybe he wouldn't. Talk about bullshit. Mary Kay was just learning.

Stick said, "Listen, let me get back to you, okay? I think we need some ice."

He got out of that one, for the time being, but missed the scene with Frank and Sonny, which he'd have gotten a kick out of.

Sonny had had a glass of milk all evening; nothing else, no potato chips and dip or Pinconning cheese. She was out on the balcony with Barry Kleiman and one of the junior executives, the quieter of the two Rons. He and Barry were standing with their fingers in their tight pockets, posing with the poser, very cool and serious about it.

Frank had nothing personal against Sonny. He kind of liked her style, the fashion model put-on and all that. He liked it even though it pissed him off. Look at her. She was skinny, no tits to speak of; bony hips; long, thin, dumb-looking hair she liked to get out of her eyes with a lazy little toss of her head. No personality, no real person in there Frank could see. She stood around with her box pushed out like she was daring anybody to make a grab for it. That's what got him the most.

When Frank walked up to them Sonny handed him her empty milk glass.

"How about another one?" he said. "If you think you can handle it."

"No thanks." She didn't look at him. She turned to Barry and said, "I've got to get going," like it was his place and he was the host. "Have to be at the studio by seven tomorrow. I think we're doing some Oldsmobile stuff."

"Listen," Barry said, "what we were talking about. How can I help you? Tell me."

She gave him a little shrug. "I don't know. Talk to your agency."

"I mean it," Barry said, "you'd be terrific. I don't mean behind the counter, one of the broads there in the uniform. I mean a customer...high fashion, a very chic chick. You bite into this quarter-pounder. Your eyes are saying mmmmm, great. And here's the part. You get some mustard right here, on the corner of your mouth. Jesus, you'll have every guy watching TV wanting to lick it off."

Sonny was nodding, picturing it. "That's earthy," she

said. "Or how about, just the tip of my tongue comes out?" She demonstrated. "In a tight close-up."

"Ter-*rif*ic."

"With kind of a down-under look." Sonny lowered her head slightly and gazed up with a sleepy, bedroom look in her eyes. "What do you think?"

Frank said, "You mind if I ask you a personal question?"

Sonny made it seem an effort to turn and look at him. "I think not, if it's all the same to you."

"What do you mean, all the same?"

"If you don't mind, then."

"But I mind. That's why I want to ask you something."

"All right, what is it?"

"You ever been laid?"

Sonny's composure held. She said, "Have you?"

"A few times."

"Good for you." She looked at Barry again. "You mind walking me down?"

"Do I *mind*? Does a bear—no, strike that." Barry held out his hand to Frank. "Man, it was fun, I mean it."

Frank said, "You going to try your luck?"

Barry frowned, a quick expression of pain. "Hey, come on, let's keep it light, okay?"

"He'll be right back," Sonny said. "Unless he's going home."

Frank looked at the quiet, good-looking Ron with his big shoulders and golf shirt.

"You following this?"

"Am I following it?"

"What's going on. The principle involved. The great truth. You know what it is?"

The quiet, good-looking Ron shook his head. "I guess you lost me."

"It's called," Frank said, "the myth of the pussy."

"Hey, what?" Barry was grinning. "Come *on*. The myth of the—what?"

"The myth of the pussy," Frank said again, solemnly. "It seems like a simple little harmless thing, doesn't it? Something every broad in the world has. But you know what? They sit back on their little myth and watch guys break up homes over it, go in debt, mess up their lives. It can make an intelligent man act like a little kid and do weird things . . . this idea, this myth that's been built up. Girls say, You're bigger and stronger than we are, buddy, but we got something you want, so watch it. They use the myth to get you to open doors and give them things and pick up checks. And some use it more than others." He looked at Sonny. "Some think it's really a big deal, and you know what? They don't even know what it's for."

"That's wild," Barry said, a little awed. "It really is."

"No, what it is," Frank said, "it's a fucking shame."

A little before eleven they drove over to Woodward to find a liquor store open. They needed Scotch, vodka, and beer.

"And grapefruit juice," Stick said. Stick had got to the car first and he was driving. "All the broads I think're drinking Salty Dogs. You taste one?"

"They're having a good time," Frank said. "Everybody is. I think there's only one turd in the bunch and she left. No, maybe there's two, I don't know."

"Who do you mean?"

"That Irish broad, the nurse."

"She's all right. She's going through her first change."

"I'll check it out," Frank said. "That cute little house-wife, I think she's another sleeper. Her husband's busy with Jackie, looking down her kitty outfit. Or I could steer him over to Karen. Yeah, I could do that. She'd keep him busy. Christ, her appetite, she'd eat him up."

Stick glanced over. "You wouldn't mind that?"

"What do you mean?"

"You wouldn't care if he got her in the sack?"

"Why should I?"

"I just wondered."

"Karen's all right," Frank said. "You know, nice build and all. Maybe a little bigger than she looks. I'd say she goes about one thirty-five. But she's kind of bossy. You see her there? Like she's the hostess, getting Jackie to pass the cheese and crackers. That's the way she is. In the sack she says, Okay, that's enough of that, now do this. Yeah, that's it right there. A little more. No, a little up. That's it, good. Okay, the other thing again. All right, let's try this. It's like doing it by the fucking numbers." Frank put his head back on the seat cushion, relaxed, comfortably high. "It's something," he said. "All that scratch in one place. You believe it?"

"You don't say that anymore," Stick said. "Now you say, 'Well, here we are.'"

"That's right. Well, here we are. And you say, 'You sure?' Say it."

"You sure?"

"You bet your ass I'm sure," Frank said. "That's a quiz show on TV. It isn't really, but those dumb broads, they believe anything you tell them. Hey, am I sure? You better believe it I'm sure, because we got it fucking knocked and it's going to get even better. I don't know what happened to Marlys. I saw her this afternoon, I told her stop by, she wasn't doing anything. What's tomorrow?"

"Sunday."

"All right we'll wait'll Monday, we'll go down there,

I'll show you around. It's not worked out yet, you understand, but I want you, I think you ought to start to get the
feel of the place."

"I've been to Hudson's, Frank. Lots of times."

"Upstairs, where the offices are?"

"I think so."

"End of the day," Frank said, "they leave fifty bucks in
the cash registers, everything else goes upstairs."

Stick was a little high but alert, moving along in the
night traffic on North Woodward, watching for a liquor
store that was still open. He didn't want to get in an argument with Frank or even a discussion with him now.
It would be pointless. Frank would start yelling and
wouldn't remember anything.

Stick said, "You look on your side."

He saw it then, in the next block across the street, the
neon sign and the lights inside, and felt himself relax
again.

"There's a place, Frank. It's still open."

They parked in front. Going in, Frank said, "What do
we need? J&B, vodka?"

"Grapefruit juice," Stick said. "I don't think they'll
have it. Maybe."

He asked the clerk behind the counter, a neat little
gray-haired man with rimless glasses, and the clerk said,
"Yes sir, right over there. All your juices."

Stick got four big cans and brought them to the
counter. Frank was ordering the liquor. Stick went over to
the cooler and pulled out a case of Stroh's, the brand the
young executives were drinking. Walking back to the
counter with it, where the clerk was waiting, he saw
Frank up by the front of the store.

"We got everything?"

"I'll be right back," Frank said. He went out the door.

There were three bottles of J&B and three top-priced Smirnoffs on the counter. The clerk was putting them one at a time into an empty liquor case.

"That be it?" the clerk asked.

"I guess a couple bottles of tonic," Stick said. He got potato chips and Fritos from a rack, a can of mixed nuts. The clerk was coming back with the tonic. He stopped, his eyes wide open behind the rimless glasses. Stick looked around.

Frank was coming toward the counter with a grin on his face, his Colt Python in one hand and Stick's Smith & Wesson in the other.

"What the fuck," Frank said. "Right?"

Stick almost said his name. It was right there—*Frank, you dumb shit.*

But they were into it already and it wasn't something you could call off and say, Oops, just a minute, let's start over. Or tell the guy you were just kidding.

No, he had to take the poor scared-shitless clerk into the backroom and tie him up with masking tape and paste a strip of it over his mouth, while Frank, the dumb shit, was out there cleaning the cash register. Stick didn't say a word to the clerk. He laid him on the floor and patted his shoulder, twice, telling the guy with the touch to be calm and not to move.

He still didn't say anything out in the store again. He picked up the cardboard case and took it to the car, got in and waited while Frank brought out a case of Scotch and a case of Jack Daniel's and put them on the back seat.

Leaning in he said, "You think while we're at it we should grab some more beer?"

Stick, waiting behind the wheel, said, "Get in the fuck-ing car."

When Frank's door slammed, Stick took his time pulling away from the curb and working the T-bird into the stream of traffic, his eyes going to the mirror to watch the headlights coming up behind them.

"I'd say we got five, six hundred," Frank said. "You missed the wad in the guy's pocket. I got it, I went back there for the cases. Let's see, plus a couple hundred worth of booze, just like that. Not bad for a quick trip to the store, uh?"

Stick didn't answer.

"You're not going to talk to me now?" Frank said. "Is that my punishment? For Christ sake, you saw the guy, the place is empty. You can't pass up something like that, it's too good."

"We're in a car," Stick said, "in your name. The registration, the plates."

"All right—this one time, it's an exception. There it is, you got to make up your mind that instant. So it's done and nobody saw us."

"How do you know?"

"Because I didn't see anybody. You got to see somebody for them to see you."

"Somebody could've been coming in," Stick said. "They see Twogun in there, for Christ sake, and they get out. But the car's sitting there, right? And they could've gotten the number."

"All right—we get home, we report it stolen."

"Frank, a dozen witnesses up there, they know we went out. The guy in the store, it'd take him one second to pick us out of a lineup."

"Hey, Ernest," Frank said, "don't be so fucking earnest, all right? It was a spur-of-the-moment thing. It's over, it's done. You want to live by the book all the time, is that it?"

"You wrote the book, ten rules for success and happiness," Stick said. "I didn't."

Neither of them said anything else until they reached the apartment building and Stick turned into the private parking area.

"There's a spot, right by the door."

"I already saw it," Stick said. He eased the T-bird into the space, turned off the ignition and the headlights.

Frank opened his door and paused. "You know something?"

Stick waited. "What?"

"I been thinking. I bet we end up with Karen and Jackie," Frank said. "I mean if Marlys doesn't show."

"That's what you been thinking, uh?"

"Yeah. Which one you want?"

17

THERE WEREN'T AS MANY PEOPLE, though it was still smoky and smelled of incense and the noise level was high. Somebody had taken off Loretta Lynn and put on one of Frank's Mantovanis. The quiet, good-looking Ron had passed out on Stick's bed, smelling like he'd thrown up. Stick came out to the bar and looked around as he made a drink.

Arlene wasn't there. Or the junior executive who'd been admiring her jewelry.

Frank came over to make a drink. "The place's thinning out. We'll have to get it going again."

Stick didn't say anything. He wasn't angry, he was tired. He wasn't upset about the guy passed out on his bed, he wanted to go sit down someplace where it was quiet. He thought of Arlene again. He'd like to get with her and fool around a little. Except she wasn't here.

"I don't think Marlys's coming," Frank said. "We better get a couple before they're all taken." He looked around the room, his gaze going past Mary Kay on the sofa. "I don't know, it's getting pretty thin."

He knew Sonny had left. He didn't see Donna or Arlene. Jackie was smashed. Karen—maybe.

Gordon, Donna's boyfriend, came over with two empty glasses.

"Where's Donna?" Frank asked him, "in the can?"

"She left," Gordon said. "I told her I'd be down in a lit-

tle while. It's my Saturday, but I'm having a very interesting conversation with Karen."

"It's your Saturday?"

"Every other Saturday I spend the night with Donna,"
Gordon said.

"What if you felt like doing it on a Tuesday night?"

Gordon was intently measuring an ounce and a half of
vodka into each glass. He used the stainless-steel shot
glass and had been measuring ounces and a half for over
four hours.

"Sometimes Tuesday night," Gordon said, "if there's a
special reason. See, Donna doesn't work on Wednesday."

"She rations it, uh?" Frank said. "She afraid she's going to run out?"

"No, she's got an idea about not overdoing anything.
See, Donna's very parental. Usually she's into her critical
parent. She uses *should* a lot. You *should* do this, you
shouldn't do that. Then on Saturday, every other Saturday,
she allows herself to get into her nurturing parent. Now
Karen"—Gordon looked over to where she was sitting on
the floor against a pile of orange and yellow pillows, still
in her bikini—"Karen is very visceral. She feels and acts
instinctively and has quite a lot of natural child in her."

"You're going to find out," Frank said, "she's got a lot
of mama in her, too."

Gordon held the can of grapefruit juice poised over the
glasses. He seemed interested and a little surprised.

"Are you into transactional analysis?"

"Uh-unh," Frank said, "but I've been into Karen." He
looked around to get Stick's reaction. Stick wasn't there.

There were two Arlenes looking at him, the one holding
the door partly open, wearing a man's white shirt over her

bikini, and a life-size cutout of her on the other side of the room, the one Arlene pouting, the other smiling in her silver Hi-Performance Cams outfit and white boots.

Arlene said, "I don't know if I want to talk to you. I don't see you all week, you don't call—"

"I came by here, twice, you weren't home," Stick said.

"You don't pay any attention to me, you're busy talking to the other girls, putting your arms around them."

"How about you and the guy on the floor?"

"You told me to be nice to him."

"Is he here?"

"He got sick."

"Arlene," Stick said, "I haven't been feeling too good myself all week. I went to see a doctor, he checked me over, gave me a prescription—"

Arlene was showing a little concern. "What's wrong with you?"

"I went to the drugstore, gave the prescription to the pharmacist?"

"Yeah?"

"He said, 'You want this filled?' I said, 'No, it's a holdup note in Latin, you dumb shit.'"

She laughed and he was in.

Sitting down next to Mary Kay, alone on the sofa, Frank said, "Honey, you cook any good?"

Mary Kay looked at him with filmy eyes.

"Why?"

"I'm making conversation. You tell me what you like and I'll tell you what I like. Move over a little." He pulled an LP out from under him and sailed it at the hi-fi.

"If you want to talk, why don't you talk about something real," Mary Kay said.

"Okay. How do you like that Mantovani? Nice, uh?"

"It sounds like cafeteria music."

"What do you like, then?"

"Nothing you've got, I looked. Country-western and Mantovani."

"What're you," Frank said, "you get a little high, you like to argue?"

"I'm not arguing, I'm telling you what I don't like."

"You're a nurse, RN. I thought you were very sympathetic, got along with people, like to make them happy and all."

"Where'd you hear that?"

"Really," Frank said quietly. "I bet you are sympathetic . . . kind. I can see it in your eyes, you care about people."

"I tried," Mary Kay said. "I used to knock myself out being nice. And you know what you get? You get stepped on. If you're nice to people, they're nice to you? That's a lot of crap. They use you, give you the worst jobs. 'Sullivan, take care of One Oh Four—' "

"Who's Sullivan?"

"I'm Sullivan. 'Right away, Sullivan. One Oh Four's painting his wall with shit again.' That's what I get all night, things like that."

"This person," Frank said, "actually paints with it?"

"Smears it on the wall. Sometimes he eats it."

"Jesus," Frank said. He took the smudged glass from her hand. "Here, let me freshen you up." He fixed both of them a drink—Mary Kay's in a clean glass—came back and sat down again, close to her.

"You forgot the salt."

"You shouldn't use salt. It's not good for you." Frank laid his arm along the back of the couch and let his hand fall lightly on Mary Kay's shoulder.

"Listen, let me tell you something," he said, using his quiet tone again. "People who care, people who feel, are nice to one another. They make each other happy."

"I heard that," Mary Kay said. "All my life I heard it. And if you don't mind my saying, or whether you mind or not—"

"Wait, don't say it, Mary Kay." He turned her face gently and stared at her with his nice-guy expression. "All right?" Her lips were parted; there was a fresh pimple scar at the corner of her mouth. "You have to trust people, Mary Kay. No matter what kind of deals you've been handed, you have to go on trusting and believing."

"In what?"

"In yourself, in your own right to . . . have a good time and enjoy life. People need people." Frank paused, trying to think of the words to the song. "People who need people . . . lonely people needing people—" He was improvising now. "You know what I mean? They share their loneliness and find something."

"I get so tired of it," Mary Kay said.

"I know," Frank said. He was pretty tired himself, but he moved in closer. "I know."

"Why do I have to smile all the time and be nice when I don't feel like it?"

"You don't, honey. You should do what you feel like doing."

She snuggled against him, closing her eyes. "God, I get tired. The same thing all the time. Sometimes my face aches from smiling when I don't even want to."

"Listen, Mary Kay, how'd you like to stretch out and get comfortable?"

"Hmmm?"

"Go to your place, where it's quiet. What do you think?"

"I don't know if I could make it down the stairs, I'm so tired."

"Well, I guess I could help you," Frank said.

Mary Kay sighed. "You're a nice person, you know that?"

"I try to be," Frank said.

There was one picture Stick especially liked, Arlene kneeling with her back arched, winking as she kissed the knob of a Hi-Performance Four-Speed Shifter. There were shots of Arlene at the Nationals and at hot-rod shows and conventions. Arlene said the SEMA show was her favorite. Stick said he guessed it would be. He didn't ask her what See-Ma meant. He fixed them a couple more drinks and brought them over to the couch where Arlene was holding open the big album and got to see pictures of her posing with "Big Daddy" Don Garlits, Tom "Mongoose" McEwan, and Don "The Snake" Prudhomme. She pointed them out and named them. She said she also had their autographs on a pair of her panties as a joke, if he wanted to see them. Stick said he'd look at anything she showed him.

All right, then.

The second album she got out wasn't as big as the first one and there weren't any shots of Hi-Performance machinery in it or silver outfits or white boots, either. It was Arlene in her birthday suit, skinny hips, perky boobs, and all, like a little girl posing for exotica. Stick said they were really cute pictures of her and found out her friend was a camera nut and owned three Nikons that cost about a thousand dollars each.

He wondered if she showed him the nude pictures on purpose. Whether she did or not they were working.

When she went in the bathroom to take a leak—that's what she said, "Be right back, I got to take a leak"—Stick picked up the two drinks and headed for the bedroom. He heard the toilet flush and the door open and then Arlene's voice out in the other room.

"Hey, where are you?"

He let her find him, lying on the bed in his striped shorts with the two drinks on the night table. Arlene said, "I suppose you want me to take my rings off."

The next thing she said was, "You always perspire a little, don't you?"

"Not always," Stick said. "Sometimes I do, I don't know why. It doesn't have anything to do with, you know, the enjoyment of it."

"I wondered."

Then neither of them said anything for a little while, lying next to each other in the darkness, touching but not holding. The light from the hall reached the bed, and if he turned his head he could see their outline, in shadow, on the wall close by. He liked her. He liked the way she moved, skinny little thing. She was funny. And she was smarter than she sounded. She sounded goofy, but it was just that she let it come out and didn't try to act or be someone else. He liked her a lot.

Arlene said, "I wondered, it made me think of it, something else."

"What?"

"If you were sweating that time—in the bar."

"What bar?"

"In Hazel Park."

"I don't remember any bar—" He stopped.

"The one a couple of blocks from the Hazel Park track."

Stick sat up. He knocked a glass off the night table get-

ting the light on. She was looking up at him, eyes wide
open, her hands clutching the sheet to her tightly.

"Oh God, I shouldn't have said anything, should I?"

"Wait a minute, I'm not sure what you're talking
about. Some bar I was supposed to've been at? You
thought you saw me?"

"I saw you," Arlene said. "You and Frank, you took
the money from him, I thought, God, they're cops. And
then you locked us in the room."

"You were at the bar?"

"I had on this scarf, over my hair? You looked right at
me once, I thought sure, I thought, Oh God, but I guess
you were busy, you looked right at me but didn't see me. I
didn't know whether to say anything or not. Then in the
room"—Arlene started to smile and she giggled—"it was
really funny, everybody was opening bottles and drinking
and the woman was trying to stop them. She kept hitting
the poor guy—"

"Who were you with?"

"Just my friend."

"Arlene," Stick said, as gently as he could, "did you tell
him you knew us?"

The telephone rang in the living room.

She frowned. "Who's that? I know he's out of town."
She was up, climbing over him—

"Arlene—let it ring."

—running naked out of the room.

"Arlene—"

He listened and heard her saying, "Really? But isn't it
kinda late? . . . No, but it's pretty short notice."

She'd been in the bar, seen the whole thing, and admit-
ted it to him. Christ Almighty.

"No, no, I didn't mean *that*. Hon, you know I'd love to

come.... Yeah, okay.... God, I'll have to move....
Okay, 'bye."

Arlene came back in the room, hurrying, not looking at
Stick.

"I'm going to Chicago. Calls up practically in the middle of the night—gets the big urge, I *have* to come. He's
sending the company plane over."

"Arlene," Stick said, "hold still a minute, okay?" He
watched her come out of the closet with a suitcase and
clothes over her arm.

"He's at the APAA convention. God, I didn't know it
was the APAA. Who's he had in the booth? Some girl,
must be from Chicago. But what would she wear?"

"Arlene, did you tell him about me and Frank, that you
knew us?"

She looked at him briefly. "You got to get out of here,
I'm being picked up. Why didn't he take me when he
went? The prick. No, I shouldn't say that, he's been very
nice to me."

"I'll drive you," Stick said. "We can talk in the car."

She was in the closet again, getting a green pantsuit and
the shiny silver costume. "One of his hot-rodders is on the
way over. God, the way they drive. He doesn't believe
anybody should get to the airport more than ten minutes
early. It means they don't have anything to do."

"Arlene, did you tell him our names?"

"Why would I do that?"

"Say yes or no, will you?"

"No, of course not."

He felt a little relief, just a little. It was funny, in a way,
watching her run around the room naked, taking things
out of the dresser and throwing them in the suitcase.

"Did you tell anybody else?"

She was out of the room again.

"Like the police!"

He heard the bathroom door close and lock and the water turned on. Stick put on his pants and shoes. He couldn't believe it. Carrying his shirt he went into the hall and stood close to the bathroom door.

"Arlene?"

"Hon, I can't talk now, I'm doing my eyes."

"You didn't tell anybody else?"

"God, I almost forgot. Look in the front closet, see if there's something hanging there, from the cleaner's."

Stick hesitated, then went into the living room, putting his shirt on.

The front doorbell rang.

Almost immediately the bathroom door opened.

"Get in the bedroom."

Her eyes, vividly lined and framed in silver-green, were wide open. She ran in and put on the green pantsuit before running back out to open the door. Stick waited.

He heard her say, "Larry, hi, you're a doll." She laughed at something Larry said. "No, no, get in the car, I'll be right out."

Arlene came into the bedroom with a dry cleaner's plastic bag, finished packing in less than half a minute, and picked up the suitcase.

"Arlene—"

"I'll talk to you when I get back," Arlene said and rolled her eyes at him. "God."

The front door closed and there was silence. Stick made himself a drink, Canadian Club, because her friend didn't have bourbon. He drank it and smoked a cigarette and went back to Arlene's bed for the night.

18

"**I PUT A STACK OF** plastic glasses on the bar," Frank said, "they use the good ones, have to go and *find* them so they can put their cigarettes out in the glasses—plastic ones're sitting right there."

Stick passed him, going out to the kitchen with a couple of ashtrays.

"I'm surprised you got anything in there at all," Frank said and picked up a glass. "Look at the cigarette butts. Potato chips all over, ground in the carpet, drinks spilled—like they're raised in a fucking barn."

Stick came out of the kitchen. He felt like moving, doing something, and kept picturing Arlene running around naked, packing the suitcase.

"Next morning always looks depressing," Stick said. "Especially with the sun out." He could remember hangovers in the Florida sun. He went through the open doors to the balcony and began gathering empty beer cans. "Nobody's down at the pool yet."

"And they aren't at church," Frank said. "Where you suppose all the partygoers are?"

"Throwing up," Stick said. "Hugging their toilets."

"You get the guy out of your bed all right?"

"He opened his eyes, didn't know where he was."

"You didn't come back, uh?"

"This morning," Stick said, "about half-past seven."

He didn't want to mention Arlene just yet—Arlene seeing them in the bar—so he said, "I noticed you weren't home."

"You want to know where I was?"

"With the nurse," Stick said. "I figured you were both about due."

He came in and dropped beer cans into an open grocery bag on the floor. "She any good?"

"The quiet ones," Frank said. He was resting, taking a break with a beer and a cigarette. "You know what they say about the quiet ones."

"I know what they say," Stick said, "I just don't know as it's true."

"Take my word, buddy."

"You promise to marry her?"

"We're engaged," Frank said. "I notice you went out, you must've made some arrangements."

Stick brought in more beer cans from the balcony. He didn't say anything. He let Frank believe whatever he wanted.

"Well, let's see," Frank said. "Karen was with the talker. Jackie was smashed. If you got her kitty outfit off, you might as well've put her jammy-jams on, she was through for the evening, and I can't see you doing a number on some broad's out practically cold, at least I hope you wouldn't. Arlene was already gone when we got back—was it Arlene?"

"You got another cigarette?"

"Last one. Look on my dresser. It must've been Karen, then. She got rid of the talker and you met her at her place."

Stick went into his bedroom; he might as well get his own. He was thinking maybe he should wait until Arlene got back and talk to her again. He didn't know what she really thought about it. Say she didn't tell her friend who they were, fine; but what did she think about it, seeing two guys she knew holding up a bar? She was nutty. It was hard to imagine what she might think. She might even think it was cute.

He could hear Frank in the living room.

"How you like doing it by the numbers? Now the other. Do the thing with the boobs. That Karen—she's too much. Now the one where we stand on our heads."

Stick got a pack of cigarettes from his dresser.

Tell him, he was thinking. You got to tell him sometime.

He opened the pack going out to the front room.

"She too much?"

"I wasn't with Karen," Stick said. "Arlene."

Frank raised his eyebrows, a little surprised. "Arlene—yeah? Not much there but I can see it could be very active, a good workout. Right?"

"She's a nice girl," Stick said.

"Almost all of them are," Frank said. "But is she any good?"

"What're you asking me something like that for?"

"You just asked me the same thing, for Christ sake."

"Okay, let's drop it," Stick said, "get the place cleaned up."

"You hear that? Honest to God," Frank said, "the way you think. You don't sound like a broad, but—I don't know—it's like you think like one, with a broad's mentality. I don't mean that as an insult—"

"You don't, uh?"

"No, it's just you've got a different way of looking at things."

"Wait'll I get a beer," Stick said. "We can sit down and argue for a change."

"We're supposed to be at Sportree's, four o'clock," Frank said.

That stopped it. Stick looked at Frank sitting there with his beer, Frank staring at him, waiting, sort of a little challenge in his expression.

Stick thought, Well, screw him. And then he thought, No, why fight about it?

He said, "What's that, the cocktail hour? Drinks are half price?"

"He's arranged a meeting, a special presentation," Frank said, "I think you're going to be quite interested in."

"Shop at Hudson's and be happy," Stick said. "Am I warm?"

"That's all you are," Frank said. "Shop at Hudson's and make enough to be happy for a year is the way it goes. It's all worked out. He's going to show you how we knock down the biggest department store in town and find happiness. Show you how it's no more trouble than a supermarket."

"Nothing to it, huh?"

"Not if you know what you're doing."

Stick said to himself, I'm not going to get pissed off. I'm not going to get in a dumb argument. I'm not going to say anything, no, nothing at all about Arlene.

He said to Frank, "Okay, let's go, then."

"One more thing," Frank said. "They're all going to be black. At least I think they are. Now, it's okay to call a Negro a Negro. Like with Jewish girls, they know what they are. But don't refer to them as niggers, okay?"

Fuck you, Stick said to himself. He said to Frank, "I'll try not to."

19

THEY WERE IN SPORTREE'S APARTMENT, upstairs over the bar, and Frank was telling them how Stick had shot the two muggers in the Northland parking lot.

Stick was uncomfortable, he didn't like it at all. Three colored guys and a colored girl listening to Frank describe how he'd killed two other colored guys, not telling it the way it actually happened but making him sound like a gunman: The two guys come up and try and take the bag, my partner here doesn't say a word, fuck no, pulls out his piece, .38 Chief's Special, and blows the two guys away.

Blows them away—Christ, he shot one of them in the back.

Sportree would nod as he listened and sometimes smile, but you couldn't tell what he was thinking. Or sometimes what any of them were thinking. There was Sportree in some kind of funny loose open shirt and trading beads. Marlys cool in a bare midriff, showing a dark little navel. And the two guys Sportree had brought in for the job.

Leon Woody, with a beard and moustache, looked like an Arab. He sat quietly, with one leg crossed over the other. He'd smile a little with a gentle gaze that held as long as he wanted it to. Leon Woody reminded Stick of Sportree. There was something African, mysterious, about them. Nothing was going to hurry or surprise them.

The other one, Carmen Billy Ruiz, was Puerto Rican.

His eyelids were heavy with scar tissue and his mouth looked puffy and sore drawing on his Jamaican tailor-made. A long time ago he had been a welterweight with a seventeen-and-seventeen record, then a sparring partner for Chico Vejar, then for Chuck Davey after Davey whipped Vejar. In 1955, in Detroit, he shot and killed a store clerk during a holdup and spent the next seventeen years in Jackson. (Carmen Billy Ruiz said *diez-y-siete* was a bad fucking number; don't mention it in front of him.) He resented the fact Stick had killed two men and said through a smoke cloud, while Frank was telling the story, "What is this shit? He put away a couple of kids." Leon Woody and Sportree looked at each other—Stick noticed this—and Leon Woody said, "Billy, be nice and let the man finish. Then you can tell how many you put away."

Stick was glad, God, he was glad he wasn't going to have any part of this. They could say anything they wanted. He'd listen and nod and seem to go along, and when they were through, that was it. He didn't know these guys or owe them a thing. Be nice, like the man said, and play along.

He nodded yes, he'd have another bourbon, yes please, when Marlys picked up his glass. Marlys was doing the drinks and constructing big Jamaican cigarettes with four pieces of paper each for Billy Ruiz and anybody who wanted one. The redheaded black girl who played the piano wasn't around. Unless she was in the bedroom. Or Sportree could've gotten rid of her for the meeting.

There wasn't any doubt Sportree was in charge. He sat on the couch with Marlys next to him, looking over his shoulder, and sheets of drawing paper on the coffee table that showed the floor plan of several different sections of Hudson's downtown store—including the administrative offices, with dotted lines leading to exits—and a plan of the exterior with adjacent streets indicated.

"We start with the outside," Sportree said and looked at Stick. "You—you here on Farmer Street on the back side of the building, in the bar, right here. You see the Brink's truck turn in the alley that run through the building. You know what I'm saying?"

"I know the alley you mean," Stick said. "It's like a tunnel."

"That's right," Sportree said. "They come in off Farmer, alley bends in there, they pick up the load and come out on the south side the building. Before that, soon as you see it coming, you make the call."

"What's the number?"

"You get the number when I'm through."

Sportree looked at Frank. "You by the telephone outside the men's room, north end of the toy department, fourteenth floor. You been there to see it?"

Frank nodded.

Sportree's gaze moved to Leon Woody. "You watching Frank. You got the doll box, huh, in the Hudson bag."

"Little Curly Laurie Walker's box," Leon Woody said.

Sportree began to smile and shook his head. "Come on, shit—Curly Laurie Walker. That her name?"

"Little redhead girl, three foot tall, she do everything but bleed," Leon Woody said. "Billy try to jump her. I give her to my little girl so she be safe."

"What was that?" Billy Ruiz said. "What'd you say?"

Marlys was laughing and slapped her leg. "I can see him doing it, stoned on his herb."

Billy Ruiz was frowning, puzzled. "See what?"

"Man, let's pay attention," Sportree said. "Okay? You got one minute. Bang on the door the men's room, Billy comes out in his uniform." He looked at Ruiz. "We get that tomorrow, bus driver suit, I know where we can get one. With the holster it be good enough, get you in the office. Okay, so the three of you take the stairs, here, by the exit sign. You go up to the office floor."

"How long's it take them, the Brink's guys?" Frank asked.

"About five minutes," Sportree said. "It varies."

Marlys looked up from the drawings. "You know the man down at the door, he's like a porter? He calls up the office when they come, then we know to expect them in a few minutes. He doesn't call and some dudes walk in with uniforms on, we know they not from Brink's."

"So we get to the office just before the Brink's guys," Frank said, "giving us, say, four minutes."

"Say three," Sportree said, "to get in and get out. They see Billy in the bus driver suit and the gun, they open the door. You two go in behind him, put the people on the floor, take the sacks, put them in the doll box, and get the fuck out, down the stairs to the toy department. You go in the stockroom and put the box on the shelf where all the curly what's-her-name little jive-ass doll boxes are, in the back. The box is already marked." He looked at Leon Woody. "You been in there?"

"Yesterday."

"And they still got enough little curly-ass doll boxes?"

"Whole shelf full. I put it there and see Billy get out of his bus suit."

"All right," Sportree said, "about that time the bell's going to ring and they'll be security people all over the store, at every door and exit. The police, First Precinct, could be there before you get to the ground floor, and then it's time to be cool. First thing, dump your pieces in a trash bin, someplace like that. Then split up and circulate.

They want to search you going out, that's fine, you just a dumb nigger, you don't know what the fuck is going on at *all*. They let you out, you go home. Two days later, this man here"—he looked at Stick—"goes up to the stockroom and gets the doll box with the mark on it. He goes because nobody's seen him before, clean-looking white gentleman. Tell me you see something wrong." He waited.

Frank and Leon shook their heads.

Billy Ruiz said, "How much we going to get?"

"No way of knowing," Sportree said. "I told you, I give you a guarantee, five K off the top. You said beautiful. You want something else now?"

"I want to be with him, carry it out," Billy Ruiz said. "I don't want somebody giving me some shit later—we didn't do so well, here's a humnert bills. Fuck that shit, man, right now."

Stick saw Sportree and Leon Woody look at each other again. "Hey, we trust each other," Sportree said to Billy Ruiz. "Nobody going to cheat nobody. You hear Frank saying anything? Leon? No, we all in this."

"This guy, he picking up the money, I don't even know him," Billy Ruiz said.

"He don't know you, either." Sportree looked over at Stick and back to Billy Ruiz. "You saying you want to pick it up, Billy? You don't trust nobody?"

"I go with him," Billy Ruiz said.

Stick saw the exchange between Sportree and Leon Woody again, their gaze meeting, each one knowing something.

"All right, Billy," Sportree said. "You go with him."

After that they sat around a little while. Sportree went out to the kitchen for something and Frank followed him.

Marlys went over to the hi-fi and picked up a record sleeve. Stick looked over at Leon Woody sitting there quietly with his legs crossed. There was something he wanted to ask him. It wasn't important, but if he got the chance, if the guy happened to look over.

Billy Ruiz said to Marlys, "Hey, Mama, play some of that Al-ton for me, okay?"

Marlys, reading the record sleeve, had her back to them. "You want some Alton Ellis and his Caribbean shit? I'll give you some Stevie," Marlys said. "Be grateful."

"He's all right, his soul," Billy Ruiz said. "It's very close."

"Close about a thousand miles," Marlys said. "Stevie can fake that reggae boogie shit better than Alton can do it straight."

Leon Woody was smiling, listening to them. Stick didn't know what they were talking about. He waited until the music came on. Leon Woody looked over at him, maybe to see what he thought of it.

"You have a little girl?" Stick said.

"Yeah, little eight-year-old. She small, not much bigger than the doll." Leon Woody smiled faintly. "Sportree has trouble with that name, don't he?"

"I got a little girl seven," Stick said. "She's going to be in the second grade next month."

"Is that right? Yeah, they cute that age, aren't they?"

Stick said yeah, they sure were. After that, he couldn't think of anything to say.

It was getting dark when they left. Frank drove. He was up, excited about what they were going to do. He tried to appear calm, but it showed in the way he took off from lights and wheeled the T-bird through traffic.

Stick said, "That Carmen Billy Ruiz—where'd he get a name like that?"

"He's Puerto Rican," Frank said. "He was a fighter once. Fought Chuck Davey—you remember him?"

Stick said, "What I meant to say—where'd they get him, for Christ sake. He could get you in trouble, not even trying."

Frank said, "Don't worry about it. Sportree's going to handle him."

"Is that what he's going to do?" Stick said, "because I'll tell you something, I don't see him doing anything else."

"He's been going down there—he's the one put the whole thing together." Frank looked over at Stick. "Now that you've seen it, what do you think?"

"What do I *think*? I think it looks like amateur night."

"Come on—"

"Come on where? You got a guy with a little girl used to steal TV sets. You got a crazy Puerto Rican living on dope and a guy runs a bar telling you what to do. A bus driver's suit—you imagine that crazy fucking guy walking in in a bus driver's suit? Is he going to have one of those change things on him?"

"He knows what he's doing," Frank said, "Sportree. Listen, that's why I took it to him. Everything he gets into, it goes. He doesn't touch something he doesn't make out."

Stick said, "What's he touching? He's sitting home watching the fucking ball game while you clowns are running around the store with a doll box. I thought you said it was your idea."

"It was, the basic idea, yeah, when I find out Marlys's working in the office. But it was Sportree worked it out. You got any doubts or questions, talk to him about it."

"I'm talking to *you*. I don't even know the guy, what do

I want to talk to him for, like I work for him now or something? We got a nice thing going, two grand a week, we can't even spend it all, you want to go hold up a department store."

"You know for how much?"

"He said you didn't know."

"He told Billy we didn't know. We're talking about minimum, I mean *minimum*, a hundred grand."

"You're crazy," Stick said. "It's all charge accounts there, and checks."

"Uh-unh, not the downtown store. Half the people go there are colored. You think they all got charge accounts?"

"I don't know—" Stick said.

"I know you don't. Listen, fourteen floors of cash registers, every floor the size of a city block. People come in, buy all kinds of things, some on charge, some pay with a check, and a bunch of them, man, a bunch of them, have to pay strictly cash, because that's all they've got."

"Anybody ever do it before?"

"Not the whole thing," Frank said, "that any of us can remember. Ten years ago, maybe more than that, a guy got twelve hundred from a cashier on the mezzanine. All small stuff."

"Small stuff like what we've been doing." Stick said, "and getting away with. Now all of a sudden you want to do the whole fucking thing at once."

"I'll talk to you when you calm down," Frank said. "It's staring you in the face and you can't even see it."

"Relax, huh?"

"Right. Relax and think about it. We walk in—it's waiting there in little gray sacks—and pick it up. Christ, you're outside, what're you worried about?"

"I'm outside—till I go in with that crazy Puerto Rican."

"I told you, what're you worried about him for? I talked to Sportree, he said, Don't worry about Billy."

"I'm not worried, because I'm not going to have anything to do with it," Stick said. "Nothing."

20

STICK LINED UP FOUR PAY phones on Farmer Street, behind the J. L. Hudson Company.

He did this after he'd given in and told Frank okay, but this was the last one, and found out this part of the plan hadn't been thought out at all. What if he went in the bar to call and some guy was using the phone? What if he went in the doughnut shop or the drugstore, the same thing? What if all of a sudden the Brink's truck comes and everybody around there decided to make phone calls? Sportree hadn't planned it at all. He'd gone through the motions. If they made it, fine; if they didn't, well, it wasn't his ass, he wasn't out a thing.

Stick didn't like relying on other people he didn't even know.

He didn't like Arlene knowing about them—Christ, just to add a little more to it—and not knowing where Arlene was and what she was thinking. She hadn't been home all week and he hadn't told Frank about her yet.

He told himself he was dumb. He should've stayed out of this, not learned anything about it. If he wasn't afraid of Frank and he didn't owe him anything, then why was he doing it?

Maybe he felt he did owe him something. Frank could've put him in jail, but he didn't. Shit no, Frank needed him.

He should've left for Florida. Right after shooting the two black guys, the next morning, he should've left and not said a word to Frank.

Now he was into something with three more black guys. Christ, everybody on the street, half the people anyway, seemed to be black. He wondered where everybody was going—if they had someplace to go. Or if they were out of work and just walking around downtown. It was a nice day, mid-seventies, the sky fairly clear. Maybe because some auto plants were shut down. What do you want, a job or a clear sky? He looked across at Hudson's—old, dark-red building filling the block and rising up fifteen floors, then narrowing into a tower that went up another five stories. He wondered where they kept the flag they displayed across the front of the building on some of the U.S. holidays, the biggest American flag ever made.

The Brink's truck was coming south on Farmer, the way Sportree had said it would. Stick went inside the bar on the corner. Nobody was using the phone. He stepped into the booth and made the call.

When the phone rang, Frank turned from the wall, ripped off the sheet of paper that said OUT OF ORDER, and picked up the receiver.

"Toy department."

That was all he said. A moment later he hung up and nodded as he turned.

Leon Woody was playing with a game called Mousetrap, watching the little metal ball rolling through a Rube Goldberg contraption that set off a chain reaction of things hitting things that finally dropped a plastic net over the mouse. Leon Woody left the counter, carrying a big greenish Hudson's shopping bag with a doll box inside, and walked down the main aisle to the men's room.

Frank watched him go inside. He started down the aisle.

Leon Woody came out of the men's, followed by Carmen Billy Ruiz in the Air Force blue bus driver's suit and peaked cap. Frank was ten feet behind them when they went through the door beneath the exit sign.

The stairway took one turn to the fifteenth floor. None of them said anything; the sound of their steps filled the stairwell. Leon Woody opened the door and stepped back to let Billy Ruiz go ahead of him. Billy hesitated.

Leon Woody said, "Take out the piece, hold it flat against your leg, you dig? Go past the elevators, down on the right side. That's this hand here. You see the door, credit department. Don't say nothing. Nod your head, they say anything to you."

Frank, waiting on the stairs, watched Billy Ruiz take out the gun he had given him, Stick's .38 Chief's Special. He could feel his own, the big Python, in the pocket of his safari jacket. The store was air-conditioned, but it was hot in the stairwell. Leon Woody glanced back at him and went through the door.

Frank hurried to catch it before it closed—like he didn't want to be left behind. He went out on the fifteenth floor, cutting diagonally across the main aisle, past the bank of elevators. Billy Ruiz was thirty feet ahead, taking his time. Leon Woody paused by the optical department to look at glasses frames. Frank came up next to him.

"What's he doing?"

"He's all right," Leon Woody said. "Be cool."

They moved on, past theatrical display boards and ticket windows, past the travel service and portrait studio. There were no customers anywhere. Billy Ruiz turned into the credit department. They were fifteen feet behind him now. A face appeared at a teller's window. The door next to the window opened. Billy Ruiz went through. Leon Woody sprinted the last few yards and caught the door. Frank went in behind him, pulling the Colt Python.

He heard Billy Ruiz say, "Turn around, everybody. I mean *every*body, get down on the floor."

Frank saw their faces briefly, their eyes with the startled expressions, two older women and a young man. Marlys wasn't in the room. They got down on their hands and knees, the women awkwardly, and lowered themselves to the carpeting. Billy Ruiz covered them, holding the .38 straight out and down. Leon opened the doll box without taking it out of the shopping bag and set it on a table against the wall where five gray-canvas sacks were waiting. Leon looked at them a moment, then walked over to a door with a frosted-glass window and opened it a little at a time, looking in.

Marlys's eyes rose from her typewriter, but her fingers continued to move over the keys for another few moments. The door beyond her desk was open to an office where a man sat half turned from his desk, talking on a phone and gesturing with his free hand. They couldn't hear his voice. Leon Woody stepped away from the frosted-glass door. Marlys came out, closing it behind her, and Leon nodded toward the sacks.

Frank watched her walk over to the table. She paused, then touched three of the sacks and looked up at Leon Woody. When Leon nodded, she walked back to her office, went in, and closed the door. Like that, not a word.

Leon dropped two of the sacks into the doll box, then the three Marlys had indicated. Frank watched him, not understanding. What difference did it make which ones went in first? He wanted to touch Leon's arm, get his attention, frown at him or something.

He heard Billy Ruiz say, "Jesus!" Like he was sucking in his breath.

Frank looked over and saw him raising the .38-it didn't make sense—raising it up to an angle above his head.

Leon Woody yelled at him, "Hold it!"

And Frank didn't know what was going on, until he looked up, in the direction the .38 was pointing, and saw the window above the row of file cabinets and the guy outside, strapped in a safety harness with a cloth over his shoulder and a squeegee in his hand, standing on the window ledge.

The guy had been there all the time and they hadn't seen him, concentrating on the three people getting down on the floor. The guy standing there, leaning out away from the window, trying to get away from it, fifteen floors up and no place to hide.

Frank wanted to run—seeing the guy staring at them scared to death—get the hell out of here and keep running, forget it, call it off, the whole thing, like it hadn't happened.

Leon Woody said, very quietly, "Shit . . . man seen the whole show. I don't know where my head's at." And he shook it from side to side, almost as if to make sure he was awake. He said then, "Billy—"

Billy Ruiz shot the guy twice, through the glass, shattering the pane, and they saw the red spots blossom on his white T-shirt and his head snap back, maybe screaming—there was a sound, a woman screaming—the guy straining against the harness before his feet slipped from the ledge and his legs and hips dropped away and they could see only the top half of him in the shattered window, his head hanging forward, motionless. The woman inside the room was still screaming.

Billy Ruiz went for the door and Leon said, "Walk, man, don't run. Same way we came." Frank was right behind him, then stopped as Leon shoved the Hudson's shopping bag into his arms and took the Python in both hands.

"Let me have it."

"What for?"

"I'll get rid of it."

"Where you going?"

"Hey, be cool, we all going together."

Frank didn't understand, but he couldn't argue. He let go of the gun and held the Hudson's bag in front of him, his arms around it. It wasn't as heavy as he had thought it would be.

There were a few shoppers down toward the end of the aisle, by display cases. None of them seemed to be looking this way. The rest of the aisle was empty.

The three of them were close together going through the exit door to the stairway. Then Frank had to stop. Holding the box in front of him, he almost piled into Leon Woody standing at the top of the stairs looking down, waiting. Past him, Frank could see Billy Ruiz reaching the landing where the stair made its turn.

"Go on, for Christ sake."

Leon Woody didn't move or say anything. He raised the Colt Python, aiming it down, and shot Billy Ruiz between the shoulder blades, the explosion filling the stairwell as Billy Ruiz was slammed against the wall and slid partway down the rest of the stairway.

Leon Woody moved now. Frank watched him, his profile, bending over Billy Ruiz. He told himself to drop the box or throw it at him and get out, back through the door. He knew he wouldn't make it, though. Leon Woody was looking up, the Python in his hand pointing at him but not aimed at him.

"Come on, man," Leon Woody said, "what you waiting for? You know where to put it, back behind. It's already marked. Then go down the fourth floor, get the escalator. Maybe I see you outside."

Frank watched him go through the door to the toy department. By the time Frank got there, stepping over Billy Ruiz, not looking at him, Leon wasn't anywhere around.

The voice inside Frank Ryan wasn't in condition; it had gone to fat and was pretty weak when it told him he had fucked up and the whole thing was an awful mistake. The voice did get through, and in those words, but Frank barely heard it and it didn't take much to smother the voice completely. A couple of Scotches-on-the-rocks.

Stick said, "Well?"

Frank stood at the bar, between two of the bamboo stools, holding onto the drink. He heard the faint sound of a girl laughing, coming from the patio below, then silence again.

"Well what? It's done."

"I never saw so many police cars," Stick said. "I would say within ten minutes of the time I called, no more than that, they're all over the place, completely around the store, and these guys are running in with their riot guns."

"Don't tell me," Frank said. "They're waiting at the bottom of the escalator, four of them with their guns out. Anybody looks suspicious, 'Would you mind stepping over here?' They're going through packages, searching people, even women."

"How'd you get out?"

"How'd I get out? I walked out. What're they going to find on me? 'Hey, what's going on, Officer?' And they give you something about a routine investigation—five hundred cops in the place, shotguns, riot outfits, everything, it's a routine investigation."

"You ditched your gun all right?"

"Leon took care of it."

"How come Leon?"

Stick was sitting forward in his chair, holding a can of beer between his hands. He watched Frank go over to the coffee table to get a cigarette.

"Weren't you carrying it?"

"I carried the doll box," Frank said. Lighting the cigarette gave him a little time. He walked back to the bar and took a drink of Scotch.

"Yeah? So you gave him your gun?"

"We had a little problem." The whole thing would be in the evening paper—Frank realized that—still, he wanted to tell it the right way, like there was really nothing to it, or Stick was liable to go through the ceiling.

"What kind of problem?"

"Billy shot a guy."

"Jesus—I *told* you."

"Wait a minute, a witness," Frank said. "A guy washing the window."

"Christ Almighty—"

"We look up, the guy saw the whole thing, sees Marlys, so Billy had to shoot him."

"I told you. Christ, didn't I tell you? That guy's going to fuck the whole thing up, not even trying?"

"Will you wait a minute?" Frank said. "Take it easy, okay? and listen." He paused to make sure his voice would sound calm. "Billy pulled something else."

Stick was staring at him, waiting.

"He tried—we're going down the stairs—he tried to grab the box from me. See, he wants the whole thing, probably had it planned all the time and that's why he was going to settle for five. He shoots a couple times and misses, luckily, Christ, and Leon, he's got the Python, he shot him and that was it."

"You left him there?"

"He was dead, for Christ sake."

Stick shook his head slowly and let his breath out and shook his head again. He said, "Oh, boy—well, how do you like the big leagues?"

"We still did it," Frank said. He was being earnest now. "We got the money, five sacks, waiting there in the stock-room."

"Hey, Frank, come on—"

"I'm not shitting you, we got it, it's there. Everything went according to the book except the thing with Billy Ruiz. Okay, Billy's out of it, put his five K back in the pot, you never liked the guy, anyway."

"Frank, you got two dead men—you want to go back in there for the walkie dolly box?"

"I look at it this way," Frank said, getting into it and feeling more at ease, in control. "Whether two guys are dead or not, the money's sitting there waiting. The two guys don't change anything—you think Sportree, Leon Woody's going to say, Yeah, well let's leave it, then? Bull-shit. This is armed robbery, man, and you know what I'm talking about, you go in with a gun and sometimes you have to use it or else you'd carry a fucking water pistol, right? When it's you or him, buddy, you know who comes first or you're in the wrong business. Listen, I saw you blow away two guys in that parking lot. You ought to know what I'm talking about better than I do."

"It's different now," Stick said. "We're not talking about armed robbery, ten to a quarter, we're talking about murder, maybe life."

"I can't argue with you," Frank said, "or quibble about the degree. Yeah, it's different now. But the odds, the odds are the same. You go in, look around, take your time. You don't like the feel, you smell something isn't right, you walk out. Nobody's going to blame you for being careful. You don't like it, get out. If it looks okay, pick up the box. Anywhere along the line something doesn't look right, dump the box, get the fuck out. But remember one thing, my friend, Ernest Stickley, Junior, there's over a hundred grand in the box and it's no heavier than you're carrying the doll in it, a present for your little girl."

There was a silence. Stick took a sip of beer. "I'll think about it," he said.

"What's there to think about? Your part, what you said you'd do, hasn't changed any."

"I said I'd think about it."

Frank put on an act of being calm, in control. He said, "Take your time. But if you turn chickenshit before day after tomorrow, let me know, okay? I'll go get it myself."

Leon Woody came in while Frank was at Sportree's, the two of them sitting in the living room upstairs. Frank saw Marlys in the doorway for a moment: she looked in, didn't nod or say anything and kept going down the hall. Leon Woody said, "How you doing?" and sat down. Frank frowned, looking over at Sportree sitting there in his Afro-Arabian outfit and a big Jamaican smoke held delicately between his fingers.

"She upset about the man wash the windows," Sportree said.

"How upset?"

Sportree shook his head. "Uh-unh, little girl's fine."

"I can't keep up with you," Frank said. "Last week, no, the week before, it was the redheaded girl plays the piano."

"Yeah, she still playing, she happy," Sportree said. "The one I'm worried about is your friend, if he's got his shit together on this thing."

"Well, you say don't worry about Marlys," Frank said. "It's the same thing, you don't have to worry about Stick. I remind him he said he'd get it and he will, I'm sure of it."

"I like a man like that," Sportree said. "Can take his word. I mean if it's true."

"I don't know, I'm saying the same thing to him all the time. I'm in the middle of you two guys, I trust both of you, naturally, so I just assume you trust each other."

"You like him," Sportree said, "hey, then I like him. You give me a Stick, I give you a Leon Woody." He looked over at Leon, who nodded but didn't say anything.

"And take away a Billy Ruiz," Frank was saying. "That was a setup, wasn't it? You knew he wasn't coming out."

"No, he could've made it. It was up to Leon. I told Leon to use his judgment."

"But what for? I mean if you don't trust the guy, what'd you bring him for?"

"Let me explain something to you," Sportree said. "See, Billy's fine for how you use him. Say to him, Billy, here two hundred-dollar bills. You keep one, if you can make that policeman over there eat the other one, tied on your hog. He'd try it, think it was easy money. But see, Billy was very, very dumb. He could go one two three four, no trouble. But something happen he had to go one three seven five, shit, you don't know what the man was going to do. So I told Leon, Hey, you come to where you got to travel light, then dump the excess baggage, man. See, another thing, if Billy was picked up, you got to hold your breath all the time he in there. They could punch him, he wouldn't say a word. As I told you, I trust him. But that man, he so fucking dumb they be getting things out of him he don't even know he telling."

"I guess so," Frank said, "but Christ, killing him like that—I wish we could've got rid of him some other way, put him on a plane to San Juan or someplace."

"Not easy, is it?" Sportree said, in his Afro-Arabian robe, the Jamaican toke between his fingers, watching the gray smoke curl up. "Sometime we have to make sacrifices."

Leon Woody was at the window, watching Frank's T-bird pull away, making sure. Sportree was smoking. He yelled out, "Hey, baby!"

Marlys came in behind the three-foot doll box she was carrying, smiling back there, and placed it on the coffee table by Sportree.

"Little Curly Laurie. You want to know how much she got in her box?"

"Tell us," Sportree said.

"Exactly eighty-seven thousand four hundred and twenty-five."

Sportree smiled in his Jamaican smoke. "You have any trouble?"

"Walked out with it in the bag, Leon's waiting," Marlys said. "I didn't see anybody giving me looks, but I wouldn't want to do it again."

"Divide three into eighty-seven," Sportree said, "you would."

Leon, coming over from the window to sit down, said, "Now this Stick goes in tomorrow, comes out with the box still there, marked. Frank pick him up, they come here all smiling—what do we say then?"

"We say—they open the box," Sportree said, "two sacks in there. Two? Open them, checks. Checks? What's this shit, checks? Where the money sacks? He looks at us, uh? We look at Frank. Hey, Frank? You put the box there the day before yesterday? Frank say yeah, he put it there. He start to look at his friend. His friend start to look at him. One put it there, the other pick it up. But what do they have? Bunch of checks made out to the J. L. and Hudson Company. Somebody begins to say—they looking at each other—Hey, fuck, what is this? What's going on, man? They don't know shit what's going on."

"So maybe they go after each other," Leon Woody said. "One say, You put it there, five sacks in it, or not? The other say, You pick it up, but you don't come out the store with everything."

"That's the way I like to see it," Sportree said. "Now after a while, sometime, they going to look at us. We can look back at them, our eyes saying what is this ofay shit going on? Somebody trying to fuck somebody? Or we can look back at them and not say anything. Frank say to me, You wouldn't be pulling something, would you? Not wanting to come right out and accuse me, you understand? Finally I say to him, Frank, maybe everybody better forget about the whole thing and not think of hurting each other, because if anybody gets hurt, you know who it's going to be. And none of us can go to the police, can we? Because we all in it. So why don't we quit talking about it, dig? And you all go home."

Leon said, "You think he do it, huh, go home and be good?"

"Why would a man want to die at his age?" Sportree said.

Stick got two sets of Michigan plates off cars parked on the roof of the Greyhound bus station and wrapped them in the morning edition of the *Free Press* that ran two follow-up stories on the Hudson's robbery.

There was a graduation-looking photo of a smiling, dark-haired guy, the window washer, and a twenty-year-old shot of Carmen Billy Ruiz in a boxing pose, on the front page, wrapped around the license plates. On page three there was a photo of the window washer's wife and two small children, and on the sports page a column devoted to Billy Ruiz's seventeen-and-seventeen record and how he had been Chuck Davey's sparring partner. Davey, now of the Chuck Davey Insurance Agency, Southfield, recalled that Billy Ruiz liked to eat ice cream—he ate ice cream all the time—but was not much of a puncher.

The two sets of license plates went in the trunk of the T-bird to be transferred to Stick's suitcase. He might use them on the way to Florida, he might not, but extra plates were good to have. He'd pick up a car that afternoon sometime.

He'd decided, finally, to tell Frank his plan and Frank had said, Wait'll you see your cut and you're holding it in your hand before you start talking about leaving.

Stick said don't worry, he was taking his cut, he wasn't going up to the toy department for nothing; but this was the end of it. After, he'd go home get his bag and if Frank would drop him off at a shopping center he'd appreciate it.

Frank said, What about your share in the bank deposit box? Stick said, We can pick it up after, or you give me the same amount out of your cut from the Hudson's deal and keep all what's in the bank. That was all right with Frank. He said, All right, if that's what you want to do. You'll get down there, play on the beach with your little girl, and I'll probably see you in about a week. He said, If I'm in Hawaii or Acapulco or someplace, I'll leave word with the lady, the manager. Frank was in a pretty good mood.

That was about all that was said between them that morning in the apartment and driving downtown. It didn't seem like much after being together three months. Frank drove up to the rooftop parking lot over the bus station and waited for him while he got the license plates. Then drove him around to the Woodward Avenue side of Hudson's and said, "I'll see you in about fifteen minutes."

That was the last they saw of each other for six days.

Stick took an escalator up as far as he could and then a local elevator to the fourteenth floor. It still took him less than five minutes. He located the stockroom first, in an arcade that connected with another section of the store. He roamed through the toy department then for a few minutes. There were only a few customers around—one guy very intently fooling with some kind of a target game, a young guy in jeans with fairly long blond hair—and hardly any salespeople.

He watched the stockroom door another couple of minutes. Nobody went in or came out. He said, Okay, let his breath out slowly, walked over, and pushed through the door.

Frank had said the third aisle over. But he hadn't said which side. The sectioned metal shelves reached almost to the ceiling and it looked like there were boxes of dolls on both sides, all the way down to the end.

America's Little Darling, Baby Angel, Playmate for a Princess, Baby Crissy, Crissy's Cousin Velvet, Jean Marie, Tender Love...Christ, Shirley Temple...Rub-a-Dub Dolly, Saucy, Wendy, Cutie Cleaner, Cathy Quick Curl, Peachy and her Puppets, Beautiful Lee Ann the Dancing Doll...there, Little Curly Laurie Walker. She wasn't bad-looking.

The one he wanted had a little red dot near the bottom of the box. Which wasn't on any of the ones in front. He had to pull them out one at a time to look at the boxes in the row behind. Then two at a time, Christ.

It was in the third row, the fifth one. Stick got it up to the front and shoved boxes in to fill the space. He picked it up. Frank was right, it wasn't heavy at all. He wondered if he should look inside, make sure.

That was when he glanced to the side.

It was strange, recognizing the guy in the quick glance and wanting to do something with the box, not knowing the guy, but knowing who he was—even if he did have long hair and jeans on—and knowing, shit, it was way too late.

"Drop it and put your hands on the shelf, man, right now."

The guy had a big gun like Frank's, some kind of a Mag, the same guy who'd been fooling with the target game.

Stick didn't have anything to lose. He said, "What's going on? What is this, a holdup?"

"It sure looks like it to me," the guy said. He had a little leather case open in his other hand, showing a badge.

Another guy, in a suit, came around the corner from the other side, at the end of the aisle, and that was it.

Stick said, "I was in here looking—I thought it was the men's room."

"You piss on dolls?" the young guy said. "Man," and whistled. "Hey, Walter, he says he thought it was the men's room."

The one in the suit was next to him now. He said, "I can see why he'd think that. All the toilets."

"No, I mean I was looking for a doll for my little girl. Then I had to go to the men's room. I came in here, I saw it wasn't, of course"—Stick was giving the young guy a nice grin he knew already wasn't going to do him any good—"but then I saw these dolls, see, and started looking at them . . . for my little girl."

"You like the one with the red dot on it best?" the young guy said.

"You can read me my rights if you want," Stick said, "I'm not saying another word."

21

STICK REMEMBERED A TIME ONCE in Yankton, South Dakota, standing around back of the chutes at a rodeo,
watching the contestants drawing the bulls they'd ride.

He remembered one especially, a skinny guy with his
big scooped-brim hat and tight little can, spitting over his
hip and saying, "If I cain't ride 'im, I'll eat 'im." He lasted
about three and a half seconds on a bull named Candy-
man and came back through the dust limping and hitting
his big curly hat against his chaps.

The young guy, the cop, reminded him of one of those
bull riders or a saddle bronc rider. Long hair, no hips,
faded jeans, boots. It was the badge and the foot-long .44
Mag under his left arm that made him something else, a
Detroit police officer.

Frank had said it, you couldn't tell the cops from the
hackers and stalkers anymore.

Stick kept his eyes on the young guy while they were at
the First Precinct police headquarters, but didn't say anything to him or answer any of his questions. Shit no, he
was standing mute. He didn't say anything getting finger-
printed and photographed and the only thing he said at
the arraignment was not guilty. They set a bond of five
thousand dollars and asked him if he wanted it. He said
no. They asked him if he had counsel. He said no. They

asked him if he wanted the court to appoint counsel for him. He said no. He'd sit it out and take his chance at the examination. If he didn't say anything, if he didn't call anyone for bond money, if he didn't talk to a lawyer or to the young guy even about the weather, he knew they couldn't do a thing to him—not for picking up a doll box, even if it did have a red dot on it.

Stick sat in the Wayne County jail with all the colored guys awaiting trial. He had never seen so many colored guys. He didn't say much to them and got along all right. The place smelled—God, it smelled—and the food was awful, but he'd been here before. He'd made it.

It was funny, sitting in jail he remembered the ice machine at the motel in Yankton and the sign on it that said: WE CANNOT PROVIDE ICE FOR COOLERS. He remembered thinking at the time, But how do they know if they don't try?

He remembered going into the place next to the motel, walking up to the two girls at the bar, and saying, "Good evening, may I buy you ladies a drink?" One of them said, "You dumb bunny, we work here." He said, "Oh, then would you bring me a drink?" And she said, "Certainly, sir, what would you like?"

Sitting in the Wayne County jail. He remembered telling Frank, coming out the last time, they didn't serve cocktails in there.

Most of all a Porter Waggoner song kept going through his head, about a hurtin' behind his left eye and a tiny little bee buzzin' around in his stomach. Porter was all tore down because of too many good, good buddies and bad, bad gals.

Stick didn't know about the gals, but the buddies were something to think about.

Every once in a while he'd think about the doll box,

too. He had only held it a moment, but he remembered, in that moment, the box was a lot lighter than he'd expected it to be.

And he kept thinking about the cop who'd arrested him, the young guy. He could tell the guy was eager.

The young cop's name was Cal Brown.

Once he said to a superior, "But look, I've learned that already. I know it. Responsi*bil*ity? Having people under you? Giving them paychecks and shit? I had sixty guys under me and I kept them fucking *alive*. I've done that, man, what, when I was twenty-three."

He had been a combat infantry officer in Vietnam and had been with the police department seven years, since trying out with the San Diego Chargers as a free-agent wide receiver and ruining one of his knees before the season started.

Today he was having lunch at the Hellas Cafe on Monroe with Emory Parks, the young little fat black assistant from the prosecutor's office. Cal Brown ordered the stuffed grape leaves, feta cheese salad, and a glass of retsina. Emory Parks ordered roast lamb and lima beans and hot tea. They were waiting for the food to come. Emory Parks was fooling with his tea bag. Cal Brown was hunched over the table on his elbows.

"You read up on it yet?"

"I haven't had time, man. I probably won't read it till we're in court."

"You met the guy before, three months ago. Three and a half."

"Refresh my memory."

"Ernest Stickley, Junior, auto theft. Charge dropped at the exam, no positive ID."

"Shit," the little prosecutor said, "you know how many Ernest Stickley, Juniors, there are?"

"This one was in on the Hudson's thing."

"You'd like to believe that."

"His roomie," Cal said, "the guy he lives with in a four-hundred-and-fifty-dollar-a-month apartment out in Troy—listen to this part—is the same guy who was the eyeball witness to the auto theft and lost his memory."

Emory Parks stopped fooling with his tea bag. "Is that so?"

"Interesting?"

"Where's this boy Stickley now, out?"

"In. Passed on the bond, passed on the free lawyer. He gives you his name, rank, and serial number and raises his hand when he has to go to the bathroom."

"What's he arraigned on?"

"Larceny from a building. Conspiring."

The little prosecutor frowned now. "Larceny? Shit, you got a murder in there, haven't you?"

"Murder? We got two murders. We got all fucking kinds of numbers going. That's why we're talking. Listen—the gun used on the window washer? Same one killed the two guys out at Northland. In the parking lot."

"Well, you don't need him for that. Man did the community a favor, as I recall."

"That's not my question. Right now I'm giving you facts, okay? One of the guys killed at Northland—I don't remember which one—had a piece of a grocery bag in his hand, and a few bills. From a store that'd been knocked over about an hour before. But the guys that knocked over the store weren't black."

"This one, Stickley—you show his picture out there?"

"With the Southfield police. Manager says no, he never

saw him. One of the checkout girls, she cocks her head, well, maybe. She couldn't say for sure."

"So you got to stay with Hudson's, which is better anyway."

"Not necessarily," Cal said. "Yes, it's better, but I mean there're other possibilities, at least two dozen robberies out there, all armed, same everything, two guys come in, very polite, but no bullshit. We can go that way, right? Follow it up and probably get a conviction."

"You mean hand it to all the little police departments out there, they ain't cutting their grass they can work on it, and the first one off his ass and gets an ID gets an armed robbery bust. That saves you some work, doesn't it?"

"Look," Cal said, "since I'm buying the fucking lunch, don't tell me things I know, okay?"

"Excuse my friend," the little prosecutor said to the waitress putting their plates in front of them. "He likes to talk dirty, he wasn't insulting the food."

The waitress looked at him but didn't change her expression. She either didn't know what he was talking about or didn't care. It was one thirty and the place was crowded.

Cal didn't look at his stuffed grape leaves. He said, "We can send this clown out to the country. There're a dozen circuit courts he can get lost in."

"Or?" Emory Parks was starting on his lamb and lima beans.

"Let me tell you the rest. A different gun was used on Billy Ruiz. We found it in a trash thing, a Colt Python three five seven."

"Belonging to whom?"

"Guy out in Bloomfield Hills. Registered—you listening?"

"I can eat and still listen, Calvin. It's a trick I learned."

"The Colt's registered to this guy and"—Cal paused—"you ready? So is the thirty-eight they used on the window washer."

"That's impressive." Emory Parks nodded, chewing his lamb. "You're keeping it neat, but you're still out in suburbia with the two guns."

"They were stolen three and a half months ago, in May," Cal said. "Stickley was acquitted in May. The two dozen or so robberies that all smell alike go back to May. Two guys get in the business, liquor stores, supermarkets, doing pretty well—you follow me?"

"And they decide it's time to go big time."

"And they get greedy, right? and go for the big banana."

"Bring some friends in."

"Bring *some*body in. A white guy and two gentlemen of the Negro persuasion go into the Hudson's office. Not Stickley, though, an unknown male Caucasian, Billy Ruiz, and another black gent with an unhappy childhood. One of whom shot Billy Ruiz in the back on the way out. Why?"

"Shit, anybody'd shoot Billy Ruiz in the back if they got the chance. That's not the question. Ask the right one," the little prosecutor said. "No, let me ask you one. How'd you know the money was still there, in the box?"

"Not the money, checks. Just checks."

"Not the money?"

"Let me tell it," Cal said. "We're looking all over the fucking store, top to bottom, and we find a little something—this is the next day—in Billy Ruiz's street clothes. They're in another trash thing, on the same floor we found the Python."

"Something in his clothes."

"In a pocket. A little toy soldier, thing's two inches high, costs nine and a half bucks. No sales slip. Where's it from? The toy department. One floor below the office. What was Billy Ruiz doing in the toy department? We start looking, two o'clock in the morning—this is the second day after, now—we found the doll box with the checks in it."

"The question," the little prosecutor said, "what would he want with just checks?"

"He comes in the *second* day after," Cal said. "Keep that in mind. What if he thought the money was there, too?"

"I see that," the little prosecutor said. "Like maybe somebody's fucking somebody over."

"Like maybe somebody came in the day before," Cal said, "and picked up another dolly box with a mark on it, but they don't tell Mr. Stickley. He's supposed to come out, they open the box and they say, Yeah—giving him the dead eyes—now where's the real stuff? But he doesn't come out. He looks around and he's got a forty-four Mag in his ass. He doesn't know he wasn't picking up the money, because he doesn't know what was in the box."

"And you haven't told him."

"Not yet. That's why we're having the lunch."

The little prosecutor paused. "The store, they haven't released the news yet that any money is missing."

"They don't want to advertise for any repeat business."

"How much?"

"In the neighborhood of eight-seven."

The little prosecutor smiled. "And you got this boy for larceny from a building, which I doubt will even get to trial. He says, 'I didn't know what was in the box besides a doll,' and you didn't let him look, or walk out with it."

"We figured, we were *sure* he'd be identified in the office."

"You haven't mentioned what his roommate was doing that day. What *do* they do, both of them?"

"Yes indeedy," Cal said, "how do these two pay the rent? Stickley, unemployed, drives a cement truck when he isn't behind the wheel of a stolen vehicle. Frank J. Ryan, that's his roomie, is a car salesman. Last place of employment, Red Bowers Chevrolet. You ready to hear it again? Three and a half months ago."

"You got a sheet on him?"

"Frank's been a clean liver up to now, or else he's never been caught. He's a dude, with the hair and the mod suit and shit. I present myself at the apartment with a search warrant and tell him his buddy's been arrested. Oh my, he says. I don't believe it. Stick? But he's a nice guy. I'm thinking, Not Johnny, he was always such a good boy, good to his mother."

"What'd you find?"

"The search revealed nothing unusual or incriminating other than nine hundred bucks under the sink in an Oxydol box. Clever? Ryan goes, Gee, how did that get there? I said to him, Don't you ever do the dishes? He goes, Oh yeah, Stickley won it at Hazel Park, but he never knew where he'd put it."

The little prosecutor kept his plate neat and didn't let anything touch. He moved a few lima beans away from his mashed potatoes before slicing off a piece of lamb. He said, "Why don't you have the Hudson's people take a look at him?"

"Because the only one they saw—the only face—was Billy Ruiz. The other two, all they're sure of, one was black, one white."

"Well, maybe there's some liquor store and supermarket people out there can identify Ryan as well as Stickley."

"That could be," Cal said, "but then I wouldn't have anything, would I?"

"Your grape leaves are going to get cold."

Cal started eating and neither of them spoke while Emory Parks finished his roast lamb and poured himself more tea. He said, "I agree we should save them for the Hudson's job and get a murder conviction, besides find the money. We're building a new Renaissance Center, getting downtown all fixed up, we can't have this kind of shit going on. Doesn't look good, does it?"

"It fucks up our image," Cal said, "not to mention people getting killed."

"All right, you got two male Caucasians," Emory Parks said, "but no lead on the brother. What I've been wondering, if somebody might've bankrolled this deal."

"Bankroll? What's to bankroll? They get a secondhand bus driver suit from the Goodwill."

"How about the people in the office?"

"That's a possibility. They knew when to walk in. Two, the check sacks were sealed, hadn't been opened. So we assume they knew the money sacks from the check sacks. I don't want to sound racially biased, Emory, but there's a cute little black chick up there that's sort of caught our eye."

Emory Parks was thinking again.

"You didn't tell me where this Frank Ryan was the day of the robbery."

"He said he was home sleeping, but he thinks Stickley went out for a while in the morning. That afternoon, they got three broads can swear they were out sitting by the pool."

"Must be nice to be unemployed," Emory Parks said. He looked thoughtful again.

"I talked to the broads," Cal said, "asking them what

they knew about the two guys. Every one of them: Oh, they're business consultants. They have something to do with sales training or something like that. Nice guys, and they throw keen parties. I go back to Ryan. What's this I hear you're a business consultant? He says oh, that was just a little patio bullshit they handed the girls one time. They didn't want the girls to know they were unemployed. Oh, is that why you throw these big parties? He said they'd bought a lot of stuff one time and had a little bit left. The little bit, two cases of booze. There was one girl"—he took a small notebook out of his pocket and turned a few pages—"Arlene Downey. I asked her if she knew the two guys. Yeah, she knew them, but just slightly. I asked her if she knew what they did for a living. Right then, just for a second, her expression—like the light went on and her mother caught her doing it on the couch. Then she was evasive, had been out of town a lot, hadn't seen much of them."

Emory Parks was smiling a little. "Right there, aren't they? But you can't quite reach them. I think...what you're going to have to do...first thing, tell Ryan his partner needs somebody to post his bond. I think, playing Mr. Innocent Nice Guy, he'll run down there and do it."

"Yeah," Cal said, "I think he would. He knows I know he's got some money. Yeah—"

"Then you got the two of them looking at each other, the one guy facing a conviction. What's the other guy going to say to him?"

"He's going to say, Jesus, it's a shitty deal, but hang in there, man. It's like, Gee, I'm sorry you got leukemia, but there isn't anything I can do about it."

"And what's Stickley thinking, feeling his temporary freedom? He's already served time, he knows what it's like in there."

"He's thinking, Why me and not them? See," Cal said, "the trouble is I can't mention the money to him, let him know he's been fucked over. We can't let that out yet to anybody."

"You don't have to tell him," Emory Parks said. "His buddies, maybe his roommate if he's one of them, they don't know what's in Mr. Stickley's head. They don't know what he knows or doesn't know. He was in jail, they couldn't touch him, they hold their breath. But if he's out—can they take a chance letting him go to trial? Won't the cops try and plea-bargain with him? They already shot poor Billy Ruiz. They going to take a chance on this cat telling stories about them?"

"It's interesting," Cal said.

"It's not only interesting," the little prosecutor said, "it's all you got. Unless you find out one of them's been jumping that cute little black chick in the office. Then you got a lead on something else."

"Listen," Cal said, "I think I've got enough to work on for a while. Yes sir, I believe this could open it up."

"If you plant a little seed with this Stickley before you turn him loose."

"Yeah"—Cal was nodding—"make sure he realizes what a shitty deal he's getting."

"Not only a shitty deal, make him realize life can be dangerous out there. Man disappears for a time, they find him in the trunk of a car out at the airport. Say to him he ought to be very careful where he goes, where he meets his friends."

"Yeah," Cal said, "get him to reconsider who his friends are, who can do him the most good."

"That's it." Emory Parks smiled then. "You're going to take all this back to Thirteen hundred and Walter's going to say, 'You've been talking to that fat little nigger again, haven't you?' And you'll say, 'Well, I just picked at his brain a little.' "

"Your ass," Cal said. "I'll tell him I figured it all out myself. You got a free lunch, you fat little nigger, what more do you want?"

22

"WHY DON'T YOU JUST NOT say anything?" Stick said. "If you don't talk for a while, it's okay with me."

"Look, I'm sorry," Frank said. "You think I'm blaming you, for Christ sake? I'm trying to find out how it happened."

"How it *hap*pened? I reach for the box and the guy, the cop, puts a fucking gun in my face is how it happened. They're waiting there—this great idea—they know exactly where it was."

"But how could they?"

"How do I know? They found out or somebody told them—shit, I don't know. This fucking great idea—I should be in Florida right now, I'm facing a robbery conviction."

"Conspiring to commit larceny from a building," Frank said.

"At the moment. But the cop, you know what the hotshot cop says? 'Maybe at the exam we'll change it to robbery armed. And if we do that, we might as well go all the way to murder, right?' "

"The guy's blowing smoke up your ass. I think they'll go in on the larceny thing and get it thrown out."

"Yeah, well I'll tell the judge that, you don't think I'll get convicted. I'm facing the fucking thing and you're sitting home with your nice thoughts."

They walked along in silence, away from the Wayne County jail building down St. Antoine toward the parking structure. It was four in the afternoon, warm and sunny. They had walked down this street once before—it seemed a long time ago—on their way to the Greek place, the Bouzouki.

Frank said, "You want a drink?"

"I want to take a shower and change my clothes," Stick said.

Frank was silent again. Everything he said came out wrong, not the way he intended it, or Stick would turn it around. He didn't know what to say to him, but he kept trying anyway. Walking along in silence, Stick next to him, was worse.

"There was a cop, a hippie-looking guy," Frank said, "he was out a couple of times. Came with a search warrant the first time. I said, You don't need that, we got nothing to hide. He found the dough under the sink. I told him it was our nest egg, we'd won it at the track."

"He talk to anybody else there?"

"He talked to everybody. The ladies told him we're consultants."

"How about Arlene? He talk to her?"

"I don't know, I guess so."

"She was away," Stick said, "in Chicago or someplace."

"She's back now. I've seen her a couple of times."

"But you don't know if he talked to her."

"You afraid he told her something? What's the guy know? There's one little piece in the paper about you. It said you'd been arrested, but it was only speculated, in connection with the Hudson's thing. See, they're not playing it up because they don't have a case against you. They start bragging they got the guy and then you walk out, they don't look so good."

"Who'd you talk to?" Stick said. "I mean the girls there."

"I talked to Karen and I talked to Jackie. They say, What's this with your buddy? I told them it was all a dumb mistake. You walk in, you're going to buy a doll, send to your little girl, they think you look suspicious for some reason and they arrest you. They get it cleared up, you'll be out, we'll all be laughing about it," Frank said. "Don't worry about the girls, they don't know anything."

"Arlene does," Stick said.

"What? There's nothing anybody could tell her."

"I'm saying Arlene knows about us."

It took Frank a moment. He almost came to a stop. "Wait a minute, you mean *you* told her something?"

"I didn't tell her anything," Stick said. "The bar in Hazel Park, we took the money from the guy? She was there."

"Come on—"

"Sitting at the bar with her friend."

"Jesus Christ—you sure?"

"Am I *sure*? She told me, she's sitting there. We push her in the room with everybody, we didn't even see her."

"But—she didn't go to the cops?"

"I think we'd of heard."

"Then what's she doing? She want something?"

"I don't know. I'm going to have to talk to her."

"You don't *know*? You discuss this with her—when was that?"

"Just before she left. I haven't seen her since that night."

"Jesus Christ," Frank said. "That's all we need."

Stick felt a little better. Frank wasn't his calm, casual self anymore.

* * *

"Latest development," Detective Calvin Brown said into the phone, "I didn't get to him soon enough. While we're having the lunch, his roomie put up the bond."

He took a sip of coffee as he listened to the little prosecutor and put the cup down on the metal desk in the little gray partitioned room that was called his office: Criminal Investigation Division, fifth floor, 1300 Beaubien.

"It could be all right," the little prosecutor said, "if the man's been thinking and he realizes they could be worried about him and that's why they wanted him out. But you don't know, do you, the extent of his imagination."

"I don't know," Cal said. "He sounds like a country boy, but I really don't know."

"You don't want to find him dead before he has a chance to learn who his true friends are, do you?"

"No, I sure don't."

"Then you better see about talking to him pretty soon. Maybe go so far as to mention some money being taken. I've been thinking about that."

"I have, too," Cal said. "I just wanted to hear you say it."

"This other Ryan, man used to work with me a long time ago," Leon Woody said. "His name was *Jack* Ryan. We work for this man was in the carpet-cleaning business? Get in a house, we see some things we like, we leave a window unlocked, come back at night. He was a nice boy, Jack Ryan."

Sportree came in from the kitchen with a drink in each hand. Frank Ryan thanked him as he took his and waited as Sportree handed the other drink to Leon Woody and went out again.

"No, I don't think I ever heard of him," Frank said.

"He wanted to be a baseball player."

"Is that right?"

"Play in the major leagues. Nice boy, but he couldn't hit a curveball for shit."

"I guess it's pretty hard," Frank said, "you don't have an eye."

Sportree came in with a drink for himself and sat down.

"See, what I'm thinking," he said, "man was in the joint once, he sure don't want to go back."

"There's no reason he will," Frank said, leaning forward now, sitting on the couch. "All they got on him, he might've been *think*ing about robbing the place. How do they prove he knows there's money in the box?"

"I'm thinking I don't know what he's thinking," Sportree said. "Maybe he believes they can put him away. He does, he might want to tell them things, give them some names, uh? And they tear up his piece of paper."

"He wouldn't tell them *any*thing," Frank said. "I know he wouldn't."

"Thing that bothers me most," Sportree said, "man was in the joint. See, he think different after that. He finger his mama to stay out in the fresh air."

"Look," Frank said, "if they had something on him, it'd be different. If they were really going to hit him and he saw he was going to take the whole shot. But he knows if he waits them out, keeps his mouth shut, they're going to have to let him go. All he did, he picked up a box."

"*The* box."

"Yes, and they assumed things too quick, he'd been in

on the hit and somebody in the office would identify him. Otherwise they'd have let him walk out with it and then nailed him. But they were too eager, little too sure of themselves."

Sportree looked over at Leon Woody.

"That'd be nice he don't say nothing," Leon Woody said, "and they say to him, Thank you, we sorry we bothered you, man, let him go. That'd be nice. But the way I see it, they going to take him down in the basement and whip the shit out of him and pull his fingernails out 'less he start to talk to them."

"Come on," Frank said, "they don't, they can't get away with that stuff anymore."

"Hey shit, they don't," Leon Woody said. "If he the only one they got, they going to do something with him, drop him out a window on his head, he don't start to talk to them. Say he try and run away."

Frank looked at Sportree. "How about I bring him around, you talk to him?"

"Might be an idea."

"I think you should," Frank said. "You got any doubts at all, talk to him. You trust me, don't you?"

"You not arrested," Sportree said. "Not yet."

"I mean wouldn't you trust me? If it was me instead of him? It's the same thing. I give you my word the guy won't talk."

Sportree said, "He knows about Billy getting hit, don't he?"

"I told him Billy wanted it all for himself and it was something had to be done."

"You make up a story, you not too sure of him either."

"No, it was so he'd go in and get the box, not change his mind."

Sportree and Leon Woody sat in silence, staring at him.

Frank shook his head. "Hey, come on, what're you thinking about? You're not sure you can trust the guy, you want to kill him, for Christ sake?"

"Frank," Sportree said, "we known each other a long time, longer than you known him. He start mentioning names, your name's going to be on the list, too. Everybody's name. Next thing, they got us in there for murder. Something a dead man did, and we didn't even make it, did we? Got nothing. But nothing is better than being in there for murder, and the only way we can have some peace of mind is to know your friend isn't going to tell them anything. You agree?"

"But he won't," Frank said. "I give you my word he won't talk."

There was a silence, and again they stared at him. Leon Woody took a sip of his drink. Sportree's fingers fooled with his trading beads.

"I'll bring him here," Frank said.

Sportree nodded. "I be anxious to see him."

23

"**I THOUGHT WE WERE COMING** right back," Arlene said, "but we went to St. Louis for the Gateway Nationals and I spent three days in the courtesy trailer passing out beer and soft drinks. Least it was air-conditioned. God, it was so hot and dusty at the track you wouldn't have believed it. But the only times *I* had to go out was when they gave out an award and I'd pose with Larry Huff and Chuck Hurst and Bob Amos and those guys. I got a lot more pictures. Oh God, but there was a terrible accident. This Pro Stocker went out of control about nine hundred feet down the track, went through the guardrail, flipped over—fortunately there weren't many people in the stands that far down—"

"Arlene."

She stopped.

"Have you told anybody about seeing us?"

"What?"

"You know what I mean."

"I shouldn't have mentioned that to you, should I?"

"You did," Stick said. "I've been a little anxious wondering if you told anybody."

"I haven't. Honest to God, I haven't told a soul."

She was afraid of him and afraid of showing it. He saw it in her expression again, in her eyes, as he had seen it, momentarily, when she had opened the door and he was standing there. Then covering up quickly with a smile that must have ached: Come on in, stranger. Gosh, it's been awhile, hasn't it? And getting rapidly into what she had been doing the past two weeks. Busy, God, she'd never been busier.

They were alone in her apartment in the quiet of a sunny afternoon. Arlene had come up from the pool a few minutes before—Stick had watched her from the balcony—and she was still in her lavender little two-piecer with her beads and rings and damp, tight-curly red hair, looking fragile and afraid. He wanted to touch her, put his arms around her, and feel the calm settle in her body as she realized there was nothing to be afraid of. But he knew he had to approach her gradually, that if he raised his hands she might scream and run from him.

"I believe you," Stick said. He tried a little smile and meant it. She was still tense but trying not to show it, standing in the middle of the room with the photographs and the life-size cutout of her in her silver Hi-Performance Cams outfit. They were both awkward standing there, not knowing what to do with their hands. Arlene touched a Maltese cross hanging from a thin gold chain and held on.

"How about the guy you were with? You didn't tell him you knew us?"

"Honest to gosh, I really didn't."

"Why not?"

"I don't know. . . . Well, I knew he wouldn't want to get involved, and you know, his wife finds out he was there with somebody. So I didn't say anything."

"Why didn't you tell the police? Leave him out of it."

"Well"—she made a face, frowning—"it's hard to explain. You want to sit down and have a drink or something? I don't know why I told you before. Maybe because I'd had all those drinks and wasn't feeling any pain, but I could sure use one now."

Stick made her a Salty Dog and then changed his mind and fixed one for himself, something to sip on. They sat down on the couch, Stick anxious but covering it pretty well, showing her she didn't have anything to worry about. He remembered telling Frank about Arlene knowing. It popped into his mind with the realization, an instinctive feeling, he shouldn't have; he should have waited at least, talked to Arlene first. Dumb, telling Frank because he had wanted to give him something to worry about. Would Frank tell the others? He said no, there wasn't any reason for him to tell them. But it continued to come into his mind, wondering about it and not being sure. Arlene sitting there, not knowing—he wanted to hold her.

"I liked you," Arlene said. "I mean I *like* you. The way it happened, it was funny, and it wasn't like you were robbing the bar, you were taking it from, you know, taking it from the one who did rob the place, like it was his then, and taking it wasn't a bad thing, it served him right. It was *funny*." She smiled a little. "God, I can still see it."

"Well, did you wonder," Stick said, "if we did it all the time? I mean, if that was what we did?"

"I didn't think about it."

"You must've, a little."

"I didn't. I said it wasn't any of my business. I thought—this may sound funny—I thought if you wanted to tell me, it was up to you."

"But if I had, then what would you think?"

"Well, I'd think that . . . you trusted me. You felt close enough that you could tell me something like that and know you didn't have to worry about it."

"You mean you wouldn't care?"

"Well, it isn't I wouldn't care. It's—see, I *have* thought about it and I always think, well, there's a reason. Like you have to have money for something. You need it desperately and nobody'll loan it to you, so you're just doing it for, whatever the reason is, and you're not going to do it anymore after."

"Arlene, I've held up a lot of places."

"Don't tell me, okay?"

"See, I can say I did need the money, as desperately as anybody needs it who doesn't have any. But I stole it."

"Why do you keep saying that? I don't want to know, okay?"

"You know about the Hudson's robbery?"

"Oh God. Don't." She squeezed her eyes closed with an expression of pain.

"I was in on it," Stick said. "That's why I got arrested. It wasn't a mistake."

He told her about it, describing what he did, his part in the robbery, trying not to minimize or make excuses, telling it quietly and seeing her eyes open to watch him with an expression that gradually lost its tension as her face, with its delicate features, became composed and her eyes took on an expression of calm awareness, as though she were looking into him and seeing more than a man involved in a robbery, someone else inside the man. He was aware of this as he spoke, feeling an intimacy between them that was different, softer yet stronger than what he had felt making love to her, and he knew why he was telling her about himself. He needed her.

He said, "I don't know what to do."

She moved to him on the couch, still looking into his eyes, and took his face in her hands and kissed him, then put her arms around him and drew him against her body.

They were in darkness now, in her bedroom, lying beside each other. He had slept and was awake, staring at the ceiling, at a faint reflection of light from the other room.

He said, "Can you go away for a while, till we see what happens?"

"Why?"

"Maybe some race or a convention coming up?"

"I'm not going to do that anymore." She sounded a little mad and surprised. "God, what do you think I am?" When he reached over and touched her she waited a moment and said, "Don't you love me?"

"I really do."

"Say it."

"I love you." He made his voice softer and said, "I love you—I never loved anybody so much."

He felt funny hearing himself and felt her breath come out in a little sigh as she turned to cling tightly against him and that part was good. He could feel her and knew by the touch who it was, the firm little body against his. He felt good. But God, he ought to take one thing at a time and save the best, put it someplace where it wouldn't get hurt. He knew he loved her. Like waking up and being somewhere else. He could hardly believe it.

"I'm not going to stay here," Arlene said. "I'll move out tomorrow, the stuff's not mine anyway. But I'm not going away—unless you want to and we go together."

"I got to stay for the pretrial thing, I can't jump bail. You get brought back with handcuffs on and they got you cold."

"Okay, I'll get another apartment, then," Arlene said, "something cheaper. I've got enough to live on for at least a month."

"I can help you out there."

"No, I'll get another job if I have to. Tell you the truth,

I'm awful sick of that silver outfit." She paused a moment. "It's funny, I just feel different with you."

"Everything could work out," Stick said. "They drop the charge and we get out of here and that's it. Clean living from now on. I'm liable to even get a job, too."

Arlene laughed, a muffled sound close to him that he liked.

"That'd be nice of you," she said.

They held onto each other in the darkness. Pretty soon he'd get up and see if the car was downstairs. If it wasn't, he'd pick up a car somewhere, one last time. Everything could work out, that was true, it was possible.

As long as he stayed alive.

When Emory Parks walked into Cal Brown's drab gray partitioned office on the fifth floor, Cal looked surprised first, then turned on a little grin, and Emory knew he had something good to tell him.

"I saw Walter downstairs."

Cal's grin faded. "He told you?"

"He was in a hurry. He said, Stop up and see the boy if you get a chance. All right, boy, what you got?"

Cal was happy again. He said, "The guy out in Bloomfield Hills with all the firearms? He got broken into again last night."

"They know where to go, don't they?"

"Maybe not *they* this time," Cal said. "One gun was taken, a Walther P-38, nine millimeter. The family was upstairs sleeping, didn't hear a thing."

"It could've been somebody else."

"You want to bet?"

"You're going to assume it's one of the whities. All right, if it makes you happy, but which one?"

"I like Mr. Stickley."

"That's a good first choice," the little prosecutor said. "But what if Mr. Ryan's in with the brothers—assuming there's more than one brother, which I'm inclined to believe—"

"Me, too," Cal said.

"—and they say to him, 'Hey, man, he's your roomie, you do it.' Then Mr. Ryan might have to get himself a weapon."

"I don't like it that way," Cal said. "Then it isn't divided up right. I want to see Frank and Ernest on the same team. I mean if the brothers are going to fuck over one of them, why not both?"

"You know what?" the little prosecutor said. "I believe you just said the magic word. *Both*. Why not? It wouldn't be any harder to take two whities as one, would it?"

Cal smiled. "But the whities have a gun now. Somebody's been doing some thinking and I like it."

"You talk to them yet?"

"It's on my list of things to do," Cal said. "I want to talk to one of the young ladies out there, too, Miss Arlene Downey, the one that was a little edgy. I've been looking into their friends and acquaintances through the computer, a nifty little machine, and you want to hear a it's-a-small-world story? Miss Arlene Downey, we find, was a witness to a holdup a month ago, the Saratoga Bar in Hazel Park. And the Saratoga Bar? Why it's on the list of twenty-five or so that fit the style of our friends Frank and Ernest."

"It certainly is a small world," the little prosecutor said, "You don't suppose she's working with them?"

"I don't know," Cal said, "but I'm sure anxious to find out."

24

I GO DOWN TO GET the car last night," Frank said, "it's not there. I thought maybe I forgot where I parked it. I looked all over. Christ, I thought, I parked it right in front, it's gone. I thought somebody stole it and I got to call the police."

"You call them?"

"No, I go back out this morning, it's there. This afternoon it's gone again. Then just now—I don't know what the hell's going on."

"I had the other set of keys," Stick said.

"Why didn't you tell me? I'm thinking. Am I going crazy or what?"

"I got to get permission?"

"Save me some trouble, that's all. Where'd you spend the night?"

"With a friend."

"I didn't know you had any." Stick didn't smile and Frank said, "I'm kidding. What's the matter with you?"

"I didn't think it was funny."

"How about this one? We were so poor when I was a kid if you didn't wake up Christmas morning with a hard-on you didn't have anything to play with."

"You been talking to Barry."

"I just saw him outside. He was asking about you."

"How about Sportree, he been asking, too?"

He slipped it in and caught the startled look on Frank's face.

"Well, sure, he asked about you. He called me, in fact. He said, Why don't you make the bond on your friend? You want him sitting in jail?"

"Wanted me out, uh? In case I start getting too friendly with anybody? I can hear him: 'We don't know your friend, man. We don't know where his head's at on this thing.' He wants to talk to me?"

"Naturally he's concerned," Frank said. "Right, because he doesn't know you. But listen, I was the one suggested the two of you have a talk. He wasn't anxious or anything, he said maybe that was a good idea."

"I'm supposed to go down there? He must think I'm out of my fucking mind."

"As a matter of fact," Frank said, "put your mind at ease, he's not too hot on you coming to his place. And he's not going to come here, for obvious reasons, or anywhere the police or somebody might see you together."

"How about down by the fucking river late at night?" Stick said. "Jesus, he must think you're as dumb as I am. Or you think the same way he does, I don't know."

"I'm standing in the middle," Frank said. "I know both you guys, but I can't convince either of you to trust me, take my word. He doesn't care where you meet. He said you name the place you want to. He doesn't care at all, long as it's, you know, private, away from where you could be seen."

"You going to be there?"

"If you want me to, sure."

"I mean does Sportree want you to come along or am I supposed to show up alone?"

"*I* suggested it. I said *I'd* bring you. Why? What difference does it make?"

"I'm trying to find out what side you're on," Stick said.

"What *side* I'm on? For Christ sake, what're you talking about *sides*, there aren't any *sides*."

"Frank," Stick said quietly, "the guy wants to kill me."

"Come on—"

"Listen to me!" Stick waited, getting himself in control again. "I say two words, Sportree . . . Leon, they're in the can for murder, maybe life. He can't take a chance."

"What about me? I can say the two words. He want to kill me, too? He could've done it. I was with him."

"Maybe you are with him," Stick said. "Or he knows you stand to lose as much as he does, or he doesn't give a shit. I don't know, but I'm the one going to trial. I'm the one stands to lose if they can build something against me, and I'm the one stands to gain if I was to mention names."

Frank waited, staring at him. "They make you an offer?"

"Not yet, but I can see it coming. I wasn't in on the hit, they know that. So maybe they reduce it to some kind of accessory or shoplifting or throw it out altogether. They want somebody for murder, Frank. And they know I know who did it."

"Are you saying—let me get this straight." Frank walked over to the bar and poured himself a Scotch. "Are you saying you're willing to make a deal with them? Cop down to shoplifting or some fucking thing?"

"No, I didn't say that," Stick said. "I'm going to ride it and keep my mouth shut and not get anywhere near that witness stand and I think I have a pretty good chance of making it, if they stay with the larceny thing. If they don't, well, tough shit, I've thought it over, I went in with my eyes open, nobody forced me, I still won't say a word. But Sportree, Leon, they're not going to hold their smoke in waiting to see what I do. Leon shot Billy Ruiz, you were standing there."

"He tried to take it all, sure, Leon didn't have any choice."

"Frank, don't shit me. A very reliable source, that hot-dog cop, one of the first things he told me, Billy Ruiz was shot in the back. They didn't need him anymore and it's that simple. You make up a story he tried to take the goods, why? Frank, you're either with them or your head's all fucked up and you don't know what you're doing."

Stick watched him drink his Scotch and pour another one.

"I don't know," Frank said. "I have some doubts, yeah. It's, well, it didn't work out. It looked easy, but things happened, things you couldn't plan on. You said we should've left it alone, stay with what we're doing. Okay, I have to agree with you, it got all fucked up and complicated. But it *could*'ve worked and we could've had an awful lot of money."

Stick said, "It never had a chance, Frank. You know why? Because you thought you knew this guy, but you don't."

"Take my word," Frank said, "okay? You don't trust him, then trust me."

"No," Stick said, "you take *my* word. Tell Sportree and Leon I've already shot two colored guys, so I know how to do it. They're always saying. Be cool. Well, tell them to be cool."

Arlene did a dumb thing. She was expecting some glossies taken at the Gateway Nationals and she wanted them, just to have, the last shots of her taken in the silver outfit. So she rented a box in the Royal Oak post office and told the lady manager of the Villa Monterey to forward her mail there. She thought it was safe because she'd just be a number, with no name.

That's how Cal Brown found Arlene, in three steps, from the manager to the post office to the name and apartment address in Clawson.

Arlene opened the door, thinking it was Stick. She could feel her expression change. God.

Cal smiled and said, "How you doing, Miss Downey?" He had his notebook open in his hand and looked down at it.

"There's something here I wanted to ask you. About this holdup you were a witness to?"

25

THE YOUNG GUY, THE COP, was straddling the leg-rest part of the lounge chair with his boots on the cement deck. Hunched forward in skinny faded Levi's and a corduroy sport coat and tie. Stick couldn't tell where he was carrying his gun.

He was relaxed, his hands folded in front of him, facing Frank, and seemed to be interested in whatever Frank was saying. Frank was lying back in his chair scratching his belly, being cool, his sunglasses raised to the hot four o'clock sky.

Stick watched them from the balcony. He went into the living room and walked to the Formica table and back to the balcony a few times, pausing to look down over the railing. They were the only ones at the pool. On the fifth pass, Stick said, "Shit," and went into his bedroom. He could either hide under the bed or put on his new bright-blue swimming trunks. He put on the trunks.

"I believe you two know each other," Frank said. He'd had enough to drink to be relaxed or able to fake it; or else the guy, for some reason, wasn't scaring him. "He was just mentioning a friend of ours," Frank said to Stick walking up to them, "Arlene Downey."

"I thought she moved," Stick said. He pulled a chair around and sat down facing Cal Brown, showing him he didn't have anything to hide.

"That's what I told him," Frank said. "I haven't seen her around."

"Yeah, she moved," Cal said. "She's got an apartment in Clawson. But see, that's not the point. I'm not looking for her, I already talked to her. About twenty minutes ago."

Stick had his knees up in front of him, a barrier between him and the policeman.

"How's she doing?"

"She'll be okay, I think. The thing that's bothering her is that holdup she saw in a bar not too long ago. It's stuck in her mind."

"I don't believe I heard about that one," Frank said. Stick kept staring at the guy. It was coming now.

"She said it was two guys. They take the bills off this first guy that went in with a shotgun. Weird, uh? A shotgun."

"What're you trying to say?" Stick said.

"Okay." Cal straightened up a little, looking over at Stick. "Everything I say is off the record. Everything you say, same thing. No recorders, no bullshit. You know who I am, I know who you are. Let's talk things over."

"So talk," Frank said.

"All right, first thing," Cal said. "We could bust you on a couple dozen robbery armed. Listen, shit, just the cars you used could get you a hundred years apiece."

"What's he talking about?" Frank said.

"The two spades in the Northland parking lot, you can have them," Cal said. "It reminds me of an old saying, Don't ever shit a shitter. Don't ever try and hustle a couple of ace hustlers either, especially right after a job. But what I don't understand, on the Hudson's thing—"

"What Hudson's thing?" Frank said.

"The J. L. Hudson Company Hudson's thing," Cal

said. "Is why you want to take just checks. What're you going to do with them? You got some guy named Hudson you're going to lay 'em off on?"

Frank didn't move. His face remained raised to the sky. But his eyes were open now behind the sunglasses.

"That's all they got in that one, just checks?"

"That's all your buddy was picking up," Cal said. "Two Brink's sacks in the doll box."

He waited, letting the silence lengthen.

"This was the second day after, right? What I been wondering, a theory of mine, is what if somebody went in there the next day, right after, and switched some other sacks to another box? Boy, that would sure fuck over the guys left with just the checks, wouldn't it?"

"I didn't read in the paper," Frank said, "about it being just checks in the box. I think—I believe it said whatever was stolen was recovered."

"Well, they don't like to publicize anything that'd make them look bad, or look dumb, you might say."

"You mean there's some money that was stolen, hasn't been found, recovered?" Frank said.

"Well, actually, I'm not at liberty to say. Normally there'd be seventy-five, a hundred thou in the cash sacks. And considerably more than that in checks." Cal grinned. "But the checks aren't worth shit in comparison, are they? And if you don't even have the checks, you ain't got nothing at all."

Stick said, "You want to come right out and say what you're trying to say?"

"I can spell it for you," Cal said. "It's a-s-s-h-o-l-e-s. That's what your associates, your black buddies, are making you look like."

"This is wild," Frank said. "Shit." He was sitting up now, pulling himself up and taking off his sunglasses to look at the guy. "You give us all this like we're supposed to know what you're talking about. Our black *buddies*—what black buddies? Who? Give us some names. Shit, you start to make accusations, give us some proof. What? You're talking about the Hudson's thing?"

"Frank—"

Stick waited. He looked from Frank to the policeman and said, "What's the deal?"

Cal Brown took his time. He put on a pleasant, innocent, sort of a surprised expression as he looked at Stick. He said, "Deal? Who's talking about a deal? I'm just telling you how I see it. The question is, do you want to go to Jackson for a while or do you want to take a chance on getting shot in the head by your buddies? It's entirely up to you, man."

There was a silence. Cal waited. He said then, "Well—" and got up to go, starting to move off, timing it, stopping and looking at Stick.

"I almost forgot. Your pretrial exam's been moved up."

It caught Stick by surprise. "How come nobody tells me?"

"I'm telling you," Cal said. "Day after tomorrow, nine o'clock. Frank Murphy Hall of Justice."

Frank was still in his trunks, pacing now, following the route from the balcony to the Formica table and back again. Stick had on a shirt, unbuttoned. He sat at the table with a cup of coffee, looking at it, looking at the wall, looking at Frank when Frank got in the way. Frank had a Scotch on the bar and would stop off there every few minutes. He had two cigarettes going, one on the bar, one in an ashtray on the balcony he'd forgotten about.

"You didn't look in it at all?" Frank said.

"I didn't have time," Stick said. "I told you I thought it felt light."

"Five sacks went in the box, I saw them. Marlys came out—" Frank stopped. "Jesus, I'm standing there—Marlys *told* him. She pointed to three sacks, he put the other two in first. I watched him do it. The whole thing was set up, Billy Ruiz, everything. Leon, Marlys, somebody goes in the next day, takes out the three sacks, leaves the ones with the checks—Jesus."

"The cop spelled it right," Stick said, "didn't he?"

"We show up the next day," Frank said, "we got checks, that's all we got, checks. Sportree says, 'What's this shit?' Turns it fucking around on us. We say—we don't know what to say. We can't believe it."

"Your old buddy," Stick said. "He gives it to you, he puts it in all the way, doesn't he?"

"The son of a bitch," Frank said. "Like we're a couple of little kids. I'd like to have that Python right now—or get my hands on one."

"Don't do anything dumb," Stick said. "They're not going to let you walk in there with a gun. Take it easy. As your old buddy would say, be cool."

"I'm going to cool him," Frank said, "the son of a bitch, sitting back, all that time blowing smoke at us."

"Sitting back ready. I'm not trying to talk you out of anything," Stick said. "I'm saying you got to be careful and do it right. Put yourself in his place. If he's smart enough to pull this deal, he's not going to let you walk in and take it away from him. One advantage, he doesn't know what we know and he must think we're pretty dumb to begin with. I'm saying put yourself in his place and look at it as he sees it before you run out and do anything dumb. See, that's what's bothering you right now. You don't like the idea of him laughing at you, thinking

you're dumb. Like when I swiped the car from you out
there. You don't want to prove he's right, so let's think on
it awhile."

"We walked into places thirty times," Frank said, "no
problem. How about once more? What's the difference?"

"The difference, they were guys in aprons and A&P
coats. This guy's a pro. He's into, Christ, probably everything you can think of. He has people *killed*."

"And he thinks we're a couple of hicks," Frank said.
"That's what I keep thinking about."

"I know you do, and maybe there's a way to use it, if
you know what I mean. But it's something we'd have
to give some thought to. Remember, I'm going to court
the day after tomorrow and I might not be around for
awhile. We'll have to wait and see." Stick got up from the
table and took his cup into the kitchen. When he came
back in he said, "I'm going to see Arlene. Hang onto that
Scotch bottle till I get back."

He spent the night at Arlene's, patting her, saying, "Come
on, it's okay," telling her as calmly as he could not to
worry, the cop didn't know anything—that's the way they
were, they showed their badge and were very official and
serious and tried to scare you into admitting things, but it
was all fake. Arlene said she hadn't told the cop anything.
Good. Thank God, good, she hadn't slipped him anything, not knowing she was doing it. He got Arlene
calmed down and lay there in the dark most of the night
staring at the ceiling, hoping Frank was in bed and not
out looking for a gun. He had a pretrial exam to face that
could be the first step to putting him away and he had to
worry about Frank and Arlene and the jazzy colored guy
that had really fucked them over and they hadn't even felt

it. It was a terrible mess, but it was also kind of interesting, exciting. He was getting to the point, feeling it, that he didn't have much to lose and maybe a lot to gain. What he had to do, lying there in the dark, was consider his options. Like:

Run.

No, don't run. Maybe don't move at all. Don't even look around. Forget about the money, somewhere between seventy-five and a hundred grand, the cop had said, implied. He believed the cop. So write it off.

To what?

The principle: Don't ever do business with a colored guy, especially one who's smarter than you are.

The funny thing was he still kind of liked the guy, Sportree—Maurice Jackson, his real name—Sportree in Detroit's black ghetto "Valley" and out on West Eight Mile. He admired him, the way he pulled it, and really didn't blame him. Why not? Sportree didn't give a shit about them one way or the other. Shit, if you're going to knock down a department store, get involved in murder, what was surprising about fucking over a couple of poor dumb white boys? Sportree didn't owe them anything.

They owed him something, though.

He sure hoped Frank was in bed.

He knew how Frank felt because he felt the same way. You could admire a guy's method, but you didn't have to grin and look dumb when the guy was putting it to you. You could *act* dumb, yes, if it helped the cause. And the cause was him and Frank, nobody else anymore. Except Arlene, but that was different.

All right, the options.

Sit tight. Don't say a word. Hope the larceny charge is dropped and go back to pouring cement and drinking beer and watching TV. Thank God you made it through and promise never to do it again.

Or, go for the prize. Get the fucker, sitting there blowing his Jamaican smoke.

Take the Luger P-38 and put it in the guy's face and say, "Give me the money; man. Be cool, man." All that *man* shit. "Be cool or else you're a dead nigger."

That sounded pretty good lying in the dark. Next to him, Arlene moved and he could hear her breathing.

Make sure Leon Woody was there and give him some of it. See it? The Luger, a good-looking, mean-looking, no-bullshit handgun. "Hey, man, you know what we do down in Oklahoma to guys like you?"

No, keep it straight. Who gives a shit where you came from or what they do in Oklahoma? He didn't even know what they did.

Keep it personal. He liked both of them. Leon Woody, too, with his little girl, he seemed like a nice guy and couldn't picture him shooting Billy Ruiz in the back.

He respected them.

But he also wanted them to respect him. And that was the whole thing. His only option.

It was about four thirty in the morning by the time he figured out a way to do it that might work.

At seven thirty he woke up Arlene and said, "Come on, you're moving to a motel. And this time don't leave a forwarding address, okay?"

"They're sitting there in their swimming trunks taking a *sun*bath," Cal said. "These two assholes, it hadn't even entered their heads something was funny."

He was talking to his superior now, Detective Lieutenant Walter Shea, in the lieutenant's office at 1300.

"How about the stolen gun?" Walter said. "Somebody's been doing some thinking."

"I'm pretty sure it was for protection," Cal said. "Stickley's. In case the blackies came after him. But now things are different, a little more interesting."

"You didn't search his place, then."

"What do I want to find the gun for? I'd have to arrest him."

"I'm grateful you're telling me all this," Walter said, "so I won't feel my twenty-seven years were wasted."

Cal nodded politely. "Yes sir, I can use all the experienced advice I can get."

"Emory suggest you go for a deal?"

"What's to make a deal about? I think they realize now they don't have anything to sell. Names, yes. Except that if Frank Ryan starts naming names, somebody's going to name his name right back. Because I'll bet you eighty-seven thousand bucks he was in the office when the window washer got it."

"So where are we?"

"Still watching," Cal said. "But I think the clowns are about ready to come out and put on a show."

26

"**YOU TELL HIM MY COURT** date's tomorrow," Stick said, "so if he's worried and wants to talk, it's got to be today."

"You were right there, you should've picked up two of these." Frank was sitting hunched over, examining the Walther, hefting it, feeling its weight, looking at its Luger profile in his hand. The box of cartridges was on the coffee table.

"Why would I get one for you?" Stick said. "I don't even know what fucking side you're on. I believe you told me more'n once you knew him a hell of a lot longer than you'd known me."

"That's what we should do," Frank said, "get in an argument. It just seems like, I don't know, we need more time to get ready."

"If he's setting up a hit on me, it's got to be today," Stick said. "Tomorrow I'm on the stand, you know that."

"But he doesn't know it," Frank said.

"Right. That's why he's going to have to move fast once you tell him and he finds out, I mean if he still wants me. I'll tell you something else I've been thinking," Stick said. "If he wants me, I bet he wants you, too. Why not? He's not going to split with you, he's already jacked you out of a cut. But if you found it out—he doesn't know what you'd do. So if he sets me up, why not set you up, too?

Two birds. Two dumb fucking dumb white birds. I bet he says he wants you to be there."

Frank called Sportree and told him about Stick's court date.

Sportree said, "Yeah? Hey, yeah, I'd like to talk to him, as I told you. Let me get back to you."

Frank hung up.

Stick said, "He calls back, then we wait, then we call him back."

Frank said, "Jesus, I hope it works."

Stick said, "You hope it *works*? If it doesn't work, we're fucking dead."

"He didn't say anything about me being there."

"Wait," Stick said.

Sportree called back in twenty minutes. He said, "How about I meet both of you—"

Holding the phone, Frank looked over at Stick.

"—but I prefer you didn't come here, your friend going to court and everything, you understand?"

"Where?" Frank asked.

"How about—I mean you sure you can do it, nobody following you—how about this motel, call the Ritz Motel, out Woodward near that hospital, almost to Pontiac. Look for Leon's car, light-blue '74 Continental. Make it nine o'clock."

"Just a minute." Frank put his hand over the mouthpiece and looked at Stick. "He wants to meet at a motel out by Pontiac, tonight."

"We walk in and Leon or some jig steps out of the can shooting," Stick said, "while Sportree's home watching Redd Foxx. I thought he was going to say some back alley, or an empty building. Tell him we'll meet him in front of the police station, talk in the car."

"Come on," Frank said. He was nervous holding the phone with Sportree on the other end.

"Tell him we'll think it over and get back to him. That's good enough."

Frank told him.

Sportree said, "Hey, don't be too long. I send somebody to pick you up."

Frank hung up. "He says he'll send somebody for us."

"I bet he will. One thing we know," Stick said, "no, two things. He can't take a chance doing it at his place. He's got too much going on there. And we're not going to get in with a gun. So you see any other way?"

"No, I don't guess so."

"Let's get going, then."

"Okay," Frank said. He laid the Luger on the coffee table and got up. "What're you going to wear?"

A half hour later Frank called him again from the Graeco-Roman lobby of the Vic Tanny on Eight Mile Road, almost directly across from Sportree's Royal Lounge.

"We decided it'd be better if we came to your place," Frank said.

"I *told* you," Sportree said. "Man could be followed, he bring 'em here. You want to get me in the shit? Frank, hey, use your head."

"No, we decided," Frank said. "Get Leon there so he can listen. We'll leave now and be very careful of tails and be there in about a half hour."

"Frank, listen to me—"

Frank hung up. He reached into the big pocket of his safari jacket for a pack of Marlboros.

"He doesn't like it."

"I bet he doesn't," Stick said. Stick was wearing his light-green sport coat he'd bought in Florida. The right side hung straight, tight over his shoulder, with the Luger filling the inside pocket. They lighted cigarettes and stood by the showcase window, looking out across the parking lot and the flow of traffic on the wide, parkway-divided lanes of Eight Mile. It was a long way over there to Sportree's and the traffic was getting heavier. They concentrated on the cars that, every once in a while, pulled into Sportree's side lot.

A young guy with a build came over from the counter in his tight Vic Tanny T-shirt and tight black pants and asked them if they were members. Frank said they were thinking about joining but were waiting for a friend. The Vic Tanny guy invited them to make themselves comfortable and when their friend came he'd be happy to show them around and describe the different membership plans.

"It might not be a bad idea," Frank said. "Work out two, three times a week, get some steam or a sauna."

"I could never do pushups and all that shit," Stick said. "I don't know, it sounds good, but it's so fucking boring. The thing to do, just don't eat so much."

"I don't eat much," Frank said.

"You drink too much. You know how many calories are in a shot? What you put away, those doubles, it's a couple of full meals."

"What do you do, count my drinks?"

"I can't," Stick said. "I can't count that fast."

"Jesus—" Frank said and stopped, looking out the window. "There we are. Light-blue '74 Continental. Son of a bitch, how does he afford a car like that?"

"Maybe he lives in it," Stick said.

They watched the car pull off Eight Mile into Sportree's

parking lot. A half minute later Leon Woody appeared, coming around front to the upstairs entrance, and went in.

Frank said, "What if there's a guy in the lot parks the cars?"

"I haven't seen anybody," Stick said, "but if there is, we go home and think of something else quick—"

"Maybe we should give it a little more time. I told him a half hour." Frank looked over at the Vic Tanny guy behind the counter, talking on the phone now. "Let's let him give us the tour. Maybe there's some broads in the sauna."

No parking-lot attendant, no one coming in behind them or going out. There was nothing to it. Frank pulled the T-bird into an empty space next to Leon's light-blue Continental. They got out. Frank waited, standing by the rear deck of the T-bird.

Stick walked around to the right side of Leon's car and opened the front door. He looked at Frank.

Frank nodded.

Stick took the Luger out of his coat pocket, felt under the seat to make sure it was clear and there was enough room, and slipped the Luger under there, carefully, and closed the door. He opened the rear door and reached in to feel under the front seat, closed the door and nodded as he walked out to where Frank was waiting.

"You're sure?" Frank said.

"You can reach it from both sides."

"I mean that we'll take his car. Shit, or if we're going anywhere."

"I can't see Sportree driving, exposing his plates," Stick said, "I can't see him letting us drive, meet them. What if we made a stop at the hardware store?"

"If we go anywhere," Frank said. "That's the big *if*."

"No, we're going somewhere," Stick said. "That's the only thing I'm sure of. Probably after it gets dark. And we're going to make it easy for him by acting as dumb as he thinks we are, playing into his hands and giving him a *reason* for taking us out, so he won't have to use force."

They were walking out of the lot toward the front.

"There's an old Indian saying," Stick said: "You can't judge a guy until you've walked a mile in his moccasins. I haven't been able to do that, but last night, all night long, I imagined being in that fucker's red patent-leather high-heel shoes, remembering everything I could about him—the way he talked, the way he moved, how he's kept himself out of the whole deal. He's not going to have a lot of noise in his place and get blood on his carpeting. We're going somewhere."

"And I'm supposed to offer to drive," Frank said.

"Don't forget that."

"And what if they say okay?"

"We're fucked," Stick said.

Leon Woody opened the door. He said, "How you doing?" and stepped aside. Sportree was in the doorway leading to the kitchen, pointing a pump-action shotgun at them.

Frank said, "What're you doing?" getting fear and amazement in his voice and not having to fake much of it.

"I want to make sure we still friends," Sportree said. "Leon's going to check you out, if that'd be all right."

"I don't get it," Frank said. Stick liked the dumb look on his face.

Leon did a good job. He felt every part of them where a gun or a knife could be hidden, and felt their coats, under the arms and the lining as well as the pockets. They let him, not saying anything, Frank staring at Sportree.

"Look like they still friends," Leon said.

Sportree turned with the shotgun and went into the kitchen. He came back out with two bottles, glasses, and a bowl of ice, saying, "Since you all're here." When they were sitting down and had their drinks, Sportree looked over at Stick.

"What kind of deal they make you?"

"As a matter of fact," Stick said, "they haven't said a word about a deal. They haven't made an attempt, physically, to get anything out of me either. The way it stands, I'm going to the exam tomorrow with no reason to say a word about anything that's not any of their business. All they got on me, I lifted a doll box off a shelf. If I was conspiring to walk out with it, they have to prove it."

Sportree got a Jamaican out of a gold-leaf box and lit it, looking at Stick.

Leon Woody said, "They know you part of something else."

"They got to prove that, too," Stick said.

"They ain't going to let you go."

"Then they'll have to make up something, and they'd still have to prove it."

"You saying you pure and they ain't nothing to worry about?"

"I'm saying I've played this straight so far," Stick said, "but I'm not saying you don't have anything to worry about. There seems to be a discrepancy in how many Brink's sacks were in the doll box originally and how many were there when I picked it up."

"Say what?" Leon Woody sounded a little surprised without changing his bearded African expression.

"Five went in," Stick said. "Three came out sometime before I got there."

"How you know that?" Sportree asked him.

"Because I can add and subtract," Stick said. "I think two from five is three. There were two sacks in the box when I looked in it, right before they stuck the gun in my face."

"This comes as something new," Sportree said, at ease with his cigarette. "You never mention it before."

"I wasn't there," Stick said. "I didn't know how many sacks went in. Frank and I arc talking yesterday, not till yesterday he mentions five. I said, 'Five? There were only *two*.' "

Sportree smiled and shook his head, his gaze moving to Frank.

"What'd you think, Frank, he said that?"

"What'd I *think*?" He had a good on-the-muscle edge to his tone. "First I couldn't believe it. Then I thought, Shit, somebody's fucking somebody. Guy I thought was a friend of mine."

"Oh my," Sportree said, shaking his head again. "It can get complicated, huh? People get the wrong idea." He looked at Stick. "What the police think?"

"I don't know what they think," Stick said. "They didn't discuss it with me. Maybe they think it's still in the store somewhere, I don't know. The thing is, we know it isn't." He kept his gaze on Sportree.

"Yeah, maybe they think it is," Sportree said, squinting in the smoke, thoughtful. "But I doubt it. See, that's why we have to be so careful—you coming here—man, they could be watching every move you make."

Frank said, still on the muscle, "I think we're getting off the subject, how we got fucked by a guy I thought was a friend."

"Frank, did we know Stick was going to get arrested?" Sportree waited, patient, like he was speaking to a child.

"No."

"So he'd come up here with two sacks, wouldn't he?"

"Yeah."

"What do you think I was going to do?"

"I don't know—shit, I don't get it at all. But you took the three sacks."

"As a precaution," Sportree said. "Marlys walked out with them in a box the next day. This was something I thought of after. If she can do it, fine. If they too many cops around, we wait to do it like we planned it. But see, then we have two chances and two's better than one."

"How come," Frank said, "you didn't call us after, say you had it?"

"Frank, you never give us your number till the other day. Unlisted, right? Marlys went out there to look for you. Said she couldn't find you. Probably out with those chicks."

"Shit."

"Come on, Frank, ain't no scam. We get it, man, we busy counting. Shit, you want to know what eighty-seven thousand look like? You and him supposed to come by the next day. Only he get arrested."

"*I* came by," Frank said, "the day after. You never mention it. Shit, we're sitting here talking, you already got it."

"Hey, man, listen to me. I'm telling you now, ain't I? Because I know I can trust him. But he's in jail, good friend of yours, I don't know what he's going to say. I don't know you two been talking or not. So I keep quiet till the smoke begin to settle and I see where I'm at, see where you and him are at. Okay, now everything's cool. He don't say a word tomorrow, he walk out and we split the kitty."

"Not tomorrow," Stick said, "right now. I can still go to trial. I could get ninety days, shit, a year, I don't know. I don't want to come out and not find anybody around."

"We be here," Sportree said. "Man, nobody's going nowhere."

"Today," Stick said. "Right now. I take care of mine, you take care of yours."

"I'd just as soon do it now," Frank said. "I get nervous thinking about that much money sitting someplace, not making any interest."

Sportree grinned. "How you know it's not in the bank?"

"Shit," Frank said. "Where is it, under the bed?"

Sportree's finger caressed the little bebop growth on his chin, thinking, making up his mind. He looked over at Leon Woody.

"You can understand they want to see it."

Leon didn't say anything.

"Well, we might as well drive out there, make them happy. All right with you?"

"They own as much of it we do," Leon said. "I feel better, though, we wait till it gets a little dark. People won't see us walking in and out of places."

Sportree looked over at Frank. "We can relax here awhile, have something to eat—"

"Where we going?" Stick asked.

Sportree grinned. "We all going together, man. You'll see."

27

IN THE PARKING LOT, WALKING past the cars, Frank and Stick were following Leon Woody. Stick thought Sportree was right behind them. But when he glanced around, Sportree wasn't there, he hadn't turned the corner.

Leon was walking toward his light-blue Continental. Frank said, "Hey, Leon, I'll drive."

Leon looked around. "How you going to drive, man, you don't know where we going?"

"You tell me," Frank said.

Stick was thinking, Shit. He wanted Sportree to be here.

But it was all right. Sportree came around the corner, some kind of coat or jacket over his arm. Leon waited for him. He said then, "Frank say he want to drive."

Sportree looked happy, going out for the evening to have a good time. He said, "Shit, Leon drive. Then we come back, have a drink, get your car. Frank, you ride up with Leon, me and the Stick here will sit in the back."

Stick saw it, Sportree and Leon looking at each other, quick little look in the dreamy African eyes, telling each other something. They never let down, Stick thought.

They went out North Woodward as far as Norwalk Freight Lines, past the semis lined up in the dim-lighted yard, and U-turned around the island and came back south a few blocks to the Ritz Motel, VACANCY in orange on the big, bright-lighted Las Vegas sign. There were heavy-duty truck cabs in there, Macks and Peterbilts, and a couple of vans and a few new-model cars with Michigan plates. The swimming pool was lighted and empty in the half rectangle; most of the units were dark. Leon Woody let the Continental glide quietly into a parking space in the far corner of the rectangle, in front of Number 24, away from the motel office. Leon cut the ignition.

Sportree said, "Hey, shit, listen." And Leon turned the key back on so Sportree could hear the radio.

Leon got out, taking the motel key out of his pocket. Frank got out. Stick waited in the back seat with Sportree.

"'Feel Like Making Love,'" Sportree said. "Bob James, hey, shit. Idris, listen to Idris, uh?" Sportree sat there listening. Stick sat there. Sportree wouldn't get out of the car. It was pretty good, it melted over Stick with a nice beat, but it wasn't Merle Haggard and Stick wasn't sure how long he could sit there.

Sportree said, "That's a number, you know it? Man used to arrange for Aretha." He opened the door and finally got out of the car, then reached into the front for the key and turned off the ignition.

Stick waited.

Sportree looked back at him. "You coming? You don't seem too anxious."

Stick said, "What? I dropped my cigarettes."

When Sportree turned, Stick reached under the seat. Jesus, where was it? His hand touched the grip and he got it out, stuck it in the waist of his pants, and pulled the jacket down over it.

They went inside, into Number 24, a big room with a double bed and two twins and a refrigerator that had a cooking range and sink on top. Stick knew it wasn't going to take too much time. There wasn't anything to talk about, nothing to look at, no faking anything. No, it'd be done quick. Sportree had the poplin jacket over his arm. He looked around, as if picking a place to sit down, but he didn't. Frank was standing there, too, waiting for it. Leon Woody went into the bathroom and closed the door.

Stick said to himself, Here it is.

In the bathroom, Leon Woody took a Colt .45 automatic out of the medicine cabinet and wrapped a towel around it loosely. He flushed the toilet.

Stick was ready. When he saw Leon come out with the towel wrapped around his hand, around something in his hand, Stick pulled the Luger, pointed it at him, at the white, surprised look in Leon's eyes, and shot him in the face. Stick turned the Luger on Sportree and shot him twice in the body, dead center, above the jacket falling away and the revolver in Sportree's hand. Sportree made a grunting sound, the wind going out of him, and fell back against a chair, turning it over and going down as he hit the wall.

Stick said to himself, I don't believe it. You've killed four colored guys.

"Jesus Christ," Frank said. "Holy Christ Almighty."

Stick got down on one knee over Sportree and took the car keys and another ring of keys from his side pocket. Frank was saying, Jesus Christ.

"We'll leave them," Stick said, "we might as well. And take Leon's car."

"We got to get our car," Frank said.

"You bet we do," Stick said, "and that ain't all. It's got to be in his apartment someplace."

*   *   *

Marlys was in the bedroom with the air conditioning going, lying on top of the bed in a short little slip she used
for a nightgown, reading *Viva* and listening to Stevie coming out of the bedroom speaker. She heard the door to the
apartment open and close and looked over the top of the
magazine, waiting.

"Hey, I'm in here. Where you been?"

She was looking at the magazine again when Stick
came in, the Luger in his hand, not pointing it, holding it
at his side. He saw her slender dark legs extending from
the slip, her ankles crossed.

"Hey—"

Marlys jumped and sat up quickly, swinging her legs
over the side of the bed.

"What you want?" Not about to take anything
from him.

"A doll box," Stick said.

"Where's Sportree? You come walking in here—what
kind of shit is this?"

They heard Frank call from the other room, "I found it.
Come on." He appeared in the bedroom doorway with
the Little Curly Laurie Walker box under his arm and
smiled at the girl. "Hi, Marlys."

"I think you better put that back and talk to Sportree,"
Marlys said. "I mean if you have any sense at all."

"I think he'd want us to have it," Frank said.

Marlys frowned at him. "What you talking about?"

"You're going to find out anyway," Frank said. "He
died. And you know something? You could, too."

They didn't say anything walking out to the parking lot or
while Frank dropped the doll box in the trunk of the

T-bird—not until they were driving away from the place, in the night traffic on Eight Mile.

Stick said, "Slow down."

Frank said, "Jesus, the steering wheel of Leon's car, you had your hands all over it."

"I wiped it off," Stick said, "the keys just in case, the door handles, different places we might have touched."

Frank kept watching the rearview mirror. He said, "I'm trying to see how we could've messed up. What do you think?"

"I think we're halfway home," Stick said. "But we got to make one stop."

"You think she'll do it?"

"She said she would."

"I don't know—bringing her in."

"You got somebody else in mind?" Stick looked over at him. "I think we're lucky the way it's working out. She's a good one, which is pretty nice, since we sure as shit can't take it home and that hotdog cop drops in to visit again. I don't see any other way."

28

STICK WAS AT THE FRANK Murphy Hall of Justice, fifth floor, before nine the next morning, and found out examinations would be held in Judge Robert J. Columbo's courtroom. He told the clerk who he was and sat in the seats with the waiters and spectators two and a half hours, listening to examinations: a rape, a complicated dope-related shooting, and a felonious assault, watching the little fat black prosecutor, whom he remembered from the time before. The judge didn't say much; he seemed patient, sitting back in his chair against the light wood paneling, but would interrupt in a relaxed way when the defense attorneys took too much time, and he kept it moving.

When the judge took the envelope from the clerk and called Stick's number, he walked in through the gate and was sworn in, gave his name, sat down at the table facing the witness stand, and didn't say a word after that.

The young guy, the cop, took the stand, told about arresting Ernest Stickley, Jr., in the storeroom of the J. L. Hudson Company toy department, and identified Stick as the one. There was no mention of the holdup. After Cal Brown had testified, was questioned, and stepped down, the little prosecutor talked to the judge for several minutes in conference, then turned and walked away from the bench shaking his head, knowing it was going to happen, but making a show of being surprised after His Honor asked him if he actually wanted to bring this one to trial; he had said yes, and His Honor had said he didn't. He dismissed the charge and called a noon recess.

Frank was there in the audience, getting up now with the rest of the people, starting to move toward the door. Stick was coming through the gate to join the crowd. Frank was grinning as he caught Stick's eye, and Stick grinned.

Cal Brown was waiting. He held the gate as Stick swung it open and said, "Be good now." He was grinning, too. Everybody seemed happy.

Cal watched them move out through the courtroom doorway, seeing their Caucasian heads among the pimp hats and naturals.

The little prosecutor came over to watch, too. He said, "Now, about the real business."

Cal said, "Their place was searched while they were here. I was hoping we'd come up with a P-38, like the one caused the death of the brothers and was stolen from that guy's house in Bloomfield, and of course I was hoping we'd find the eighty-seven. Nothing."

"What if they run out on you?"

"We got somebody watching their place. The two guys' clothes, the money still there in the Oxydol box and about a grand in an old beat-up suitcase—they run, they're going home first."

"You hope."

"That's all I got is hope," Cal said, "that somebody fucks up."

Stick called Arlene from a phone booth on the first floor of the Frank Murphy Hall of Justice. When she answered he said, "I'm out. No shit, it's all done, no trial. . . . Okay, call Delta, it'll have to be that five-something flight, five forty-five, I think, nonstop to Miami. Make the three reservations—your name, Mr. E. Stickley, Mr. F. Ryan. . . . Sure, you can use real names, we haven't done anything. . . . No, you won't have any trouble this time of year. Find out how much and take enough out of the box to cover it and fifty or a hundred for yourself, for magazines and gum and. . . . Right. Take a cab out to Metro. Pick up, pay for all three tickets but only pick up your own. Leave the other two at the Delta counter with our name on it. You got a suitcase that'll hold it? . . . Good, put it all in the suitcase, nothing else in with it, and burn the box. . . . In the bathtub, I don't know, someplace you won't burn the goddamn motel down. Then, listen, check the suitcase through with your own stuff. Don't carry it on, you know, they look at everything. . . . That's right. . . . No, we'll see you in the Miami airport. You get there, check the suitcase in one of those boxes, you know, and meet us in the bar in the Miami airport near the Delta counter. It's way down at one end. At Metro, waiting for the plane, you see us, don't say anything or act like you recognize us at all. . . . No, shit no, we won't be sitting together. . . . I know. . . . Listen, I can understand, I'm a little nervous, too, but don't worry. There isn't anything to worry about. . . . Right, a few more hours it'll be over. . . . I do, too. . . . You'll hear me say it plenty. . . . All right. Arlene? I love you. . . . 'Bye."

Frank dropped his cigarette and stepped on it. "It took you long enough."

"I wanted to go over it again."

"She got it cold?"

"I don't see how we can miss," Stick said.

"I don't know, I think maybe we ought to put it in the car and just go."

"How far?" Stick said.

Burning the doll box made a mess, left a tubful of black ashes that dissolved under the shower spray but left a dark, smeary-looking stain in the tub. Arlene wished she had some Ajax. The bath soap just seemed to smear it around more. The maid would probably think she'd been awfully dirty, greasing a car or something.

The money—God, eighty-seven thousand dollars and a little more, in all kinds of bills—was stacked neatly in the small light-blue suitcase, with a few inches to spare. She thought about laying one of her photograph albums on top—it would fit perfectly—but she remembered what Stick had said. Just the money. So she'd have to jam her albums and manila envelopes of photographs in with her clothes.

You don't need them anymore, she thought.

Or the silver costume.

The pictures would be fun to look at later, years later. Here's Mommy when she was a model. Here's Mommy at the Indy Nationals. Cute?

The NHRA Grand Nationals were going to be in Los Angeles this year. September 5–6–7. She could picture it on posters and in ads that ran in hot-rod magazines. They'd get some other girl. In Los Angeles that probably wouldn't be hard at all.

The silver costume didn't take up any room; it didn't even have to be folded, it was so skimpy. The boots were soft and rolled up and could be stuck down in the corners.

The life-size cutout—smiling at her—God, what was she going to do with it?

She had made Stick bring it along with all her stuff. He'd said, Why? What did she need it for? She remembered she had been surprised at him asking and had said she just wanted it, that's all.

She would have to leave it now and she wondered what they'd do with it and if they'd be mad. Well, they could just throw it out. She saw her life-size reinforced cardboard image cracked and folded in a trash can, her face looking out. She was glad she was getting out of here. She hated being alone and thinking so much. God, how did a person stop thinking when they wanted to?

Arlene finished packing, called a cab, and paid the motel bill. When the cab came she walked out with her purse, following the driver carrying the two suitcases, and closed the door on the smiling life-size cutout in the silver costume.

The lady, the manager of the Villa Monterey, said she wished she could take a vacation sometime. Frank said well, they'd been working pretty hard and needed a chance to take it easy and recharge the old batteries. The lady, the manager, said she'd have thought they got enough rest sitting around the pool every day. Sitting, yes, Frank said, but they were always thinking, and thinking was hard work. He paid her four-fifty in advance for the next month, September, and she smiled and said she hoped they had a nice time.

Stick, waiting there, was glad she wasn't a talker. He was starting to get awful antsy.

Cal Brown had volunteered and taken over the watch. Surveillance of suspects.

He was parked across from the Villa Monterey and down a hundred feet in a dark-brown Chrysler Cordoba they had taken off a smack dealer the week before. Cal was in love with the car, his first time in it, and he was trying to think of ways to keep it for his own personal-official use.

He watched them come out of the Villa Monterey with their suitcases and open the trunk of the white T-bird. The one guy, Stickley, with a cardboard suitcase, looked like he was going somewhere to pick sugar beets. The other one, Ryan, had on a suit that glistened in the afternoon sun.

Well now, Cal Brown said to himself. Hit them now or wait? He had warrants in his pocket for search or arrest, with the dates left blank.

Is the eighty-seven in the suitcase?

No. Probably not.

So why hit them now?

Are they going to pick it up and keep going?

Probably. Yes.

Might you need more help than just yourself, rather than maybe blow it and get your head cut off, not to mention other parts?

Bet your ass.

But he did not turn on the newly installed radio until he had followed the white T-bird for fifteen minutes and finally they hit the Southfield Freeway, going south.

He said into the mike, after describing the cars and their location, "Get me some very quiet state police backup. Give them my code and let me have theirs. We could be heading for the Ohio line, but I got a feeling we're going to turn off on Ninety-four."

That's what they did, south of the Veterans Hospital, took the off-ramp down through the tight curve to the right, past the sign that said AIRPORT. It was about twenty minutes from here, out the old Willow Run Expressway.

Cal got on the mike again. "We'll need two men at each terminal, International, North Terminal, and West. Give them descriptions. They're to watch for the suspects and keep them under surveillance, but are not to collar them unless they attempt to put their luggage on a flight. I'm going to be right behind them—but just in case."

The T-bird crept along in the dimness of the cement structure, past the lines of cars that seemed to extend without end, up one lane and down another, from the first to the third level.

Stick was driving. He said, "Come on, let's go up on the roof."

Frank said, "I don't *want* to park it on the roof. Twice I parked up there, I come back, my wheel covers're gone."

"They can take the wheel covers anyplace you park," Stick said. "Right in front, in the no-parking zone, they can take your fucking wheel covers."

"There's more chance up there," Frank said. "Sitting up there away from everything a couple of weeks."

Stick said, "You worried about the car, then come back in a couple of days and get it. How long you think it'll take us to make the deposits? Say eight banks, North Miami to Lauderdale. You drive it in a half hour, less."

"Maybe we'll want to rest awhile. *Maybe*? Christ, I'm tighter now than when I went in that fucking store."

"What I'm really saying," Stick said, "what difference does it make how long we leave it or if it gets stripped or not or even gets stolen, so what? Buy a new one."

"I like this one," Frank said. "I don't want to see it get damaged."

"Then come back tomorrow." Stick paused. "Wait a minute. What're we arguing about?"

"I don't want to park it up on the roof," Frank said.

Arlene paid the cabdriver and turned around to see a porter picking up her two suitcases. The porter asked her, What airline, ma'am? Arlene said thank you, but she'd take the bags herself, they weren't heavy. The porter, without a word, set them down and turned away as she picked them up. Arlene was afraid to let the bags out of her sight. She had never been so tense. She went through the automatic doors that opened in front of her, beginning to angle toward the right as she entered the terminal, knowing Delta was over there, the counters running the length of the right wall. She had come in and walked over that way before, going to Atlanta and Daytona Beach for NASCAR races.

But this time Arlene stopped.

Directly in front of her, high above the American Air Lines counter, was a giant black rectangle with white lighted letters and numbers that listed departures. It was strange the way her gaze saw, not a list of flight numbers and cities, but only one.

LOS ANGELES.
FLIGHT 41.
5:30 P.M.
ON TIME.

She looked over at the clock high above the Delta counter.

A quarter to five.

Arlene thought of her friend in Bakersfield. She thought

of the Grand Nationals coming up, the week after next. She thought of Hollywood. That was strange, Hollywood. She thought of the silver costume. And she thought of her age, twenty-six. In a month, twenty-seven. Why'd she think of that?

Arlene walked over to the American counter.

Frank and Stick came across the enclosed overpass that joined the parking structure to the main entrance that was on the second level of the West Terminal, Detroit Metropolitan. They had walked from the parked T-bird, carrying their bags, about two hundred yards.

Frank said, "You got the keys?"

Stick said, "What keys?"

"The *car* keys."

"Jesus Christ," Stick said.

Maybe he wouldn't be coming back with Frank in a couple of weeks. Let him get the car by himself, he loved it so much.

They crossed the roadway and passed the cars being unloaded and the porters and the hand trucks—none of the porters offered to take their bags—and entered the terminal through the automatic doors.

"I don't see her around," Stick said.

Frank's gaze followed Stick's, studying the people walking around and waiting, most of them waiting at counters, some sitting down in the rows of seats. The place didn't seem very busy.

There were several lines at the Delta counter. Frank picked the shortest line, behind two people. Stick waited with him a minute, then stepped over to a line of three people. Frank gave him a look. Ten minutes later Frank was still behind the two people. Stick was at the counter.

Frank came over. He said to the reservations clerk, "Mr. Ryan and Mr. Stickley. I believe you're holding a couple of seats for us. The Miami flight."

The clerk stepped over to a machine, punched a few keys, waited while the thing clicked back at him, and punched a few more. He did it again and stepped back to them saying, "Yes, you're confirmed on Flight Eleven-eighty, departing at five forty-five from Gate Twenty-nine. Will you be checking your luggage through?"

"Yes, we will," Frank said.

Behind him, Stick said, "I don't see her anywhere."

Frank said, over his shoulder, "She's probably at the gate already, picking her seat."

The clerk was holding up an American Air Lines ticket envelope, looking at it. He said, "I see this was left for you. It has your names on it." He handed the envelope to Frank.

Stick saw the names, written in ink, as Frank took the envelope. *Mr. E. Stickley, Mr. F. Ryan,* one above the other.

The clerk said, "If you'll put your luggage up here, please—" He was holding the luggage tags.

Frank shoved the American Air Lines envelope into his inside coat pocket and reached down for his suitcase. Behind him, Stick was picking up his ratty-looking bag. Behind Stick, somebody said, "Just a moment, please."

They both looked around. Frank said, "What?"

There were two of them, thirty-year-old guys in neat, summer-weight suits, no hats. They looked like pro football players. No they didn't, they looked like cops.

One of them had his badge case open already, giving them a look at his shield. He said, "State police. I'd like you, please, to pick up your suitcases and go around the

counter over there to that door you see marked AUTHOR-
IZED PERSONNEL ONLY."

"What is this?" Frank said, indignant. "What for?"

The state policeman said, "Pick up your bag,
buddy, *now.*"

"I just want to know what's going on, for Christ sake. I
mean what is this? You accusing us of something, or
what?"

Frank stopped as Cal Brown came in and walked up to
the two state cops and showed them his credentials. They
nodded and said something to him.

Stick was watching. He said mildly, "I hope this doesn't
take too long. We got a flight to make."

Cal Brown turned to them sitting at the metal table in
the bare, brightly fluorescent-lighted room, and gave
them a nice smile.

"You got a flight, I got two warrants," he said, taking
them out of his jacket, giving them a flash of the Mag holstered under the jacket, and holding the warrants up for
them to see. "This one's for search. You mind?"

"If we miss the flight, you got to pay for it," Frank said.

"No, the airline'll put you on another one free of
charge," Cal said. "I mean if you're going anywhere."

Stick said, "If you want to look in our bags, go ahead. I
mean maybe if we hurry up, we can get it done. What do
you think?"

They watched as the two state cops came over and
opened their suitcases and began going through them,
taking out each item of clothing separately and feeling it.

Frank sat back and lighted a cigarette. He said, "I
hope, when you're through, you guys put it all back the
way it was."

Stick said to Cal, "You mind I ask what you're look-ing for?"

"Yeah, I do," Cal said.

They unrolled socks and looked inside shoes and stud-ied their toilet kits very closely. The one going through Stick's bag took out a wad of bills and looked over at Cal. Cal shook his head. Frank stared at the money, then at Stick, but he didn't say anything to anybody, not until the two state cops were finished.

"Is that it, Officers?"

Cal Brown said, "Now if you'll stand up please, gents, and empty your pockets—lay whatever you have on the table."

"Come on," Frank said, "pat us down if you want. You think we're carrying guns, for Christ sake, on an *air-plane*?"

"Get up," Cal said.

Stick took out his wallet, the car keys, a pack of Marl-boros, matches, and a comb.

Frank started with his coat. He took his sunglasses case and the American Air Lines envelope out of his inside coat pocket. He pulled out his wallet and a clean, folded hand-kerchief.

Cal looked at the American envelope. Why, if they were flying Delta—He picked it up.

Stick was watching him. Frank was digging for loose change in his pants pocket.

Cal took a piece of paper out of the envelope. He un-folded it and a locker key fell to the table. He looked down at the key, then at Stick, then at the piece of paper for a moment, and handed it to Stick.

Stick looked at the two words written in ink in the neat, slanting feminine hand.

I'm sorry.

He kept looking at the words.

Cal handed the locker key to one of the state cops, who studied the number on it as he walked out.

Frank was frowning, not knowing what was going on. "What's it say?"

Stick handed him the note. He said to Cal, "Maybe somebody left that, we got it by mistake, you know?"

"With your names on it?" Cal said.

Walking through the terminal, the two state cops were behind them carrying their bags. Cal was right in front of them, holding tight to the small, light-blue suitcase. No one they passed stopped or turned around or seemed to notice that the two in the middle were handcuffed together.

They went through the automatic doors and down the sidewalk, away from the entrance, to wait for the police car to pull up.

Frank said, half whispering against his shoulder, trying not to move his mouth, "Of all the ones, all the broads that'd jump at the chance, I mean *jump*, you pick that turkey. Christ, and I let you, I go along. What'd you say, the great judge of broads? 'She's a good one.' Your exact words, 'She's a good one.' "

"She didn't mean this to happen," Stick said. "It's not her fault."

"Whose fault is it, mine? What'd I say? Let's put it in the car and go, take the swag and run, man, and not get anybody else in the act. Remember that? Hey, remember the rule? Don't tell anybody your business. Nobody. Especially a junkie. Shit, especially a broad. One you pick."

The police car was pulling up to them.

"What do you think I went to the trouble to think up all those rules for? You remember the ten rules? We act like businessmen and nobody knows our business. You remember that?"

Stick said, "Frank, why don't you shut the fuck up?"

Read on for an excerpt from

ROAD DOGS

A NOVEL

ELMORE LEONARD

Available in hardcover in May 2009 from

WILLIAM MORROW

An Imprint of HarperCollins*Publishers*

THEY PUT FOLEY AND THE CUBAN TOGETHER IN THE BACK-seat of the van and took them from the Palm Beach County jail on Gun Club to Glades Correctional, the old redbrick prison at the south end of Lake Okeechobee. Neither one said a word during the ride that took most of an hour, both of them handcuffed and shackled.

They were returning Jack Foley to do his thirty years after busting out for a week, Foley's mind on a woman who made intense love to him one night in Detroit, pulled a Sig Sauer .38 the next night, shot him and sent him back to Florida.

The Cuban, a little guy about fifty with dyed hair pulled back in a ponytail, was being transferred to Glades from the state prison at Starke, five years down, two and a half to go of a second-degree murder conviction. The Cuban was thinking about a woman he believed he loved, this woman who could read minds.

———

They were brought to the chow hall, their trays hit with macaroni and cheese and hot dogs from the steam table, three slices of white bread, rice pudding and piss-poor coffee and sat down next to each other at the same table, opposite three inmates who stopped eating.

Foley knew them, Aryan Brotherhood neo-Nazi skinheads, and they knew Foley, a Glades celebrity who'd robbed more banks than anybody they'd ever heard of—walk in and walk out, nothing to it-until Foley pulled a dumb stunt and got caught. He ran out of luck when he drew His Honor Maximum Bob in Criminal Court, Palm Beach County. The white-power convicts accepted Foley because he was as white as they were, but they never showed they were impressed by his all-time-high number of banks. Foley sat down and they started in.

"Jesus, look at him eat. Jack, you come back 'cause you miss the chow?"

"Boy, you get any pussy out there?"

"He didn't, what'd he bust out for?"

"I heard you took a .38 in the shank, Jack. Is that right, you let this puss shoot you?"

"Federal U.S. fuckin' marshal, shows her star and puts one in his leg."

Foley ate his macaroni and cheese staring at the mess of it on his tray while the skinhead hard-ons made their lazy remarks Foley would hear again and again for thirty years, from the Brotherhood, from the Mexican Mafia, from Nuestra Familia, from the black guys all ganged up; thirty years in a convict population careful not to dis anybody, but thinking he could stand up with the tray, have the tables looking at him and backhand it across bare skulls, show 'em he was as dumb as they were and get put in the box for sixty days.

Now they were after the Cuban.

"Boy, we don't allow niggers at our table."

They brought Foley into it asking him, "How we suppose to eat, Jack, this dinge sitting here?"

Right now was the moment to pick up the tray and go crazy, not saying a word but getting everybody's attention, the tables wondering, Jesus, what happened to Foley?

And thought, For what?

He said to the three white-supremacy freaks with their mass of tattoos, "This fella's down from Starke. You understand? I'm showing him around the hotel. He wants to visit with his Savior I point him to the chapel. He wants a near-death-experience hangover, I tell him to see one of you fellas for some pruno. But you got this stranger wrong. He ain't colored, he's a hundred percent greaseball from down La Cucaracha way," Foley looking at the three hard-ons and saying, "Cha cha, cha."

Later on when they were outside the Cuban stopped Foley. "You call me a greaseball to my face?"

This little bit of a guy acting tough.

"Where you been," Foley said, "you get stuck with the white-power ding-dongs, the best thing is to sound as dumb as they are and they'll think you're funny. You heard them laugh, didn't you? And they don't laugh much. It's against their code of behavior."

This was how Foley and Cundo hooked up at Glades.

———

Cundo said Foley was the only white guy in the joint he could talk to, Foley a name among all the grunge here and knew how to jail. Stay out of other people's business. Cundo's favorite part of the day was walking the yard with Foley, a couple of road dogs in tailored prison blues, and tell stories about himself.

How he went to prison in Cuba for shooting a Russian guy. Took his suitcase and sold his clothes, his shoes, all of it way too big for him. Came here during the time of the boatlift from Mariel, twenty-seven years ago, man, when Fidel opened the prisons and sent all the bad dudes to La Yuma—what he called the United States—for their vacation.

How he got into different hustles. Didn't care for armed robbery. Liked boosting cars at night off a dealer's lot. He danced go-go in gay bars as the Cat Prince, wore a leopard-print jockstrap, cat whiskers painted on his face, but scored way bigger tips Ladies Night at clubs, the ladies stuffing his jock with bills. "Here is this middle-age mama with big *tetas*, she say to me, 'Come to my home Saturday, my husband is all day at his golf club.' She say to me, 'I give you ten one-hundred-dollar bills and eat you alive.'"

Man, and how he was shot three times from his chest to his belly and came so close to dying he saw the dazzle of gold light you hear about when you approaching heaven, right there. But the emergency guys see he's still breathing, blood coming out his mouth, his heart still working, man, and they deliver him alive to Jackson Memorial where he was in a coma thirty-four days, woke up and faked it a few more days listening to Latina voices, the nurse helpers talking about him. He learned he was missing five inches of his colon but healed, sewed up, good as new. When he opened his eyes he noticed the *mozo* mopping the floor wore a tattoo on his hand, an eye drawn at the base of his thumb and index finger, a kind of eye he remembered from Combinado del Este, the prison by Havana. He said to the *mozo*, "We both Marielitos, uh? Get me out of here, my brother, and I make you rich."

Foley said, "You thought you'd be cuffed to the bed?"

"Maybe I was at first, I don't know. I was into some shit at the time didn't work out."

"A cop shot you?"

"No, was a guy, a picture-taker in South Beach, before it became the famous South Beach. Before that he was a Secret Service guy but quit to take pictures. One he did, a guy being thrown off I-95 from the overpass, man, down to the street, the guy in the air, Joe LaBrava sold to a magazine and became famous."

"Why'd he shoot you?"

"Man, I was gonna shoot *him*. I know him, he's a good guy, but I was not going to prison for a deal this woman talk me into doing, with this dumbbell hillbilly rent-a-cop. I didn't tell you about it? I pull a gun and this guy who use to be in the Secret Service beats me to the draw, puts three bullets in me, right here, man, like buttons. I should be dead"—Cundo grinning now—" but here I am, uh? I'm in good shape, I weigh the same now as the day I left Cuba. Try to guess how much."

He was about five-four, not yet fifty but close to it, his dyed hair always slicked back in a ponytail. "A hundred and thirty," Foley said.

"One twenty-eight. You know how I keep my weight? I don't eat that fucking macaroni and cheese they give us. I always watch what I eat. Even when I was in Hollywood going out every night? Is where I went when the *mozo* got me out of the hospital, to L.A., man, see a friend of mine. You understand this was the time of cocaine out there. All I had to do was hook up with a guy I know from Miami. Soon I'm taking care of cool dudes in the picture business, actors, directors—I was like them, I partied with them, I was famous out there."

Foley said, "Till you got busted."

"There was a snitch. Always, even in Hollywood."

"One of your movie buddies."

"I believe a major star, but they don't tell me who the snitch is. The magistrate set a two-million-dollar bond and I put up a home worth two and a half I bought for six-hundred when I was first out there, all the rooms with high ceilings. I pay nine bills for another worth an easy four and a half million today. Both homes on the same canal, almost across from each other."

Foley said, "In Hollywood?"

"In Venice, California, like no place on earth, man, full of cool people and shit."

"Why do you need two homes?"

"At one time I had four homes I like very much. I wait, the prices go up to the sky and I sell two of them. Okay,

but the West Coast feds see Florida has a detainer on me for a homicide, a guy they say I did when I was in Miami Beach."

Foley said, "The *mozo*?"

Cundo said, "Is funny you think of him."

"Why didn't you trust him?"

"Why should I? I don't know him. They say one time we out in the ocean fishing I push him overboard."

Foley said, "You shot him first?"

Cundo shook his head grinning just a little. "Man, you something, how you think you know things."

———

"What I don't understand," Cundo said, walking the yard with Foley, "I see you as a hip guy, you smart for a fucking bank robber, but two falls, man, one on top the other, you come out you right back in the slam. Tell me how you think about it, a smart guy like you have to look at thirty years."

Foley said, "You know how a dye pack works? The teller slips you one, it looks like a pack of twenties in a bank strap. It explodes as you leave the bank. Something in the doorframe sets it off. I walk out of a bank in Redondo Beach, the dye pack goes off and I'm sprayed with red paint, people on the street looking at me. Twenty years of going in banks and coming out clean, my eyes open. I catch a dye pack and spend the next seven in federal detention, Lompoc, California. I came out," Foley said, "and did a bank in Pomona the same day. You fall off a bike you get back on. I think, Good, I've still got it. I made over six grand in Pomona. I come back to Florida-my wife Adele

divorced me while I'm at Lompoc and she's having a tough time paying her bills. She's working for a magician, Emile the Amazing, jumping out of boxes till he fired her and hired a girl Adele said has bigger tits and was younger. I do a bank in Lake Worth with the intention, give Adele the proceeds to keep her going for a few months. I leave the bank in the Honda I'm using, America's most popular stolen car at the time. Now I'm waiting to make a left turn on to Dixie Highway and I hear the car behind me going *va-room varoom*, revving up, the guy can't wait. He backs up and cuts around me, his tires screaming, like I'm a retiree waiting to make the turn when it's safe to pull out."

"You just rob the fucking bank," Cundo said.

"And this guy's showing me what a hotdog he is."

"So you go after him," Cundo said.

"I tore after him, came up on the driver's side and stared at him."

"Gave him the killer look," Cundo said.

"That's right, and he gives me the finger. I cranked the wheel and sideswiped him, stripped his chrome and ran him off the road."

"I would've shot the fucker," Cundo said.

"What happened, I tore up both tires on the side I swiped him. By the time I got the car pulled over, a deputy's coming up behind me with lights flashing."

"Tha's called road rage," Cundo said. "I'm surprise, a cool guy like you losing it. How you think it happen?"

"I wasn't paying attention. I let myself catch a dye pack in Redondo Beach, something I swore would never hap- pen. The next one, seven years later, you're right, I lost it. You know why? Because a guy with a big engine wearing

shades, the top down, no idea I'd just robbed a bank, made me feel like a wimp. And that," Foley said, "is some serious shit to consider."

"Man, you got the balls to bust out of prison, you don't have to prove nothing."

"Out for a week and back inside."

"What could you do? The girl shot you, the chick marshal. You don't tell me about her."

Karen Sisco. Foley kept her to himself. She gave him moments to think about and look at over and over for a time, a few months now, but there weren't enough moments to last thirty years.

Foley's conviction didn't make sense to Cundo. "You get thirty years for one bank, and I'm maxing out seven and a half for killing a guy? How come you don't appeal?"

Foley said he did, but the attorney appointed by the court told him he didn't have a case. "If I can appeal now," Foley said, "I will. If I have to wait too long, one of these nights I'll get shot off the wire and that'll be that."

Cundo said, "Let me tell you how a smart chick lawyer can change your life for you."

———

"I was told by the Florida state attorney, the federal court in L.A. gave me up 'cause I can get the death penalty here or life with no parole. But this cool chick lawyer I got— and I thank Jesus and St. Barbara I can afford to pay her— she say the reason L.A. gave me up, they have a snitch they don't want to burn."

"One of the movie stars," Foley said, "you turned into a drug addict?"

"Miss Megan say maybe because they like his TV show. Plays a prosecutor, busts his balls to put bad guys away. You have to meet her, Miss Megan Norris, the smartest chick lawyer I ever met. She say the Florida state attorney isn't sure he can put me away on the kind of hearsay evidence he's got. She believe he's thinking of sending me back to the Coast. They find me guilty out there I do two-hundred and ninety-five months, man, federal. You know how long that is? The rest of my fucking life. But Miss Megan say they don't want me either if they have to give up their snitch, the famous actor. So she say to the state attorney here, 'You don't want Mr. Rey?' She say, 'Even if he was to plead to second degree and does a good seven for you straight up, no credit?' Man, the state attorney is tempted, but he like me to do twenty-five to life. Miss Megan tells him she can get that out on the Coast where they have new prisons, not old joints full of roaches, toilets that back up. No, she sticks to the seven and adds, okay, six months, take it or leave it. She ask me can I do it. Look at me, I already done five years at Starke. It got crowded up there, the state prison, man, so they send me to this joint, suppose to be medium security, 'cause I don't fuck with the hacks or have snitches set on fire. Ones they can prove. Can I do three more less five months, all I have left of my time?"

"Standing on your head," Foley said. "What's the runout for the federal action?" He saw Cundo start to grin and Foley said, "It already has."

"They have five years to change their mind and bring me to trial if they want. But I'm doing my time here in Florida by then, safe from falling into federal hands. I said to Miss Megan, 'Girl, you could have made a deal, six years, I be almost to the door right now.' Miss Smarty say, 'You lucky to max out with seven plus. Say thank you and do the time.' "

"You get out," Foley said, "you're free, they can't deport you?"

"Fidel won't take us back."

"You glad you came to America?"

"I'm grateful for the ways they are to improve myself since I come to La Yuma. I respect how justice wears a blindfold, like a fucking hostage."

"Where'd you find Miss Megan?"

"I happen to read about her in the Palm Beach newspaper. I call her and Megan come to look me over, see if I can pay her. She like my situation, a way she sees she can make a deal. I tole her I pray to Jesus and St. Barbara. Those two, man, always come through for me. You ever pray?"

"I have, yeah," Foley said. "Sometimes it works."

"You want to appeal?"

"I told you one guy turned me down."

"Let me see can I get Miss Megan for you."

"How do I pay her, rob the prison bank?"

"Don't worry about it," Cundo said. "I want you to meet her. Ask what she thinks of me, if she goes for my type."

New York Times bestselling author Elmore Leonard is back, and so are three of his favorite characters, **Jack Foley, Cundo Rey, and Dawn Navarro!**

"*Road Dogs* is terrific, and Elmore Leonard is in a class of one. Not only does he have no equal, he doesn't even have a legitimate contender. He makes it look so effortless that if he wasn't the greatest crime writer who ever lived I might have to hate him. But he is, so I just tip my hat." —Dennis Lehane

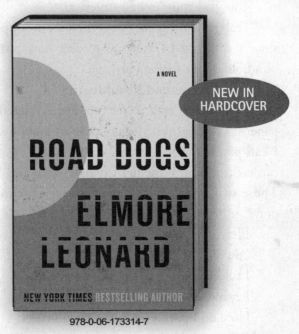

978-0-06-173314-7

"When you read Elmore Leonard, you enter Mr. Leonard's world. A trip like that is its own kind of vacation." —*New York Times*

"A superb craftsman . . . his writing is pure pleasure."
—*Los Angeles Times Book Review*

To learn more, please visit: www.elmoreleonard.com

THE UNDISPUTED MASTER OF THE CRIME NOVEL

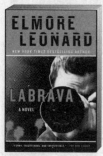

LABRAVA
A Novel

978-0-06-176769-2 (trade paperback)

Ex-Secret Service agent Joe La Brava gets mixed up in a scam involving a slew of eccentric characters.

SWAG
A Novel

978-0-06-174136-4 (trade paperback)

Used car salesman Frank Ryan has a surefire way to get rich quick: armed robbery.

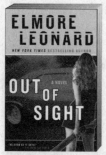

OUT OF SIGHT
A Novel

978-0-06-174031-2 (trade paperback)

Minutes after pulling into a prison parking lot, a Deputy U.S. Marshal meets a legendary bank robber—that's when the fun begins.

THE COMPLETE WESTERN STORIES OF ELMORE LEONARD

978-0-06-124292-2 (trade paperback)

This collection is a must-have for every fan of Elmore Leonard.

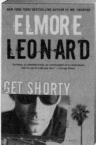

GET SHORTY

978-0-06-077709-8 (trade paperback)

A mobster goes to Hollywood—where women are gorgeous, men are corrupt, and no one can be trusted.

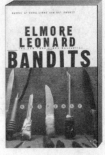
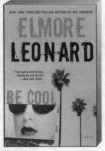
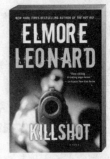